I0550129

HAPPY ALWAYS

HAPPY ALWAYS

John Fraser

AESOP Modern Fiction
Oxford

AESOP Modern Fiction
An imprint of AESOP Publications
Martin Noble Editorial / AESOP
28 Abberbury Road, Oxford OX4 4ES, UK
www.aesopbooks.com

First paperback edition 2017, revised 2020
Copyright (c) 2017 John Fraser

www.johnfraserfiction.com

The right of John Fraser to be identified as the author of this work has
been asserted in accordance with sections 77 and 78
of the copyright designs and Patents Act 1988.

A catalogue record of this book is
available from the British Library.

Condition of sale:
This book is sold subject to the condition that it shall not, by way of trade
or otherwise, be lent, sold or hired out or otherwise circulated in any form
of binding or cover other than that in which it is published and without a
similar condition including this condition being imposed on the
subsequent purchaser.

ISBN: 978-1-910301-32-6

Contents

~ Here and Back Again ~

I've finished another one. A bison. Done in lampblack. Come on!
   ... This cavern roof's so low. Mind your head!
   We have to swim here. Hold your breath. It's pitch black, I know. You have to fight the current . . .
   On your stomach now. We have to crawl. Head down – don't get stuck, or we'll be here for ever, both of us.
   Oh dear. The torch is wet. Well, anyway, you get the idea ...

'The door! There's people come. To tell me the secret of the universe.'

She hopes the old guy doesn't die while she's away. But, on the other hand . . . She comes back up.

'Yes,' she says. 'They have the secret. No spoof! The other guesses were all wrong. Not strings. The universe is made of things that look like snails. Or love knots.'

'What's a love knot?' asks the old dying guy.

'Leli the cat, she's looking bad too,' says the lady.

'Oh fuck this fidgeting!' shouts the old guy. 'This is the moment for some becoming immortal. Some go to hell. Others qualify for paradise. Mostly – it's transforming into places and objects, passing reluctant into other people's heads, and all the blur and shimmer that entails. Find the right mode! It's my moment! Music! A play of light! Birth and death – they say those are unimportant – screwing, pay packets: those are supposed to be revealing moments. Crap! This is my most important day . . .' He leaps up off the bed, his catafalque, and runs off down the street. 'You lie!' he shouts at two types in black, holding the secret. 'In the universe, the needle's stuck – "no change". It isn't made of anything at all. It's an exploded void. Nought banging into nought.'

The lady tells me, 'Your father's demented. He ran off down the street, like those three-legged wheels. Into the wood, under the escarpment. No one said anything. They all saw.'

'He's just excited,' I say. 'Probably those pills. There's always couples in the wood. They'll know where he is. He isn't voyaging. He's tripping.'

All the same, I stand outside the house a while, looking up and down. There's a youth, with a guitar, electric. I say, 'That's a beautiful red, your instrument. Like cherries.' In white letters on its horn it says, 'To the sea.'

'Why that?' I ask.

'Oh,' he says, 'I don't speak English. We did that at school.'

There's an abundance of civilisations here. Layer on layer. Priests, poverty, malaria. They've got rid of the malaria. The first paintings on the walls – that was tough. Now – I guess it's not.

'When I write, there is nothing other than what I write.' That's the philosophy, but we don't do much writing here. 'You could leave,' I say to the guitarist. 'Lodge in a civilisation, somewhere else.'

'It's the women leave,' he says. 'We tend to hang around, we men. We get the house.'

'Marx said the highest consciousness was species being. The awareness of us in everything. Communism, the only hope. Look what a cock-up! Last act – lured into a tragedy on the mountains of Afghanistan,' I say.

The lad's embarrassed. So am I.

'Go fuck yourself off!' he says, trotting away. That's what I meant.

*

Her house is clean but skinny.

Dana tugs off her sweater: in sequins, it says, 'No lingering' across the chest.

'You know,' says Dana, 'you can suckle on me. The rest – there's border control and shoot on sight.'

'It seems I'm just dependent, Dana,' I say. 'That "something more" there has to be, grows ever larger.'

'That's for someone else, or mister nobody,' she says. 'This is what you get. It's the best there is. There is no greater happiness. If you can't emote to match – the problem's your capacity. No use pouring wine in bottles that are full.'

'I guess it's the culture,' I say, not satisfied. 'The family . . . Baseless claims . . .'

'Yes,' she says. 'This is the full life. Get used to it.'

'Then there's the work, the recognition . . .' I say.

'Everyone has to do it,' she says. 'When they hire you, you have to sign a paper that says you resign. That way, when they fire you, the law is happy.'

Dana stows herself away. Time to leave. 'Your trouble is,' she says, 'you have good ideas, but right after someone else has had them. Try to keep up – even to inch ahead. And find out what to do with them.'

The street is hot, like a varnish.

Mirko is leaving. He speaks French, so that means Belgium. I suggested Senegal, but no . . . The illusion of work . . . promotion, even. A fat girl with good legs who makes quiches. He says,

'If you play with French cards, you know straight off – every prince is a knave. Every king is waiting to be done down by an ace. Everyone here will cheer for tyranny, because they admire the puffed-up guys, and think they can outwit them. Screw out more money, pout a bigger chest. Then, it all slumps. Melancholy, not intelligence, in play.'

I hear this all the time.

'That war,' he says, 'was just across the water. A stroll away. The ferry goes through the flat sea like a sleeping man doing breast-stroke. Throb and pause . . . We surely have the hate they had. True – we're held back. No weapons. Sentimental songs. The system's always clogged. Never a massacre to clear the pipe.'

'Everyone's mixed up. On the stairs, to go up or down,' I say. 'You couldn't manage a civil war.'

'Think of your life as story,' Mirko says. 'Where does it lead? Maybe a mafia? End as boss, or fall-guy. Repentant: or in jail for life: spat on for sure.'

'No, Mirko,' I say. 'That's what you want. Real life. Yours told by someone else. Verified in the paper. I don't want real life. I could go to the marshes of Poland with that girl from the bar. They have buffalo there, and green birds. Shacks, lots of shacks. Or to Iran, with her boyfriend, and dodge the prying and the deserts. It's all churches and mosques, everywhere. And with guys who hate the place and are sick with nostalgia and parents they never really knew . . . Fuck real life!' I say. 'Everyone is in it, they want more till they vomit . . .'

'This dreaming of scaffolds,' Mirko says, 'it's fantasy, because you'll never have the sparky life you want. What you'll have is being dragged along a flinty road, behind the donkey cart.'

That, I know. 'You're dry,' he says. 'With the wind, you'll snap.'

'We're similar,' I say. 'You, Dana, the rest. That's what binds a society.'

'Break it,' Mirko says. 'It's clear, something broke. It fell apart. Get a group together. Into the forest. Sort it out.'

'No men,' I say. 'They're picayune. They bully.'

'Women are even more acculturated,' Mirko says. 'They can't stand you. Men would tolerate you, push you aside.'

'The primitives,' I say. 'They faced all that. Still, between times, they napped, buried their dead, watched the sky and separated out the species. Died at twenty. Clubbed some comrades.'

'The forests,' Mirko says, 'are full of settlements. Already – migrants. Nomads who don't move. Your troupe would not survive.'

Mirko goes to Belgium, lives like he wants. Happy for ever. Dana says,

'There's a French woman come. She does books – she's in a cottage she says France bought for things like that.'

And here she is. A long nose, sharp, a hidden pearl in its tip, like all the thinkers have. 'I'm looking into Maeterlinck,' Sandrine says.

I don't believe her. Maybe she has broken down, inside. She shows me a picture of a road – Paris, London – there's food from Thailand. 'Inuit snax' it says too. There's busy people, never hungry, never tempted, not by anything.

'This is what our cities, rich places, once looked like,' she says. 'You imagine they still do, I bet. Really, it's your crime scene interests me. Every place must have one, else we'd all trek back and long to live in holes. It's evil that I'm after. They pinned it on the great ones – the leaders, builders, great destroyers. Then – it was passed around. We all had some. "The evil that men do . . ." That was the quote. Women too, I guess. Many think that way.'

'Sandrine,' I say, 'this is a place you spend a hundred years – they pass undimmed, just your enamel wears away, you rust, you tarnish, fray and crumble. Time will get you – not the place. Here, there's been no massacre. People leave, before the urge comes to be evil.'

'Of course,' says Sandrine. 'The Maeterlinck is just a cover.'

'You mean,' I say, 'states go round the world buying up cottages and gifting them to nationals who look for massacres, so that they can dump upon the past? Aversion therapy?'

'Oh dear,' says the French lady, fingering her long, bony nose. 'I hope you're not an extremist,' and she laughs. 'Some lost souls, I know, have a chuckle about terror. It's quite infantile . . .' She turns on me. 'Guys like you – a foreigner, yet you'll live here all your life. You could be anything – a revolutionary, terrorist, a punk. Off to fight jihad? Or – worse – you wouldn't fight for me, for us. Me – I'm a sort that's more advanced. A national culture – but quite continental. Paid in a continental coin. You – you're all covered up. Scurrying among the leaves.'

'We have to hide him,' Dana laughs at me, pinches my face, as if affectionately. 'It's not that he's ashamed of anything. I think he just enjoys it, hiding.'

'Being hidden,' says Sandrine, analytically. 'There's a difference. Vital. Which does he enjoy the most, I wonder. Hiding? Being hidden? Some think it's the same thing – it's an unhappy couple.'

'Yes,' says Dana. 'I know all about those.'

We stand, entwined. Three statues, glancing outside the ring we make.

Dana expires! We hear the bang and then a whistle – but Dana's gone already – a fish split open by a shell, revealed and speechless to the bones. Struck dead. A lightning strike.

'Friendly fire!' says someone. 'They have to practise shooting off these things . . .'

It isn't true – no accident. Somewhere there is bad intent. That's why Sandrine is here. 'Stop snivelling!' she says to me. 'Dana's death – just one of many – uncountable profusion. Remember – you're a brave soldier, we're at war.'

It hadn't seemed at all like that, though if you're informed and interested, it does, I guess . . .

*

'*Mann vergisst*,' the opera says. 'We forget'.

I say to Sandrine, 'Do you know, really close up, I mean – Cécile La France? The name alone . . . I saw her in a movie. She needs love . . .'

'I'm often asked,' says Sandrine. 'I am here for that as well. You want an introduction? She'll not come here, of course, but . . .'

I'm sure we'll never meet. In any case, it's true, that my opinions are extreme. That could be why I'm watched . . .

'Yes,' says Sandrine. 'You are extreme. It stimulates the others, who become extreme themselves. It isn't what you want; power, winning – it's how your arrogance expresses thoughts . . . Too speculative, excluding nothing. They change from day to day. I'm sure they're grounded . . . Maybe it's a question just of taste.'

'Dana said my taste was quite insipid,' I tell Sandrine. 'Like wild asparagus. The scent comes through secreted in your urine, some time after.'

'You keep staring at my eyes,' she says, irritated. 'They're absolutely a pair. Maybe Dana's weren't. You depressives . . . think nothing creates futility except your memories – usually anomalous . . .'

Not eyes: the nose, unique in this particular shape.

'That's quite wrong,' I say. 'There's no futility. On you go! You can't take stuff with you – but you can leave great piles behind.'

'What stuff did you have in mind?' she asks.

Nothing. 'Well, of course,' I say. 'I could try with wood. Objects. Sculptures. Things in a frame. No call to breathe life in – the wood has it all already.'

'Yes,' she says. 'That sounds real naff. Say it, don't do. It's beyond you and beneath you. And – you can't sell.'

'Then, Sandrine,' I say, 'what can *you* do? Your blue birds fly away. They can't be caught. Can you protect us from our loss? From all the loss? Unknown people with an unknown plan – sweeping us away. Maybe they'll find a guy to make apologies. Another generation hears, amazed. Live people – that's what we know, all we know, that's kin to us . . . not the ruins, the old symphonies, the tomes. But our lookalikes, brothers and sisters, comrades, here they are beside us – then, they spin and drift – and disappear. People – they fade away – like captains tumbling from a spaceship. No air, no gravity – a "help" won't carry. It just fills your baggy suit. There is no help, no hand. Another project, that's the most to hope. Sandrine, it must be why you're here.'

'I have my orders, that's for sure,' she says. 'And my aesthetic. Names unstuck from myths, and whirling round. I might enquire into Dana, that death . . .'

'Leave it, Sandrine,' I say. 'Put an end to it. You'd have to enter into what a person feels and fears . . . the moment of extinction. Looking down, into the void. The story she becomes; the story all around, before and after, then . . . She ends. As Dana – it's all over.

Real and ephemeral. All those stories – never end. They go on for always. You can't look for real ephemeral stuff in tales, in stories. There's only frustration if you try. The family, the state, the justice. Police, the falsity of memories, gossip – it's a thicket, Sandrine. Those are the epics, improvised and drying brown. You don't need go into all that.'

'Oh,' she says, 'I'm quite at home in stories. I'm here to nudge the plot.'

'You were sent,' I say. 'So, someone knows more "why" than you.'

'Oh no,' says Sandrine. 'These opinions. The extreme ones. Ever since those puffed-up guys wanted more land, more power, ports and peasants – all that – it's been opinions. Superior races. Higher gods. Better politics. More friends. Socialism, independence. Well – those may be extreme – they're not exactly new. I'm here to see what opinions may be called extreme – but anticipating. For the next time. Something far out. Really extreme. Maybe not punk or *pointillisme*. Ideas that mobilise, that terrorise. Otherwise – it's all cold soup.'

'I seem to have it wrong,' I say. 'Behind opinions, I thought, there's . . .'

'You do,' she says. 'Of course, there's accidents. But each accident's unique. The rest is: getting those who want to get you. Get them first. Expunge. Time's invented just for that, anticipating. No doubt you'll leave the rough stuff all to me.'

I can't believe she came here just for me, and my mistakes.

'Cécile says she'd love to meet you,' Sandrine says. 'In a while.'

'That was just a whim,' I say. 'It's all of no account.'

'Well,' she says. 'I hope none of you guys is taking arms, enlisting somewhere. I'll find you, that's for sure. Stick to the whittling.'

'Round here, we all went to school together,' I say. 'Everyone thinks the same. I went too, but didn't listen. No one has special thoughts, or invites their comrades to view their numinous works.'

'You see,' says Sandrine, 'someone like you – could be a Luther. There'd be you – and your extreme idea. And if there was, in the end –

in the beginning too – no idea at all? Just you . . . Away would fly . . . the lot. The church, the state, the land, the buildings. The opera was bad enough – the painted ladies, prancing, guys with antlers on their head. It disperses, butters up your mind . . .'

'I hadn't thought of anything like that,' I say. 'I know you have to snoop. Carry right on. But – I have no extreme idea. I haven't come to it, Sandrine. Maybe I can't. Maybe you're right – it isn't there. Or if it is – then everything would disappear. Change shape.'

'That's exactly it,' she says. 'I'm here to see if you arrive at it. I told you – it's not now. It's next year, or tomorrow.'

*

There's a Sandrine everywhere, in every hamlet. They have a grant. Maybe they all write books on the exotic too. They pry. Perhaps my friend, Romolo, would take her on? He screwed a Swiss girl, here on a vacation. When he went to find her in her home, they turned the hose on him, and then the dog. It must have been his name.

'Maeterlinck,' I say to him. '*Bluebeard and Ariadne*. Brilliant stuff. Her nose – it has the pearl of genius, tucked in the tip. She'd love to catch you, thrashing in her net . . . She collects extremes. Invent a ride, and sit her on it, a cause, try to recruit her into it . . .'

'Useless, my friend,' says Romolo. 'You can't unstick her and stick her on to me. Any cause I might one day be sympathetic to is indefensible. This side or that – anything involving other people – it's a joke. If it isn't blood, it's futility that's dripping on your head.'

'Suppose,' I say, 'there's something so grotesque . . .'

'They'll send a letter. You join up. A cell incorporated unto cells. They bury you for free. Sometimes you get a medal. There's nothing you can do, except for heroism,' he says. 'All for the cause. Sacrifice.'

'What you don't foresee is exactly what she's looking for. The offensive: the new that transforms everything,' I say. 'Sometimes you feel you have it right, your extreme, your inoffensive thought, I know.

But when it's not so fugitive? What then? Suppose you light upon an idea – that really shakes it all – the tree, the landscape, and the sky? What then? Swing along with Sandrine – the new extreme is ours,' I chant.

'No!' he says. 'No to you! And her. This time there won't be dogs that tear my pants. She rides with packs of kings and queens, all after me, no doubt. Me – I'm innocent, every time!'

*

'I fear Romolo won't have sex with you, Sandrine,' I say. 'Though you don't have a dog. He's not ready for new tricks.'

That's beyond her. 'I want to know what web I'm in,' she says. 'You have sex with a family, not an individual. And – I thought Mirko was your brother.'

'No, no,' I say. 'He lived with us a while – but who your mother is – it makes no difference to your age.'

'That's true,' she says. 'I hear your mother died quite sudden, in an accident.'

'She fell downstairs,' I say. 'An open razor in her hand. Nearly decapitated. Two accidents and one effect: – there's no intent established.'

'I'm sure that's true as well,' she says. 'Though – you'll have felt the impacts.'

'I told you, Sandrine,' I say. 'Here, it's all the same, indifferent. Whoever you live with, they tell you everything the same. Only the bad guys leave a trace.'

'It's them that interests me,' Sandrine says. 'But I don't trust you, and your telling. The people here – when fascism collapsed, they went to being communists. And then . . . tell me what happened then.'

'I wasn't born here, Sandrine,' I say. 'You should have asked my friend, Mirko. He was the storyteller. He went to Belgium, but he wasn't happy. The Flemish did for him. He wasn't understood.'

'This is good stuff,' Sandrine says. 'You, a foreigner too, and certainly not French. Disinheriting everyone, your country . . . you might be Italian, somewhere deep and dark. The language – it's easy. Stick vowels on the end of everything. Family ties all razored out. And – pimping for your mate, that Romolo! No one could invent you, not even you!'

'I'm surely not your only client hereabouts,' I say. 'You'll have a soft and tender streak . . .'

'Of course!' she says. 'Who'd not be fascinated by a Mélisande?'

'We're back to that?' I ask. 'Romance? The people here – they hunted down all living things – the furry ones, that is. Resistance ended there. They ran from power – the paladins, the churches, the fields where the mosquitoes lived. When all the furry things were dead, they put their guns into the rafters. Curled up themselves, like ammonites.'

'If you want relationships,' she says. 'You must try hard. Much harder. The future doesn't arrive if you just wait and wind the clock.'

'I know, Sandrine,' I say. 'You're not American. You have doubts. I realise – here everything requires an effort, some *rhodomontade*, exegesis. History demands it. But – you're part of the reactionary wave. Nothing to push against. Your just a mass of surf. You swallow everything. Kings, Nazis – they're all embedded here. Reaction for its own sake. There's nothing else. No one dissents. There's space, but there's no room . . . All disappears into your tide . . .

'Us – we're stones. We sleep, deep. There – forests of trees. Here – a coppice of shambly cottages. Don't wake us. You're quite other. You speak in French, but your country is the globe. Your lookalikes, your brothers – those guys you say you're trying to exterminate – the guys with black flags, breaking up the past, posturing, selling it. It's you, see: in the mirror. A small distortion. They smirk, you scowl. They massacre, you bomb. You do it from the office. They – the same. They are your jesters, your caricatures. Your caricaturists. Their religion – is the perfection of yours. They do what you keep inside. Yours a double act – the big serious guy with baggy pants is you – clowning against the clown. Pour the water down the other's trousers. Who will end up, prince of the ring? There's no *auguste*. It's a sham, my dear. The thing is – choose the winning side.'

Vanity. It sounds like vanity, my voice. Then there's her nose. The nose – where does she put it when she sleeps?

'Not sham,' she says. 'It's real. Just not how you thought. You especially – you don't need to pick a side. You're here, and what you are.'

'You're right, Sandrine,' I say. 'I give up. Everything is as it seems. The novelty – it's just the circling round. It's countries, states – all that old stuff. You should give up too, looking for what's coming next. We know what we need for our contentment. The unanswerable questions dangle on their strings above our heads. You needn't look. The next big thing – is scurrying somewhere in the forest. A creature, laden with a head so big it has to waste time doing sport – no gadgets, no telephones – but smart! High on self-protection.'

I pull Sandrine – into the forest. 'Hey,' she shouts. 'Wait! These few trees – there's nothing here . . .'

'Oh yes,' I say. 'Life! The species that comes after us – they must be very small. Billions of them – mostly eating air and drinking dew. Maeterlinck had prevision – they're his fairies, his princesses. They'll take over, if we don't poison them – one of our bright mistakes . . .'

There's guys shooting up, and making little fires, or stretched out on some foam. A wave of giggling, pleasures that fleet away, and people you'd not recognise in suits.

'This is my free day,' she says, and pulls me close against her. Her face goes out of focus – the features melt away, time on the rocks, our destiny seeking the medallions of sun that flickers through the leaves . . . 'More light, Sandrine,' I shout, pulling myself away. 'I must have brightness, see what's happening . . .'

Well, the forest's here: she hesitates.

'It's life!' I say. 'They say to cheer it, celebrate. Life is a relay. If you drop the baton – there's someone there to pick it up and run, maybe with hundreds of legs more, nearer to the ground.'

She laughs, goes further in, expecting me to follow. I let her go. So much for my date with Cécile. Wasn't it a Bardot movie she was in . . .?

Sandrine's inside – how she'll feel at home, chivvying the mushrooms, interrogating the red ants.

It's worth a song. 'Burning bride' comes to mind – 'You'll be lucky when she runs out of desire,' I sing. There's crowds around my house. It burns: someone burns it. Hard to tell.

'Go away!' I shout. 'It's stone. There is no flame.'

The floors and ceilings have flared up, and lie as charcoal in the cellar. Mine was a torch song. I possess a white stone cube, unique and warm.

My friend Remo stands beside: he says, 'Maybe something fell on it. An act of thunderbolts, a quiverful.'

It's true. The storms roll in and over, shells fall all about, the plastic powder finds the wires and blows up everything. 'The mice!' I say. 'They live in reeds below the tiles.'

*

'Oh,' Remo says, 'they hear the whistle, don't wait for the bang. Like the green birds in the trees . . . Don't worry about them. There's worse has happened, and if you looked at what's to come . . .'

'Your brother Romolo,' I say. 'He's such dry grass. Yet when I wanted – he wouldn't go on fire. Sandrine – she's tinder. Or – no, she's a spark, she's already reaching upward, wavering into dance . . . The red hair, the pale eyes, the lashes carroty . . .'

'It's the nose,' says Remo. 'That's what puts you off. Not knowing if it's sharp or like an instrument the doctor shoves, it goes right in . . .'

'I want to do her a good turn,' I say, 'because it's the best turn for me.'

'I know all that,' says Remo. 'You think she'll have to draw up constitutions for the ants. You're wrong – they already have one. It's the best. Then, there's us. The next thing coming – we'll call terror, the big guys dressed like crows who come to get us. They already came. They come quite regular, they always have.'

'No one loves them for it,' I say.

'Oh,' he says, 'you old reactionary! You have to take a side. Your crows bring truth and justice. Whoever sends them.'

It's true. It doesn't lift the heart.

'You have a heavy touch,' he tells me.

'That's not so,' I say. 'Everyone has parents, known or not. They die, all of them, in ways you haven't thought about. But it's random. You don't will it. People move away – some stand next to you: many die. It's random. They do other things as well, more vigorous. My house suffered a random hit. It happens to a mass of things. Only the intervals, the time spaces, make a tragedy, when there's a symmetry, or it all happens pouf! like that. All occurring in one day – it's common, though. I could show you on a map, or in a book . . .'

'That's so,' says Remo. 'Time is a lousy marker for the normative as well. It's not just when you're considering what is reasonable: time's not up to any scratch.'

'You know, Remo,' I say, 'a place like this – into my mind comes Smolensk. It's bigger, of course, but the market – desolation. Everybody drunk or hungry. Too big for what it has to hold, like mammoth jeans you find in charity bins . . .'

'That's bigger,' Remo says. 'And it's in Russia too.'

'It used to be in the USSR,' I tell him. 'And in the war. It's the desolation I'm talking about. It had the same whiff as here. But – I've travelled, all over. I've more to look back on and regret than most. And held executive posts, though briefly. I had a conscience, jumped ship . . .'

'We need a star to follow,' Remo says, thoughtfully. 'Ships sail by them.'

'I had this fantasy,' I say. 'Cécile La France. Saw her late one night. In a movie, I think. She impressed me with her poise. People seem to need heroines. If you forgive me, not to hurt your sensibilities – she had more poise than Jesus.'

'I'm not sensitive at all,' says Remo. 'Go right ahead.'

'We were talking about randomness, things that hit you in the middle of the night,' I say.

'You should have stuck with Sandrine,' Remo says. 'No poise, but class. You had neither, palming her off on Romolo.'

'She's in the forest, researching, like everyone does now,' I say. 'Other species, tottering but more hopeful still . . .'

We see her, Sandrine, in the trees, flickering, a menacing firestick.

'You should do some travelling again,' says Remo. 'Your luck's burnt out here. We're all thinking about it too – hoping we won't meet anyone we used to know. and have to sub them.'

'There's always characters like me from the past,' I say. 'Bearing a fear and disappointing hope from history – nothing specific, though. and no remedy for any of it.'

I hope Remo will take me up, give a criticism, maybe, that starts us talking. About me. He says,

'You say you want things to change,' says Remo. 'But you flinch from the dark things that change brings. It's just your style – pushing things away.'

*

This is the perfect city. Everybody's hostile. There's revolutionaries here, all imports – Naxalites, *Ivoiriens* and Tigers . . . some waiting for the past; and some just wait.

My room, high up, overlooks the waves of grey, grey chimneys, no-smoking muzzles pointing up, you remember from the cinema.

Americans, down there – maybe using that clinic as a front – busy as wasps, with stings and movie plots. Arms and the men. I see only –

the guys that go in for a checkup, stumble out or prance. Cécile La France – here I am, maybe I should look her up?

'I've never seen China,' says the song, '*Mais je l'imagine.*' I can't afford their restaurant down there, alongside, but the smell insists all day.

The guy in the next room, Marcel, says, 'I'll show you to my friends. They're all revolutionaries. Lay, of course: no red-head firelighters flitting in the trees. Don't mention Maeterlinck.'

'I can't see any job I want,' I say. 'I might work for the Chinese, away from all the food.'

Maeterlinck – not my strong suit. They send them – agents – seeking love, vengeance, to the villages. Sandrine – making it all up, perhaps, but a career for her as well, a job.

'They're all my friends,' Marcel says, proud and timid.

'They dress so colourful,' I say.

Marcel's impressive. I hear him not sleeping, pacing all night, something important forming there. What happens to the people here? They're like Plains Indians. You wonder what will get to them. The measles? Treaties? Cavalry – millions swept away. The animals too, all gone, and now the grass, the stones – dried out and pounded into grit. White guys, a few of them, replacing them. Coming from an undiscovered land. I guess we're white, Marcel, and me – but we don't count. We're too high up, no one will look up, see us looking down. Giving them free will, which is no use to them.

Every night – Marcel's anxiety. He says, 'I bought two whores. One you must take, and owe me for.'

The woman, Liliane, says, 'I'm not a prostitute. I need the money, though.'

'Marcel,' I say, 'think only of yourself. That's where we are, that's what we're in – ourselves.'

'I did,' he says. 'You'll need this while you await your merchandise.' A packet.

'I don't sell drugs,' I say. 'I hadn't thought.'

'That's just too bad,' he says. 'You'd deal, and I could turn you in. I need the money, that is all.'

'No criticism, Marcel,' I say. 'I'm at a crossroads. I'm like Balaam's ass. It takes a while to starve – you hallucinate, and maybe that comes out quite well. Creation. A manifesto. Poems. Something on a stage.' I hadn't thought. Liliane pouts – it's not an invite.

'"*Qui je suis, qui je suis?*"' I prompt her – "The twentieth child of a king of Tartary . . ."?'

'I was good at school,' says Liliane. 'We didn't do that. Maybe we should take a quiet pill – a blue one, qualoo something . . . so's we don't disturb Marcel. He could be an actor – those cheekbones, like Buster Keaton. We'll provide the silence, while Buster goes to, with his whore, my pal, next door. Quiet sex, as if it isn't there.'

'No, no, excuse me,' Marcel says to me. 'We're booked in here, with you. A party. You've no mother, listening in . . .'

'I've no mother,' I say. 'She went with a younger father. When I was at school, we disinherited ourselves – off to the forest: finding a temple, sex, chasing live things. You know what they say – one body, three spirits. It'll never be as good as that again.'

'You can't go to school again,' says Liliane. 'Or have another father. If you stay here, though . . . when you go to school, even if you're like me, from some forest, distant – you get a new identity. A real one. French. It can go on and on, and back too, as long as you can read, longer than you can remember.'

'Yes, Liliane, I know,' I say. 'You're cute, with your speeches.'

'Not just those,' says Liliane. 'My father is a shaman. He makes it so I don't feel things like the others.'

'Less?' I ask.

'No,' she says, 'much more. We're from Tourcoing. Our life comes from nearer the surface than it does for you.'

'Well,' Marcel says, 'you are boring me. I'm off to have some sex.' And he climbs on to my bed.

'Marcel says you must have a set of friends that's quite complete,' says Liliane. 'Nomads and ministers. Lots of maître d's and tennis coaches, but scholars and monopolists as well.'

'So – you *are* the one from Tartary, Liliane,' I say. She laughs.

Marcel terminates. 'Your friend,' I say. 'She doesn't say too much.'

'What's she to say?' asks Liliane.

'Now, you junkies,' Marcel says. 'Take your voyage of choice, and I'll sit and watch you.'

'I'm not your succubus,' says Liliane's friend, Beatrice. 'Though I'm sure you're very powerful and know everything.'

'That Beatrice has class,' I tell Liliane.

'I know,' she says.

'Doktor Caligari, working the crowd,' Beatrice says. 'That's Marcel,' and she laughs.

'That's exactly right,' Marcel says. 'You degenerates – you make it true, the part is more indicative than the whole. This room – a nutshell, we the rodents chewing it. I'm putting it together – my friends, transgressive here and there, but pure reactionaries – not to say quite ignorant. Uncaring too – of left and right – and so . . . they'll join in naturally, with all the rest. Reaction. What is progress? Guys in labs, playing with pipettes. Reaction everywhere. The Russian nats, the Arab Tories, family and festas – all those young macho guys who're scared because they have no work, no clues . . . And all the others – they'd be fascists if they read a book, but as it is . . . You need to make a pudding of it, a dough. Respect. Pomp and fear – that brings them all together. They can't hate properly what they don't know. Posturing – their enemies are their twins, they recognise them in the mirror, wearing the same shirts. Beneath it all – there's envy and illusion . . .'
On he talks.

'Your dough . . .' says Beatrice. 'I'm waiting! So – when do you pull out your purse? Eats and drinks, is first.'

'I've got the raw materials,' Marcel says. 'Here in my brain. Fizzing. What do I do with them? Let it spew out, a big molten bang?

Or keep it to myself?' He puts on some clothes. 'The fact is – you put them all together, stir them in – I'm not sure it's still me. They aren't a bunch I feel at home with. Thoughts is one thing – being in the room and hearing them aloud is quite another . . . Mamma's boys, they kill and cry . . .'

'I left because they sent a person – spying on me. My ideas . . .' I say. There's a silence, abstracted.

'Being a leader is one thing,' Marcel goes on. 'Because it's friends around you. Enemies as well, I guess. But – if you need electing . . . Surrounded by those evil shards . . . trying to grease your wheels and take a spin on you.'

He looks disgruntled. 'Those guys who said it was a life of cockroaches and caterpillars – they were right,' he says.

'Well, you've had your spin on me,' says Beatrice. 'Where's the grease?'

'Don't sound so ignorant,' Marcel says. 'Debt is healthy. Nothing's done unless you're worth a lot of it.'

Liliane settles the blankets, takes the flat bottle from beneath the bed, and drinks. It seems I've a commitment to her.

Through the window comes a primal reek. Like a wall. 'Chinese!' says Beatrice. 'Wild onions. Eats! They gather them from between the flags where the Communards are buried.'

'These women,' Marcel tells me, 'are still at school. Fuddle-doo! The stories in their heads! The thing is – never write it down. Nothing. Let your friends do what they do. The dead lie. The living – beside, on top, or underneath. It's nature. Write on no walls! That way – you're free. You have no past, and so your future's a blank wall and all potential.'

'Maybe the Chinese will give me work,' says Liliane.

*

The Chinese say they'll take her, but not me. 'Oh!' says Liliane to me. 'I'm not one of Marcel's Tory friends I'll keep you! Write nothing down so I could spy on you. Be free! You'll be my lizard, waiting in its crack till I come home from Tartary.'

'We can't screw in my room,' says Marcel. 'The mattress is quite hard, all stuffed with cash. Beatrice and I – we'll keep you company,' and so they do.

'You could lead, Marcel,' I say. 'Take responsibility.'

'These guys,' he says. 'You can't lead them. Reactionaries! They don't move! I'm at a full stop. I can't change friends because we're full up here, even taking the bed in turns . . . Besides, the high-up guys – they're dull. They organise, defend themselves. There's no fantasy in that.'

'We're fine here,' I say, 'except that smell. Before you eat . . . kills appetite.'

'That's nothing!' Marcel says. 'The people here – they have a filter in the nose . . . Consider – what happens to the other guys. The people here – they send the cash abroad, and that brings trouble. They buy the earth and water overseas, then, everywhere but here – it's scrabble time. Nails broken in the dirt.' He bounces on my bed. 'Everyone's responsible, of course. It's equally shared out. And, as they say, "The rich have fun. The poor go crying to their graves." I'm a special case, you see: rich in the next room, poor in this.'

'That sounds the best,' I say. 'If you can't be famous. Or at least a namesake.'

'No, no, it's stalemate, friend,' he says.

Liliane tells me, 'They want me to go to China – and I want to go. There's life! You're stuck here. Any excuse so's not to move!'

'They don't want me,' I say.

'That's so true,' she says.

'The forest, Liliane. It calls. The plants, the animals – a universe,' I say. 'It's memory – the earth, the resin – all is wild . . .'

'I'll think of you, when I am in Lanzhou,' says Liliane.

'There's problems here,' Marcel says. 'I'm moving in with you.'

'You are already, Marcel,' I tell him.

'No,' he says, 'financially. The cash is spent. And so am I.'

We lay him out upon the bed. 'I'll be a tiny sparrow,' Marcel whispers. 'Crumbs are enough. Just leave me quiet, and pay the rent.'

I say to Liliane, 'I thought he was a great man. Another leader, despising all he leads.'

'*Accidie*,' says Liliane. 'He has read the book. After the roses thrown – the rocks rain down.'

'I want him out of here,' I say.

'Yes, of course,' says Liliane. 'That's what the Chinese say of you. "A wise man. The wisest we have known. His forest – wilder, thicker, more concealing . . . the green and blue birds whistling in the leaves . . ." They're lookouts. "Duck!" they cry – they don't mean those with wings. They see what's coming in to land . . . The Chinese say – "A wise man knows when he must run, and when to hide his friends and bury all his cash." It is a compliment supreme. Each morning, they cook up the herbs, and send the odour through to you: it's purest spirit, it will nourish you . . . Like incense. You know that if you starve – it's wisdom too: coming by the most sapient route . . .'

'Those are inspiring words,' I say. 'When are you off to China, Liliane?'

'Oh,' she says, 'there's doubts about exactly what I have to do.'

'You can't live with those kinds of doubts,' I say.

Marcel lies on my bed all day, a plucked eagle, probably poached, lead pellets oxidised inside.

'Beatrice brings what it takes to keep him quiet,' says Liliane. 'You don't want him mouthing off while you're busy here, a-watching at the window as I work down there below.'

'No, Liliane,' I say. What would the wise man do? He'd find another room, for sure.

'If I'm there, I'll join the Party,' says Liliane. 'Help build socialism.'

'What do you offer, Liliane?' I ask. 'I know you're not a prostitute – what useful skills . . .?'

'Refreshments,' Liliane says. 'Don't be snide.'

'You're hard, Liliane,' I say. 'You rush towards responsibility.'

'I don't see any political sense at all in Marcel,' she says, finding a thread. 'All his friends . . . a tangle of squeaking twigs. Tarts and nazis – some titled, some lusted after. There was only Beatrice, worrying over him. She wanted to be the love of someone's life. He'd want to be like Sartre – coffee and cigs . . . eyeing the traffic on the sidewalk, lifting people up and dropping them, on strings. You wouldn't like that?' she asks me.

'Just that? No, I don't think so. I'd not know where to start,' I say.

'Just that!' she says. 'You hear the echoes everywhere. Those times – they went like cabaret. The music got much louder since, and now – it's dying too. Inside your ears, like those old earwigs. Ugh!'

We stare at Marcel, wondering how to pack him out of sight. His journey's done.

'When I'm in Lanzhou,' says Liliane, 'I could send for you.'

'You do just that,' I say. 'Meanwhile, we could leave him here and find another room. Higher up, perhaps.'

'There's Beatrice too,' says Liliane. 'Her friends might come along . . . Some of them are his friends too. A wild wood! You could make a sect of them. A trend, a movement. Epic guys. They cluster, and they clot. I love her, naturally. How'd we be rid of her?'

We won't be rid, I'm sure. But she should stay with Marcel. I wonder if there's forests left in China, deep in the mist, mountains like sugarloaves behind. Maybe Sartre's chosen to be there, as good as anywhere.

'Where you were,' Liliane says to me. 'You must have been the village idiot. If you ever said a word, no one would have understood.'

'No, no,' I say, 'it was not like that at all. A place immobile – it's a train station, a bus stop. If nothing comes – it's up to you to walk.'

'Fantasms,' Liliane says, 'spectres haunting Europe. Ghost walks, ghost dances . . .'

'That what there is,' I say. 'You live with them. They drip on you. Dirges and nursery rhymes. Morning fog. It's your heritage.'

'In the real life, like what we're in,' says Liliane, 'though we stroll and trudge and shop – no one cares if Beatrice loves Marcel, or he loves her. It's part of a show, a tour. Watching other people's brains – it's what works in movies, on the stage. Not here, on your mattress.'

'Maybe I should find another sage, a pal,' I say. 'Double the stake.'

'Not recommended,' says Liliane.

*

Even if . . . the best Chinese diner in the quarter nominates you 'wise' – you see there's little that a sage could do. Few places he or she would be. Not a hero, not in Leningrad, in Stalingrad, resisting. Telling on his friends, escaping the camps. Living in a peaceful zone, hoarding canned food. Cohabiting and paying tax for two. Wisdom means playing safe and losing to the dealer.

Maybe give up some wisdom for some stupidity? Trade wisdom for some knowledge, information, maybe false, attested, though, believed. 'Whistle!' 'Duck!' Maybe it's a blue bird after all . . . that ring's not on a grenade, but on Mélisande's white soft hand? Maybe epics needn't end with some unlikely triumph, a peace that justifies the macho stuff before . . .?

'Neural damage?' asks Liliane. 'Drink? Something else? Being wise – a problem, so it seems. It gives you qualities you can't explain, can't talk about . . .' She looks at me quite kindly. How does she think a touch of kindness polishes up a brain?

'No, Liliane,' I say. 'Wrong generation. Mine's the new. The old guys screwed themselves. Felt they were always falling short. Not me. Don't reflect, this city's not the place. It's smooth, you glide. Don't think you hook yourself to someone else. It isn't wanted. Brings you both down. It's like – "The poor! Help them!" say the fine thinkers. Do the poor say, "Thank you, brother"? No, they say "Fuck off!" They're right.'

'Well,' says Liliane, 'I'm not poor, nor a fine thinker.'

'You're just ingratiating, Liliane,' I say. 'Everything you say – it spills out, irreplaceable. You'll be empty in a while. Do you think I'll fill you up with bonded stuff? All I have's this room. When I leave it – there it stays behind. The rest's among the trees.'

'I feel I need engage with you, you silent bonzes. It isn't only cash,' says Liliane. 'I feel, that's all. There's no engagement, but it doesn't matter. It's like Beatrice, wondering where Marcel's wandering, in places that they've decided don't exist.'

'Now!' I say. 'That's a point! I'm thinking of the old communists back home. They loved the Soviet Union, and when it disappeared – so did they. They'd never even looked in the cellar, seeing who'd ended up in there.'

'Not everybody looks,' says Liliane. 'I'm sure you suffered from their oddness. Passing over hardships, crimes. But – if you're troubled by massacres – there's no country free of them, no idea you can hitch to that prevents. Russians, Americans – communists or liberals, atheists, believers – they make big omelettes, and leave the shells, red hot in the pan.'

'I've learnt a lot from you, Liliane,' I say. 'More than from Sandrine.'

'If this is the end, my indifferent friend,' she says. 'Remember! Your wisdom when you die – won't even wet the floor. Whatever in China they have me do – I'll carve my name on it. I'll wheedle out two bones, and limp, but write my name on them and leave them in a jar, under what mountain's left.'

*

The people here – they duel. Some pray, some sit, some hand around. They go to fight – but in some distant land. Those that come back, they haven't won. Nor have those who stay.

'I've met this guy, *Ivoirien*,' says Liliane. 'He has a forest. Real. Or part. They keep it thick and green. The animals – in such profusion, they're not culled or eaten. They are sold. Parts. Remember Hesiod – the part's worth more than the whole.'

'And does the money go to you?' I ask.

'I'm sure it will. Everywhere has its good cause,' she says.

The guy is confident. Like Marcel, he's many friends, all confident. You look at him, Hervé – you can see the trees, perhaps, behind him. 'There's no photo possible,' he says. 'Of all the good we do. The thick protecting woods. You'd need to stand back, and it's about something else entirely – earth and sky, and other forests.'

He's quite convinced Liliane: they are a couple now: he doesn't offer money . . . He's a story, certainly. 'We're a species, friend,' he says. 'How might it behave, seeing a little of itself? Eating and burning? Digging holes. Going in the dark. Storing. Fasting. Praying. Sacrificing. Don't assume you know.'

'Oh,' I say, 'I don't assume.'

'I could be the link,' says Liliane, quite timidly. 'It's all tradition. Tradition – trading: the words are cognate. Species don't decide, or change. Could I preserve the forests they no longer have in China? Send them more animals – their useful bits, the parts medicinal? The money – goes to us.'

'It's the species part that interests me,' I say. 'Once they said you acted in the interests of the whole, the species, once you see that's what you are. The idea, though, is Rousseau: the interest! The interest of all becomes the interest of each. Or is it the reverse? Assumptions! The optimism, the happy end . . .'

'No, no,' says Hervé. 'If anything, it's us – and each of us – against the rest. Our nature – doesn't think of harmony, of self-protection. No! We don't want the long haul! We'll make some bucks and use our guns. Selling off the animals – their differences, like what they say – means cutting off their nose! I just sell parts of them.' And Liliane says, 'Yes, that is right! And, maybe – you just hope you can survive . . . Just you. Not everybody. Though – why not the rest as well? It's up to them.'

'You're into heavy arguments,' says Hervé. 'You guys – you can't place my home upon a map! You paddle on with stereotypes. I'm quite unique.'

*

I tell the cops about the animals. They pass me down the line.

'Do you know how hard it is, down there?' the last cop asks. 'In Africa?'

She wears an armlet, no uniform, no gun. 'Absolutely,' I say. 'I wouldn't know how to start, to get a start down there.'

'Those guys, that country – it's always drugs,' she says. 'Far away, those animals are – what can we do about them? If they don't transit here?'

'It's really up to you to know,' I say.

I've no idea, how to make a start.

'It's hard where I come from,' I tell her. It's a softer hardness, though.

She's written down my name. Will they go to the room, find Marcel, moribund, stick him on to me? A crime?

'You could have a conference,' she says. 'That's what our species does. Or leave some money in a will.' She laughs.

I say, 'Some love destruction, some – survival. That's our dialectic.'

She twists her hands: one file of knuckles – 'Good', the other, 'Bad.'

'We have some twisted guys like you,' she says. 'They come in every day. We are their alibi for something bad they've done. If you're innocent – go and tattoo it on your skin, to show it's meant.'

She pushes me towards the door. 'If you want,' she says, pushing harder, 'I could give you citizenship. You know about Jean-Jacques. That's the question that we ask. Saving the species – that was him, and that's the mission for the French. Huddle: it's our interest.'

'I have one passport, I want less, not more,' I say.

'You're wrong,' she says. 'Lots is better than just one. And – we cops, we only eat with innocents and other cops. If you'll invite me . . .' And I feel her boots entwining round my calf.

'I know a Chinese place,' I say. That would show Liliane, I think.

'Good!' says the cop. 'Their motto's "dog eat dog", I'm sure. I am not comely. I've been called a dog. But – it's best to have me on your side, even if you are an innocent.'

They raid the place, the restaurant.

Air lifts the scrolls we see inside – sages in forests, with tigers – a screen with sages, some stringing cash, some grinding ink . . . some roasting bones, some sealing a letter to a taxman . . .

'Liliane and Hervé should be here,' says the cop, Marianne.

'I told you everything,' I say.

I only wanted Liliane to myself. Now it's a raid – they'll all be disappeared . . . 'What have they done?' I ask.

'What are you innocent of?' asks Marianne. 'You won't say. So, I can't tell you what those two are guilty of. We have them come inside. Mostly, they confess. We all watch TV. That's what you do, to move it all along. Confess. Those animals – we're animals. Are you certain it's about them, not us, the hunting and the eating? Côte d'Ivoire, China – they're both a ways off . . .'

'So, we don't eat?' I ask.

'They've all run out the back, and left the sages in the breeze,' she says.

'Perhaps it's those questions about Rousseau,' I say.

'No, no,' she says. 'Those Chinese have it in their bones, like it was seaside rock. Salvation. Species-being. No, behind it, there's some other stereotype.'

The more we wait for Liliane, the more I miss her.

'Old crimes,' says Marianne, 'They wear you down. A bore.'

'I'm sure I'll still be innocent,' I say.

I hear her whisper, 'human flesh'. 'You know,' she says, 'a species stressed – often turns to being cannibal. Those articles in the magazines – freedom, cooking. Travelling around and gawping at the poor. It's quite a class thing. And all these restaurants. The city has a reputation . . .'

'How'd you stop becoming some appetising dish?' I ask.

'The remedy? It's meth, or antifreeze, bush beer: purple Jesus. Drink it; like Alice. Your flesh is tainted. Won't get past the chef.'

'So Alice – it was all about the running to avoid becoming sacrifice and being gobbled up?' I say, amazed. 'The rabbit hole – œsophagus? Then, journeying through intestines?'

'Oh well,' says Marianne. 'We girls – we've always had the problem as a metaphor – the "being eaten up". And now – we all, you boys as well – must make ourselves inedible. I told you – it's the stress. The banquets with the leaders – the big cheeses: they sweat and eat some speciality that's overdressed and overnamed. A subject: a person and a topic too. Subjects – chewed over. What else do you expect?'

'I followed the crowd,' I say. 'I thought it was our struggle against nature, identifying problems, conferences, the solution . . . Instead, we struggle to avoid the à la carte . . .'

She leans against me. She smells rank, her hair – hot, greasy, metallic. More cops arrive, sit on the sidewalk, pass round anonymous demijohns.

'Our work is easy,' Marianne says. 'The guilty come and see us. Or they don't. It's all the same. But – it's the stress, the changes to our nature, to our flesh. From words to deeds, from metaphor to fry and roast.'

'Or raw – like in Piemonte,' I say, remembering the *carne cruda* . . .

Sweeney's pies. I push Marianne some way away.

'Liliane and Hervé – in danger, Marianne,' I say. 'But from each other? Or from us? Or from what's browsing in the forest?'

'Oh, silly boy,' she laughs. 'There's so much you sages brood about. We're all innocent, until we aren't.'

The diner's empty now. The pictures, the sages – disappeared. The Chinese – fled. The wind comes in the back, ruffles the drinking cops.

'I loved the raid,' says Marianne. 'Those bad suspicions – then . . . all innocent! Blown away. You wanted Liliane for yourself, and so – you snitched. The tale about the animals,' she laughs. 'None of them complains or witnesses. The restaurant – that was more promising: so innocent. What joy! Too late! for everything, you naughty boy. Too late for Liliane . . . for jungle beasts . . .'

'Marianne,' I say, 'you are my type.'

'You sneak,' she says, approving. 'We'll find a use for you. We're not the kind that shoots. It's anticipation that we do: prevision. Catastrophe our speciality. You're nervy too. You could be an informant, paid. Sleep free in a cell.'

We go back to her lair, her commissariat. It smells of spirits. Boxes have come. 'Aha!' she says. '*Metaxas* brandy! The Greeks – they pay their debts in kind. They don't bear gifts, not any more.'

Yves, Alain: the big chief – Apollinaire. The supercops . . . they stagger in, start on the brandy, chasing it, catching it with . . . *Fix* beer.

'We have another insight,' says dear Marianne. 'Of course – we cops are always paid and work our hours. But soon, all the rest here will be unemployed. Then they'll have to work twelve hours a day, sitting before their screens, competing with the rest. All underpaid and hunting for the cheapest stuff . . .'

I tell her about the past, the forest, and Sandrine: 'Oh, the old intelligence!' laughs Marianne. 'She must be one of us! Intelligence is quite passé. Only us cops have jobs – but when you're fired, you work on literature, you follow some poor guy and find what real life is like . . . Sandrine had chosen you, by chance, by intuition, who can tell. She's a loose molecule: she doesn't drink, so in the forest, she'll meet up with cannibals, her flesh is sweet, free-range, a leggy chicken with that beak . . .!'

'That's awful, I suppose,' I say. 'But patience! There's Beatrice – watching over her dead warrior, Marcel. A classic lover. Maybe he will rise again. And Liliane – bringing raw nature to her Chinese comrades . . . Maybe the Party will resuscitate.'

'You teeter, as you sages do, between unlikely and impossible,' says Marianne. '. . . Mostly what you know is cops or crooks. You come with us! We're cops who know our crooks, you bet! We are the best of worlds. We know what's coming next. You don't.'

'I hear the voice of high romantics, Marianne,' I say. '"Roncevaux!", those *"bruits prophétiques"* before the deaths of paladins!'

'Yes,' she says, 'but hark the voice, the breath of Corneille . . . his Roman verses, his *"verres de rhum"*! Too bad you're abstemious – we can't do without them.'

She drinks: the brandy tastes of meths. Her flesh – would burn: a flaming candle.

'Of course,' she says, 'guys who would fight – we hope to send them overseas. We're keenly orientalist, of course: we don't want fighting here!' she laughs. 'We're lay. Only those who don't believe can truly love all faiths . . . the plainsong, Kaddish, El Andalus – music alone is worth our obol . . .' and she drinks some more. 'The disputes going on around,' she says, 'are nothing, when you look at what we prophesy.'

She fits me with a cell. I'm a joyful jailbird – a lark, a mynah, face to face with judgement. Cells are so snug, so tight – the cot's a plank, a branch, a twig: there's nothing you can do in them except have sex.

'Your nose,' she says, 'it's much too sensitive for frontline tussling. I have to smell this way . . . There were the Chinese too – and Sandrine's nose . . . I fear we're stuck in the motif: the Nose. Blow it, blow it away – light my fire, huff and puff the wind, the meths . . .

Sandrine, running with her flaming hair, a torch amid the forest . . . a fox with brands tied to its tail, setting the world . . .'

'No, no,' I say. 'Keep calm. Those trees – too wet to burn.'

'It's the idea,' says Marianne. 'The renegade. The wild card, heretic. The one who's fired. Not very bright, but burning with resentment. That's where the talk of justice comes, smouldering, infiltrating . . . Getting up your nose.' She laughs and drinks.

'You guys,' I say, 'must often go to court . . . the judges and their rites . . . such bores . . .'

'Oh, absolutely not!' she says. 'We're not judgmental. If you confess, or lie – you go before the beak. Nothing to do with us. How'd we know, or care, what badness marks your history? You write it down in here – away it goes. Maybe – you end with mercy. Maybe – the guillotine, castration with the knife or pill, the dark, the yard, the rope . . . or history that's turned to time: to days and years, white, shiny as enamel, stainless steel. On, on – a perfect life. No incident, no fault, no triumph. Just . . . a duration. Too long to count, too long for mathematics. Nature ageing, in the hole and in the grave. Apotheosis. Beatification, not a sin or smirch . . .' The brandy carries her along – a riff, a long wave, a lagoon of unevent.

Marianne pulls me forward, says to the chief, Apollinaire, 'He doesn't drink. He's wise, they say. We'll stack the booze in here.' The cell is full. They lock the door. Should I enjoy the perfect life – no sin, original, banal, no good deeds, no epiphanies? It's duration, gestation without birth. It's dark in here – sometimes a cop comes in, the light goes on, they take some bottles from a case – a case that never travels, box never buried. If it's a womb I'm in – am I a foetus, do I grow tails and fins, and see them spin away? Or grow to beast size, scales or tufty hair, an appetite, spiked tail, teeth longer than a thumb – and then revert, go back to starter cells, a prison where the sentence grows – there's years to go, and then you calculate – no! there's time you've done, and time to do. One time's immense – the other tiny . . . the future; long, or just a day: the past – a milliard of years, or else . . . you can't remember yesterday.

I might draw upon these walls – they're rock-hard, though: I've my blood – the red, the white, revolution or Bourbon – like Stendhal. The Danish flag – the making of new Germanies, the blood, the oil anointing. Must I draw all that? And all the rest? Me? I've done no wrong – and if I have – here, I can do no more . . .

'Don't dramatise,' says Marianne. 'There's millions like you. You've earned a life of rest, of doing nothing. No suffering, your meals left in a trap. There's just no use for you outside. Your hands and brain are slow, you don't cheer the heroes, don't roll over, die for your country, don't donate head or heart. It won't begin! Nothing you might want . . . Just rest!'

It's true – the place is warm. Always the food is punctual, identical to all the other meals. I have a past. It seems quite trivial: I think – what was the fuel that smells like this, the brandy cut with meths: was it 'metaldehyde'? I had a toy, grandfather passed it on – a tiny sawmill, worked by steam. You heated up the boiler with the tab of meths. 'Metaldehyde'? Marianne has asked around. They don't remember it: 'A miniature sawmill? Where's the fun? Just trees?'

'Fun? No, not for that at all.' I say. What then?

Apollinaire, the chief, comes in. 'I looked it up,' he says. 'It's poison. Used for slugs. It kills all animals, and people too . . . It's not a toy. It burns, it kills, it prowls and roars and crawls – blows steam. We'll work on it. Our finest sleuth . . . Maybe we're doomed. Maybe the world comes to an end if there aren't slugs and snails . . .'

'We're proud of you,' says Marianne to me. 'This is a most unusual lead . . .'

'Marianne,' I say, 'I'm wise. I may have got it wrong . . .'

'No, no,' she says. 'It fits: a sawmill, a steam boiler. Play with it – it gives no satisfaction – but . . . The trees. The forest. Strange fuel, that poisons everything. Sandrine, the emissary – birds and blue . . .'

We cuddle on the bunk. 'A bigger cell,' says Marianne, 'means you might have to share. So what was bigger ends up smaller yet – with guys appraising what we do, the cuddling, all that stuff. It might affect your perfect life, that's best lived on your own. Though I will come to you, and you can think of me as fantasy. Keep yourself pure, unique . . .'

*

They love me here. Peoples move, new bombs are tried: new states are forged, the old ones totter, crumble into ruins, terracotta – buy your ticket here . . . look on, walk round. But my – your, everyone's – catastrophes – they hunt you down. They're quite unstoppable, and only I foresee . . . who lurks among the trees, carting us all away; its bloody jaws, its appetite – primed.

'Exchange of children, Marianne,' I say. 'The rich ones go down south. The nordics raise a swarm of swarthy urchins The parents visit – see what the good life is, and what's the hard . . . Infanticide there'll be, you bet. Quotas and fingerprints. But once again, at last, a global breed. Like at the start – the colour indeterminate, the sizes mixed. Running, painting, inventing the epics and their gods. Eating grubs and iguanas.'

'We love you!' Marianne shouts out for all to hear. 'But – don't steal our booze.'

'You know, we don't do guilt and innocence,' says Apollinaire. 'We never have. A bullet in the head, and down the cellar steps you go . . . no philosophical stuff. Or – we'll help! Away your habit! . . . Watch your health and don't do pills. It's all the same to us. And so – we guess at ends. Conclusions. What the finish is. We're the drunken kings, we trace out on our stele: 'This way? Or that? We told you so . . .' a stele made of rock so hard that when we all burn up – it will survive, take off. A meteor. Zoom round the universe – a lark ascending, dropping, always twittering. Our message, to odd beasts on other worlds . . .'

'It's genius,' I say. 'I'm proud to be alongside . . .'

'Oh no! You're not!' says Apollinaire. 'Not one of us. No comrade. We fight. You sleep. Scratch Marianne's itch, sometimes. We drink, we rule. You potter through your forest . . . Looking for Sandrine . . . she looks for you as well. She's old school. No mercy. "You're a pacifist? Try on these boots – and go! Go kill Armenians, Kurds, whatever's in your way. The trees are thick, they hide all things, you think."'

'No, I don't think that . . .' I say. He doesn't listen. Here, no one does. It's all surmise, assuming. The end is certain – the music's alcohol. It has to end, that's for sure – the singers' voices melt and crumble, they sizzle out like bacon in the pan.

Suddenly – there's light. 'Hervé was right!' shouts Marianne. 'Those animals! We call them species – they don't know a jot. It's families for them, and then you have to stop the dad from eating the new brood. Conditions too – quite primitive. Those elephants – they trek a thousand miles, just for a drink.'

I see she's holding out her glass to me. Bourbon, chased with some Schlitz so flat it tastes like pee.

'There's migrations and there's floods and droughts,' she goes on. 'You save one kind – there isn't food! Those roaches on your wall – they multiply, your shoes are worn with massacring. It isn't worth it. Vanity, oh vanity! Save ourselves – that is the clue. The animals – cut them up and ship them out. We'll keep a few – there's swimming pools – a rhino here, a hippo there to wallow in your mud. And there's an end to it. If there are tourists – they lie like seals upon the beach. Who wants to stumble through the reeds to tread on snakes . . .?'

I ask, 'And when you've cleared the places inhospitable?'

'Oh well,' she says, 'there's evolution. Maybe your bugs will grow and eat the cats.'

'So Hervé works for you?' I ask. 'And all your colleagues plan like this?'

'Oh we're the best,' she says. 'Elite. But somewhere at the top there's laid-back guys. Mission, they're called. For every continent must have a Mission – for some, it's digging holes. Others – it's building tall. Respect. Or prayer. Dams. Each has a forest – some have trees, and some have metaphor. You know our history,' she says. 'The human dialectic. Some, our distant friends, down to the abyss: the Abyssinians. The gas, the rope, the axe. Others – they got enlightenment. They all go in the forest, and we cherish them.'

'It sounds quite simple, Marianne,' I say. 'It is a splendid panoply, set out like this.'

'I know,' she says, 'we can't be satisfied. Not yet. Maybe Mission will come up with something fresh. Between us, for example: there's an obstacle. You're a genius, I've my stripes – and yet we have the grungiest hetero sex. No genius there. Pedalling the cycle of our history. Death to birth and back again. Of course, there's empire . . . being the best. But then – you worry that your savings may run out . . .'

'That sounds like Mission's job,' I say, not wanting to be involved. 'Sorting things out.'

'I'll leave the door unlocked, and you can come and see us dance. You must be quiet,' she says. 'We dance. You watch.'

They're in Reception. It's quite dark. Hervé and Liliane are sitting there, ignoring me, eyes brightly following the cops, all padding round, a soft-shoe shuffling, stooped like pelicans. There's ritual music – sounds like doors: opened and closing, tinkly keys that turn. Catchy, banal, it gives the beat and nothing more.

'Apollinaire's the genius of the song and dance – the anvil chorus gave him the idea,' says Marianne, joining the circle, plodding round. 'He saw guys do the hokey-cokey. We cops do booze, not cokey – this way, we take our leisure, slow things down. You could say it is our hocus-pocus,' and she giggles.

The tape loop goes round and round. Sometimes there's hocketing: maybe the tape is flawed. They know the rhythm from their bones . . .

They're together, in the womb – a pack, pride, gaggle – a fraternity. It is a primal scene.

'There!' says Marianne. 'It's done. We're back into our roots, the filaments renewed and sucking hard. That's how the cops began, that was the dance.'

Cops start to drop out the circle, flopping down. I hear Liliane say to Marianne, 'Hervé's a genius – and it took you to see it. Those animals – they're cannibals, just like us. Some guys go on about salvation for them – in the end, they all get ate! Some even kill more than they can eat – like us. And now you've set us up in here – a cell for two, so snug . . .'

Marianne points to me. 'It was him, started us off. His line, about our species fate.'

Liliane looks at me with interest. 'I thought he was just the common crooked sort,' she says. 'Making friends and having sex with them – leaving them to moulder in some tacky room.'

'Things that have to be, they are,' I say, lightly. 'You're in false problems, Liliane. We humans – forget the clockwork ones they make to fly the bomber planes – we can be herbivores. A snip to the intestines, and it's done. The animals will do as they have always done – fend for themselves. The problem then's a different one, it's not just putting bromide in the tea to calm the anxious soul. It's watering the grass. A major project, even if we had the wherewithal. Can grass grow watered with our oil? Probably – it can't.'

They look at me with wonder.

'Daisies,' says Marianne. Maybe it's rapture in her eyes. 'In the grass. Daisies, everywhere. Nothing to lose but your daisy-chains.'

'Hodge with his scythe again,' says Liliane. 'At school, only poetry . . . then – dinner on the grass.'

'The grassy stage,' sighs Marianne. 'The lovely green. Ensared with flowers, I fall on grass . . . The hay ropes – love binds love as hay binds hay . . . Though – how'd I choose between you and Hervé?' she asks me.

'With all that feast of grass,' I say, 'you needn't decide. You could smoke some, while you mow some. The quest – unnecessary. Peace. The wisdom of the elephants, the cows. Like we were, in the Garden. Don't eat the fruit. No steaks.'

'With this brilliance, we should send you up, our new star born, to Mission. Shining there . . .' says Marianne.

Out of the cell. Wonderful!

'Mission,' says Marianne, dreamily. Then – 'But . . . there's a warning. If they don't like you, your ideas – it's oblivion. You live – but you're invisible. Can't even spray on walls.'

'Tell me, Marianne,' I say. 'Oblivion's physical characteristics. A box? Hotel? A compound, hole or slot?'

'How should we know?' she asks. 'Oblivion means you're never seen again. How can we know what kind of space you're in? Or if it is a space: maybe it's a solid, a cone, a plastic slab, a slide for cultures. For sure – they don't break out Metaxas there.'

'Maybe . . .' I hesitate. 'Since ideas are anonymous, no given cause, effect, or source or end . . . I'd send them up to Mission, nameless. Stay in my cell.'

'That's what I thought,' says Marianne. 'That way, we get the credit if they're good.'

*

The folder comes back, quick. It's marked INOPPORTUNE.

'What does that signify?' I ask Marianne.

'We don't get given credit. We're sent out, into the field. It's better than Sandrine had. She went to the forest . . . Yours . . .' she says, 'with no way out. The field means open season. Running like hares.'

'My forest – is quite a different kind,' I say. 'Domestic. Not like . . .' I don't know any other forests. If we go to eating grass – we'll cut them down.

'Mission means,' says Marianne, 'the time is wrong. Maybe the idea is good. Or bad. Or both. Usable on friends, or enemies, or what each might become. Not now. And not to be discussed.'

'Well,' I say, 'that's pretty good for me. It's genius.'

'If that's enough for you, you're happy, dear,' says Marianne, thrusting disguises in her kitbag. 'We'll have a party; now, for us, it's sober, clean and pure . . .'

*

They move forward in the field, the cops, slow as stone-pickers, clue-hunters. I hear Marianne say to Apollinaire, 'Did I forget to open Hervé's cell before we left?'

I feel I've lost my pace. I oughtn't be here, not with them. I am not trained.

Apollinaire carries a small hunting horn, a slughorn, tight coiled, a snail's shell. There's fugitives, scampering here and there, into the trees, stumbling through the stony soil. The cops' eyes are always down. 'Marianne!' I shout. She looks towards me. Tears have furrowed down her dusty face.

'Why are you suffering so?' I ask.

'You're so evil, all of you,' she sobs. 'There's nothing to be done for you. Our futile lives – and yours.'

Sometimes Apollinaire raises the horn: he toots, and coughs. 'See,' says Marianne, 'he's bronchial. Crime seizes one more victim, innocent, as we presume.'

What can they be looking for? There's nothing there. Mystery is heavy, planned: you don't just come on it. If you're stupid, everything is mystery and unexplained. No – it must be the end. The order is to seek – not their end, or mine: just the end of that particular job, that field, that soil. They want a rest – being told they've done it well: now stop! Do something else.

I walk away. No one turns round. The fugitives outrun them, as they plod, lockstepped. In front of them – a wood.

*

A relief – standing here, reared up, the bar! . . . They give me space. I'm a police spy. It's good.

'Give me some of all of those,' I say, and point: it always tastes of meths, until it gives you wooden tongue.

A guy says, 'I oughtn't tell you this. There is a point where three states meet – Arizona, Nevada, and the big one . . . nowhere special. Void . . . There, they've made another state. It's oil. A compound. Some razor wire, a padlock, and some pumps. My brother has the key. He is its only citizen. The monopoly of force is his, the sovereign power. For cash, you could take the nationality. A passport. Photos of the trucks that come and drink . . .'

'Oil?' I say. 'A gas monkey? That's hardly cool! And – being a subject. . . what's the point?'

He moves so our shoulders touch. 'Don't you have other brothers?' I ask. 'Energy – even closer to the earth?'

'I see you like the dance,' he says. 'My Chechen brother, now . . . He loves to dance. The steps are simple.'

'I come from the trees,' I say. 'The architecture there in Chechnya . . . not organic . . .'

'We could attack your commissariat,' he says. 'They must have liquidity.'

'Liquid days, for sure,' I say. 'I'm sure it's all ingested, though.'

'My twin in Mission, then,' he says. 'That's your star to sail by . . .'

'You promise me,' I say, 'that your brothers, and the options, are all real.'

'Oh yes,' he says, drawing a glum face in spilt beer with the bottom of his glass. 'As real as I am empty.'

'The States: cash, possibly arrest?' I say.

'They don't like tiny states that bud,' he says. 'It presages a separation. They might shoot,' he says.

'Chechnya,' I say. 'It attracts. Even more – a raid on the police jail, except . . . I'd love to spring my friends, of course, but if you come from Mission, as you say – it's all a trap.'

'It's true,' he says. 'Drink lets me down. My secrets – I can't retain. It is the human touch. I fawn on you, I beg your sympathy.' He weeps.

'The mission,' he says, brightening. 'You know what they will say. "Salvation. Liberation . . ." Oh my friend,' he shouts, 'it's repetition. Millions of years, we stare into the fire and say "Take us away – out of this cave, this stony field. Show us the way." They show. Thousands of tracks. You know – I could turn my coat. Take you to my brothers – none of them's convinced it's worthwhile gazing in the fire, the forest, thumbing the clouds and turning them to see the face on the other side . . .'

'Xavier!' I cry. 'We could go to your brother with the gas. Beans in hot sauce. I hate the delicacies, the subtleties, the smears of tortured grublike droppings on a plate . . .'

'Wait!' says my friend, my Xavier. 'My brother's into zen. He weeps for *dashi* – for remembrance, spirit food . . . After a month with him, your stomach grows so small, it's saltier, sallower than – a peanut . . .'

'The trucks? The cops?' I ask.

'There'd be us three. All innocent and free. If they attack – we put a match and up! goes all the store.'

He shows a home movie: there's the guy, covered in hair, like the hairy Ainus in the books, putting a red tongue out at the camera. We see him eat some beans out of a can.

'Of course, he doesn't get to handle cash,' says Xavier. 'Those waterbutts – that's where he tries to grow his *dashi*. You could look after that.'

The guy is filling up a Routemaster – there's a line, identical, waiting, like in your toyshop fantasy.

'To me,' I say, 'it looks like once there was a civilisation. That is all that's left.'

'Don't be a fascist bastard,' Xavier says, pushing me to the asphalt. 'The best cultures pick and mix the rest. Besides – ends and starts. They are the same. In the book it says, "In the beginning was the dark. And in the end – quite similar." Except, of course, there's starlight. You could make a song . . .'

'What about the word?' I ask. 'That got things moving.'

'It's meaningless,' says Xavier. 'A shout's a shout – across the universe, it comes out like the roaring bull. It could have been a bomb, of course.'

'I guess the Indians found the gas, and left your brother pumping it,' I say. It seems improbable.

'You could dig down,' says Xavier, 'find artefacts that say you're right.'

'Your brother in Chechnya,' I say. 'What would I do there? Are they good Muslims? Do I have sheep?'

Xavier shows me photos: there's guys in black, like crows, hunching through a stamping dance.

'The architecture's big, but rather naff,' he says. 'The thing is – to choose your clan. Not big enough to have you watched, nor small, so's you're not covered.'

'It's the wide streets that scare me, Xavier,' I say.

'The trouble is,' he says, 'you want philosophy. You don't get that from touring round.'

'Then – the assault. The commissariat,' I say.

'Everyone should do one, an attack: against repression, even the symbol, that's for sure,' he says. 'Especially an empty fort. But – reflect: it could be exactly what Mission wants. You wouldn't know what side you're on.'

'We could shout the Word,' I say.

'Your trouble is nothing to do with words,' says Xavier. 'You've collected all these people. Women. Dead, in the forest, in the field, in jail. What good does all that do? Salvation? Liberation? Those are opposites, you know.'

'The cops are in the field,' I say. 'We need to help my friends. A start. A finish. We alone. The radical guys – they're bored. They don't fit in. They go to being Tories . . . They're a drag on us, no help at all. Now, what word? Who should we say we are? What is the shout?'

'Drama – you don't see it stalking round, laying a hand on what's immediate. The happening is not political. It doesn't shout. The bodies lie there, silent in the street, the ditch. No word. It's only after, someone writes it up – it's tragedy or justice. Until then – it's digging holes and keeping borders solid on the map,' he says. 'You want some drama. It won't be up to you.'

'And if you're right – what then?' I ask.

'There is no help,' he says. 'You only get the bill when you have drunk.'

'It's time for me to make a stand,' I say. 'Or else – it's having no leg, no principle.'

'I can get the key,' he says. 'A gun. You can decide which suits you best.'

'You can do anything, dear friend,' I say to Xavier: we both act drunk. For me – the first time in many years. Him – I don't know. It's not only time that counts.

We run into the fortress, waving keys and guns. My friends, my loves, Liliane, her *Ivoirien*, Hervé . . . I guess I shout to them, their names perhaps.

The cell, all the cells, they're empty, naturally.

*

'It's a rehearsal, Xavier,' I say. 'The greater hope has gone, long gone, but . . . No one is hurt.'

'You weren't ready, but we shan't try it over,' he says.

'I hardly touched my drink,' I say. 'It was vainglory in my heart: and friends owed . . .'

'Whatever drove you,' Xavier says, 'it's now an empty page. Ready for the pen. Corpses? Those abound. Some can be stuck on you. Motivations? Yours, I'd assign to history. That obscures and dignifies.'

'Blackmail?' I ask. 'And falsity? Surely, my friend . . .'

'Those may come after,' Xavier says. 'Meanwhile, give back that gun.'

Being trapped – it's always been a desire, a fancy. The king fish they all seek – caught, tumbling – he'll escape. It's certain. Traps are for that.

How to proceed? Follow a lead? A leader?

Apollinaire – straight as a stick: his face be-whiskered, mutton-chops plucked from fat ewes. His affectation – a smudge of ginger in his hair. A lord of intellect: no leader, though. But Xavier – under the fortress searchlights, I see his skull, its fuzz buzzed off reveals the bone, a red thought squirms below . . . two small blue wings impasted just above the ears. A comic nose, pores open like a pepperpot. Is it with this, this golem, Xavier, that all my life achieves its climax? Does it finish so – loves shooed away, finding new men beneath the trees, dealers from Africa . . . one day they'll all arise, directing great enterprise? Was it this Xavier – who 'cuffed the Arsènes, assassinated, and redeemed . . .'?

'Yes,' says Xavier. 'And I'm the top. You're promoted. Stand below me. Have faith. Faith in yourself – that's the best kind, inviolable, proof against all heresy.'

'What must I do . . .?' I ask.

'Forget.' says Xavier. 'You'll never embrace La France. Marcel won't start his book . . . Forget the *taiga* where you left Sandrine . . .'

'A book!' I say. 'Marcel didn't write, he just had friends. And – Sandrine's forest – it was tropical. See the birds, the salamanders . . .'

'Forget it all,' says Xavier. 'You have new masters now. You're enrolled. On plural lists. One day your uniform will come – don't fret.

We'll pay you, take some back. You'll demonstrate, to vote for me and mine . . . rewards will come.'

'This is banal,' I say, 'even if there's worse.'

'Yes,' Xavier says. 'The worst is running in the forest, eating slugs and snails. That – you might remember, friend. Live with the banal, that's what there is.'

'What exactly did you have in mind for me?' I ask. 'I sink to the bottom of things, you know. I don't have a bunch of dangerous friends . . .'

'I'm thinking,' Xavier says, 'I was hasty. I thought you were a Syrian, something similar – they all speak like you.'

'I know,' I say. 'You see people from all over, they look like you, but of course, they're not . . .'

'No!' says Xavier. 'No banality! No stereotypes. My first guess – is usually the right one. Don't say we're alike, because – a moment, and you realise that you aren't.'

'But you'll pay me,' I say. 'Even if I'm not what you thought?'

'Oh,' he says, 'I know nothing of you. You don't get paid for not being like I might have thought you were.'

'That's good, then,' I say, and remember Sandrine, who went through the same complicated argument.

I feel I must apologise – after all, we waved those arms together, shouted out the word.

'I could go back,' I say, 'though people don't seem to like me there.'

'People don't like people much, not now, not anywhere,' he says. 'It's just a fad. Like wanting to be liked. The problem is – you're not an Arab. Even Iranian would have done . . .'

'Sandrine knew that I was clean, but quite impure,' I say.

'Sandrine was just a novice, I expect,' says Xavier. 'A fugitive. Spying gives a salary. Maeterlinck does not. You get some lustre, thinking you were worth a quest. It isn't so.'

We leave it there. There is no mystery, and no unknown. Someone somewhere knows, has set things up, and sleuthed them down.

*

'We'll sign you off,' says Xavier. 'It seems you've tried a lot of things. This cash will help you try one more. And then . . .'

'Just one?' I ask. 'It could go on for years, involve a goodly company . . .'

'That's why there's not much cash,' says Xavier. 'I'm not a lucky well. You should seek out, identify, the virtues. Practise them. It shouldn't take you long, if that's your niche. Science tells us – either the universe is meaningless, or else it's part of meanings so immense we're in the wrong place to grasp what they might be. What has some sense is little things: a cause, and an effect. Conception – birth. Birth – death. Like that.'

'Maybe an enclave, then,' I say. 'Who knows where the new Soviet men have fled?'

'It sounds your place,' says Xavier. 'Maybe there's a forest near. But – those new men . . . they've gotten old. The old ones, new, then old again. You're right – the Russian people, good, courageous: fighting for the better . . . but! – watch out! the tiger's at the gates, and inside, we – kittens in the basket – bloody and mangled.'

'Those flat, empty fields,' I say. 'It's true – they frighten me. And yet – people walking down the muddy roads at dawn. The useless birch trees. It's fresh. It's my globe. The thing is – there, the bad guys, they're so rich, if you don't cross them, they don't trouble you. In the States, though, there's lots of bad guys poor as well. You're never safe. Can't get across the road . . .'

'Well, anyway, that's not your choice,' says Xavier. 'There's enclaves everywhere. No law, no faith, not many roofs to shelter you. Do I see you, with your big Russian gun, go hunting in the coppice, brown animals or grey, and blast them? Away with the frustration . . .

Then – finding they're quite inedible, unprofitable. The meat? Gone in the smoke. An animal? What can it leave, what can it give? It leaves a *boutade*: a soul, a nose, a snout, a skin, an overcoat. Like you, the joke transmogrifies, a little devil leads you in the dance, and round and round you twirl . . . To die like this – it's better never to be born. No: it isn't you. Go somewhere else.'

'Maybe,' I say, alarmed, 'I'm waiting for an Ariadne, leaving me a trail . . .'

'Hohoho,' he laughs. 'Who remembers her, the name? No, my friend – you've got it wrong. Those enclaves – don't protect you from the state – the states war over them. And you think your state will let you be! Those that don't give you any of your money back, they are the worst: you have to celebrate them, then, they send you off to war with cardboard boots . . .'

'Your views are quite banal,' I say. 'Though maybe it's as simple as all that . . .'

'Intelligence is best,' says Xavier. 'There is protection. Spies don't work too hard. It all pops on your little screen. And you get paid for telling tales. Remember – states is difficult: and just wait. It gets worse – you have neighbours, enemies.'

'Oh,' I say, 'I don't feel I'd live near anything. It menaces.'

'You haven't understood,' he says. 'We cops and suchlike – we're the good. Where you seek to live – your mates, your *potes* – is fear and crime. Profit and debt, slavery, old age – the markets where they sell your brides, exchanges where they set a price upon your kids . . . That's where you want to live? No! We're the protectors. We live parallel to your society, your pick-and-mix – making our rules, hunting you bad guys down. Stopping your tricks . . .'

'Marianne – she didn't tell me this,' I say.

'Of course,' says Xavier. 'We pretend it's all your better side come out. You think you make the rules. It isn't so. Everybody always knows the rules – it's us, the spies and cops, that live by them. Marianne – she was exemplary. Discreet. Cops are like that. They plod the fields. It's penance, and it's purity. Not what you'd boast about . . . You're still hung up on Greeks. Symmetry. Good and bad. No! There is no symmetry: you're good or bad, not both, make no mistake. Moderation. Nonsense – they were into slavery and misogyny, just like now. Beauty. Crap! Statues? Those tiny rabbits' penises on thin, unmuscled frames . . . None of that is prized. Beautiful women – definitely on the bad side. Then there's the gods. An extended family, with powers, blunting the accidents, having favourites. Screwing nymphs. They got chased away – then gods appeared who knew secrets and were good! It all obscures the work we do, and what we are.'

'What you are? Bad cops? Bad spies?' I ask.

'In theory, yes, it's possible,' he says, offhand. 'But arcane. A mystery not worth the solving. Our finger into every cake.'

I'm in confusion. 'Xavier,' I say. 'You say you're into everything, and in control. But – there's no control! The standard – what you guys have. Distrust of all enthusiasm, all expedients. I love excess. I couldn't live like you.'

'It's true. And – maybe we exaggerated right now- shooting out the glass in our own fort with our own big guns, running away, giggling. I'll atone, you can be sure. But – you've had the offer,' Xavier says. 'To enrol. Refusal means your penance will be deeper, and, let's hope, it's surer too.'

The song says, 'I'm never going to give you / Anything you wish.' That's a good sentiment. I give Xavier the gun. He stares at it, like it's a snake. He's right – those gods, saying they made all the accidents – that can't be true. What's gone – is all rehearsal. Why are there six planets? Why are they different, why don't they communicate, have the same minerals? Sandrine, Liliane, Marianne . . . The planets have French names – it takes centuries to reach the nearest. You can't say they're friends – they're like Marcel, silent on his cot, going round and round the sun.

Xavier says, 'Write down my offer to have you enrolled. Show it round. It will help you for ever.'

I sit and write it down. If it works . . . there's no opponents, no bad, no crime. We're all good guys. Who will resist? This is the best job there is, spying on people, arresting them. It convinces me. This is the path rich people follow. I'm certain. I'm not convinced . . .

A guy sits beside me. I hope I don't smell the same. I shift away. He says, 'There's many ways to fail. Only one to succeed.'

'You can't be sure of that,' I say.

'I write songs,' he says. 'Music for improvised instruments, the notes, though, rigorous. I can't handle the blobby sticks, so I write it down in sounds.'

I nod and shift further. 'They say it's the interpretation,' says the guy. 'That makes the difference. It's not. There's only one interpretation, the right one. It's the instruments that matter.'

'I see that,' I say. 'I'm going where they already have their music, instruments as well. What I need's a name. The name of the place I'm going. Or, at least, the mineral to dig, the animal to save. Something to orientate me.'

'I'll draw you a map of the world,' he says. 'And write you a ticket to your place.'

It seems far-fetched. The map is very detailed. Why shouldn't it be accurate?

'You know,' he says, 'once all the crap – dead people mostly – ended up in heaven. Now it's in a warehouse on the web. Dead flies, bundled, waiting for their spider. Don't be fooled. Don't use my ticket unless you're really gullible.'

'I guess you know the dead places . . .' I say.

'You have a category problem, my friend,' he says. 'A map is one thing. A baobab tree's another. They exist in different realms.'

'It facilitates the wilful error,' I say. 'Surrealism, for instance.'

'Ah yes,' he laughs, 'it's here, this place . . . La France . . .'

My hair arches up, hearing her name. Her place. I'm a master of coincidence. I'd be a wizard at blackjack. But – it happens everywhere, all the time. The gods make accidents and good luck. They – and you – know the difference, but . . .

'This was the centre of decapitation,' says the guy. 'Now they do opera . . . Is there a lesson there?'

'No,' I say.

'I agree,' he says. 'Now, where do you want your fortune to be made?'

Madagascar – it seems an aberrant choice. 'Everyone and everything is there,' he says. 'And see – how easily I draw it all. A shape – island, country, continent, reminding us of nothing in particular . . . You could mistake it for a sweet potato . . .'

The guy – Kaspar? Gaspard? – says, 'I could accompany you. The journey is a beast. See, on Madagascar – the first place that we land, those Japanese. It's good I taught you how to play the game. *Go*. They're here to smuggle tortoises. Of course, the lemurs have top spot. If it hadn't been for apes, we could have ended so. With soulful eyes and furry legs. All different kinds, the diets contradictory. We have those wings, remember – giant wings, those *ailes de géant*, that stop us walking where we want to go. As lemurs, we'd have had the legs, but like the wings, they are too long to let us walk. No choice but branch to branch. Flip, flop, and fly – that was the song.'

'Gaspard,' I say, 'you're the brightest guy I've ever seen. But – this place . . . It's like every poor guy in the universe has made a trip to settle here. It's like a world – the desert, trees upside down and waving helplessly their arms, their roots – and pirates everywhere, buying up and shipping out, and good and bad in wrestling mode . . .'

'It's so,' he says. 'My project is to write the Secret History of the Malgaches. Remember how they did one on the Mongols? Well, this island – continent – it has all you'd ever want to know about the planet where we live . . .'

'I understand,' I say. 'But why . . .? The Mongols – they had
Genghiz, Pony Express, all that. But what comes out of here – except
the animals?'

'That's why the History must be Secret,' Gaspard says. 'Come with
me tonight, our way lit by the lemurs' eyes, you'll start to see what it is
all about . . .'

'Evolution is a bitch,' I say.

'I know,' says Gaspard. 'Seeing those lemurs going to waste – it
burns me up. However – I've entered you for a competition. *Go.* You
could win a tortoise worth sixty thousand bucks. Just think – a buck a
day, that's twenty years, including interest. Or you could give sixty
thousand guys a day off work, or whatever it may be they do. The
tortoise doesn't give a damn. If it makes the trip all right – a good
home's guaranteed.'

We wander through the forest lit with gloaming eyes. The lemurs
hold the trees like drunks pegged on to lampposts. Long snakes dangle
down and snatch up toads. Every kind of lumpish thing orders, dines
and eats, is eaten. For sure, there's snails and slugs. Maybe we tread on
them, and others, without their light-up eyes.

'Evolution,' Gaspard says, 'is not a strategy. It's last resorts,
reaction. It's like the history, but makes you despair.'

'There must be kings and polities, all that,' I say.

'Oh yes, we'll put them in the History,' says Gaspard. 'But where
do all these guys come from? There's Chinese, even . . . And no one
herds, the animals eat all the fruit, live in the trees . . .'

I concentrate on *Go.* Gaspard shows me wondrous things. There is
no strategy, not like *go.*

We must wear white scarves. Today's a day of abstinence. The other
players drink *sake* – I have warm water – makes me gag, but my
game's strong. I win, of course, and go in the History.

The tortoise – I dump it in the forest. It disappears into the greenery,
like water draining in the sand. If it went to Asia, it would have a life
of celibacy. Maybe here, its game is sex. That will be its strategy.

'You're a success,' says Gaspard. 'That's what Madagascar's done for you. Now – my part of the plan. It isn't mad – it's odd. Like Rameau, Lully – turning it around. Something quite new and hummable. All those centuries ago: you hear it still. Not mad then – but odd now. You got your head chopped off, if you speak ill of God . . . So – invent a lot of them, gods, goddesses, have them running round, plotting, blessing: above all – they sing! I told you about my music. There's millions here. I'll have them all – singing with the birds. A massive sound – although, it'll be heard only in Madagascar. But – at least, here, heard everywhere. So, it isn't God the father's voice: it's what it should be: harmony. Resolution.'

'The story? Words? The principals?' I ask.

'Aha! Of course!' he says. 'You want to know your role. I see you as my wild card. Working the thunder sheet, perhaps: up through the trap, in spangles, a forked tail . . . As for the chorus – you never hear the words. But you can bet – all will be transformed, and not one cent is spent . . .'

'Not giving these guys some bucks? The women? At least them?' I ask.

'No, my friend, this is art. You give out coins, and there's an end. Those poor guys – they will understand. That's the whole point of being poor. Poverty's not for cash,' he says. 'It's wall to wall, not piggy bank.'

'I understand,' I say. 'There's nothing more that you can do.'

'Exactly so,' he says. 'If you see the world as problems you can't solve, you can't do anything at all. I'll get these guys to sing. You want to give them cash? It's all statistics in your head, your sludge of capitalism . . . "They don't have much, they should have more . . ." Yes! so they shall! They'll sing my oratorio. No digs, no rigs, no bottling figs, no slicing pigs . . . And – happy? You bet! They won't need work for Mister Big, or Global Corp. They'll go back to the life they know, but richer by a length or two.'

All night, there's running up and down, some shouting, whispering, lightning strikes and owls.

'It's done,' I say. 'Not odd. Not mad. Banal.'

So, here we are again, Gaspard and I. Back on our parapet. We had success in Madagascar. Friends made in abundance too, of course. It's not the place for us.

'La France!' says Gaspard. 'Back where we started, though we are not the same. Here's where they chopped off heads. There's where they do the opera. We should have brought some parrots back, given them some luxury. Out there, it's tough for them. Wait! I've maybe got an ant or two, inside my shirt – or is it just the prickly heat? Scabies, maybe.'

We pick each other over, diligent apes. 'Travel teaches history,' I say, 'Great women, and great men. But only if you're good at games.'

I can move on from Gaspard, the oratorio . . . La France, the star – surely she'd live in Paris, not knowing I'm her destiny, awaiting, like in a game of *go*. Yet – with the pleasure in the waiting – nothing can compare, least of all – a brush-off, a repulsion. Two tortoises who wait for sixty years, virgins, anxious for good sex, and blunder past each other . . . their poor sight . . .

'My friend,' says Gaspard. 'Before I leave – a word. Forget relationships. Think of some larger things. Love does not make your world go round.'

Those larger things – when I was with Marianne – they roamed past like elephants. Her commissariat too – all new, fresh people, harvested and trussed. The old mature ones – tracking on, they smell the grass and water miles away. They don't look back, can't turn their heads. The new cops, they don't know – won't say – where she has gone.

'You'll always wonder,' Gaspard says, 'what was in my oratorio. Remember that old opera – the women turned the warriors into animals. Quite stuffed. When they betrayed, or just got boring . . . Well, where we were – that had been done. Women and animals – there they are, in Madagascar. Consider mine a sequel. Those stuffed soldiers – come alive, as animals, of course. Foraging, not fighting. They sing to everything, straight from the diaphragm. Sing to themselves, and everyone.'

'And is it joy?' I ask. I don't believe it is.

'Oh no,' he says. 'There's silence, then there's song, and silence. That is it. The universe. In my music, all life is there, just as it comes. Quite orderly, of course. On a buck a day – you can't do variations. Nor harmony and counterpoint. I don't send messages, you see – just what there is. But what a scale! There's millions singing. And what scales! No bounds, no borders: what leaps, though, and what resolutions . . .'

'You are a genius, Gaspard,' I say. 'They'll never do your oratorio like it was done in Madagascar . . .'

'That is the point,' he says. '*I'll* do it – somewhere else, and differently. Why would you want it done the same?'

'Besides,' I say, 'it isn't written down.'

'And that is what is beautiful,' he says, 'though beauty wasn't what I'm aiming at.'

I imagine those cops – in line for transplants, like cats outside the butcher's: fresh liver, please. There's an urge to be normal, but you end up doing normal, day and night. If it isn't Sodom, it's Gomorrah. You have to give hope to the women, the girls, the documents, encouragement, all hanging on and wanting treats.

'No,' Gaspard says, 'you don't have to do anything. And you – you don't give hope to anyone. If they want you, they'll come for you: and if they don't want you, the same.'

'There's the girl, Varya, comes here. That's her name,' I say, 'but she prefers Lauren. Bacall – it reminds her of the lake, Baikal. She wants me to fill her forms – conceal things from the cops. But I don't understand – what she wants, and doesn't want.'

'So – that's the end,' says Gaspard.

'She's lots of friends, she says. They'll be after me, if I get it wrong, the form,' I say. 'She loves me, speaking in a Russian way. She'll not do me harm – it's all the rest, the friends . . . Though – she does threaten.'

'Run,' says Gaspard. 'It's not for you. Besides – Russians are rich. Or crooks. If she was Syrian . . . We French, once we conquered them, I guess we ought to help them out. Sleeping in tents – they're not accustomed to them any more.'

'Well,' I say, 'it's all too tangled for me. If I were a bigger boss, I could sort them out, these troubles. But Lauren Baikal – she's locked in with me – her choice.'

'You're too conventional,' he says. 'Collecting things, people, troubles. Each one has its course, its destiny. Nothing to do with you. No one will care, the day you're dead, what you said or tried to do. They'll get it wrong, on purpose, too. Why should you bother? Do something big, that only you can grasp how immense it was, how unavailing. Be master of the universe – but don't make a movie of it, don't give interviews.'

'A different scene?' I ask. 'Maybe.'

'I see it all,' he says. 'The Russians pour their money into Varya. She becomes Lauren. And you take what you want, and in return, keep her anonymous.'

'Or change the name,' I say. 'So long as I alone possess the key.'

'Blue Bird. Blue Beard. In French there's no pattern. The words are silent,' Gaspard says. 'You keep her, invisible, *la prisonnière*, but the search is on, hunting the beauty, fluttering above, waving its sky-blue tail.'

'It's all a skill,' I say, 'what I do. Don't sneer. Varya's too dangerous for desire. Best see her as a statue – no arms to embrace, a cold sex chiselled out and sanded, impenetrable. Beauty's for reverence, emulation, not desire. It can't nestle in your cot.'

'And she?' asks Gaspard. 'What feeling is there?'

'She depends on me,' I say. 'But if not me – then, anyone.'

A mistake! Gaspard could do me down and cut me out. His eyes tell everything. Better buy a ticket off him.

'That bird,' says Varya, 'it isn't blue. It's *zhar* – not a colour, it comes from within: the burning, fire. Like the burning bride you sing about. Like fire in the gold mine . . . Noranda. Red hot down there, frigid above.'

'No!' I say. 'Not Noranda. No mines.'

'I don't burn for you,' says Varya. 'You must decide – is it good for me to have trouble back in Russia? Or do the guys here think being bad's indifferent to where you live?'

'I'm quite indifferent,' I say. 'I don't do accounts, of what you say you did.'

'Or else again,' says Varya, as she has before. 'Being good – that scores no points?'

'It depends,' I say. 'What matters is your friends, who they are and do, here, now.'

'It's entertainment,' Varya says. 'That's all they do. It is the mark of luxury. Sex, drugs, those drums – that's all. Our brains – they come from Russia. All our thoughts created there, the words, all that. So, we owe nothing here. The capital is transiting here. It's resident in Russia.'

'Just be anonymous,' I say. 'Change names quite frequently. Use lots of cash, and fritter it. No signature, no name, no trace. Live rich, and don't trust Gaspard.'

'You know,' says Varya, 'we Russians are great hunters. All through history, and before. Now there's a plan to use your *Ivoiriens*, your friend Hervé. They'll ship those animals to us, we'll hunt them on the *taiga*. This is the stuff that dreams are made of. The guys back there – they enjoy a fritter: liquored up, and shooting shapes among the trees. The shamans call it exorcism – to purify the forest, wipe out irrelevant thoughts, everything that's come between us men and nature.'

'Your scheme, your trade, is better than a law or breaking one,' I say. 'It's traffic between states. So, do I go on living in your stead? Are you just a shadow from old movies?'

'I don't call you Humphrey,' she says. 'How about Humph?'

'It's just that I'm your front. A nothing. And you're your own backcloth, nothing more,' I say.

She looks at me, her lemur eyes set like coins of black caviar in her pancake face. 'I know,' she says, 'you suffer. Who can tell, if you suffer more than me? If the revolution had been done well, we'd have been French by now, not like converted Mongols. All that's left for me is suffering. Obeying the teaching.'

'Lauren,' I object, 'obeying is what I do, so that you don't have to.'

'I obey the teaching,' she says, 'not your funny revolution, so long ago. And you get the money I should have.'

'I spend it on you,' I say, 'to keep you hidden and fed.'

'You're not even French,' she says. 'You just look for women who'll betray you. It's perverse.'

'At least there's that,' I say, and we leave it so.

Later, I ask Varya-Lauren, 'What would I do in Russia?'

'What do you do here?' she asks. 'Everywhere, there's election or appointment. You choose what's easier for you.'

'I don't want a job where I can't speak a word,' I say.

'You could hunt,' she says, 'or gather. More silently, the better.'

'Just one place attracts – maybe it no longer exists – an enclave, incorporated, or gone to rest,' I say. 'Throat-singers, those beautiful stamps – there must have been another world where they wrote letters, sent packages frequently – then, shouldering imperial eagles for the hunt.'

'You see!' she says. 'It fires you up, the hunt. You don't need Gaspard with his chords to drag you, bind you to some adventure, some outlandish place.'

'It's never serious with you,' I say. 'You'd need to talk about the future. Politics. The way it all unravels . . .'

'If you want that, read a pamphlet,' she says. 'Don't trawl for anecdotes. I have all that in my bones, it's in my hair like strychnine. Go to Russia, reverse things, grow small, grow clever – I could come and hide you, I could bottle you, keep you in a jar, for sex, you – a gherkin in a pickle,' and she laughs.

'Civilian stuff,' I say. 'I have had it bad.'

'That place – the singing, eagles,' Varya says, 'it's changed. I know the postmaster. They don't write letters any more. No stamps.'

'I could act,' I say, 'if not as agent, then as actor.'

'Forget that!' Varya says. 'No stage. I should have said – there is election, merit – then, there is enrolment. Maybe as volunteer? Everyone needs those, and Russia too. The will: the People's Will. It's in the books. They'll make some movies too.'

'I'm not into risking death,' I say. 'They say at all events, it's quite inevitable.'

'I thought you were a victim,' Varya says. 'Under the lens.'

'Oh no,' I say, 'the others were the victims – not me. I don't empathise with that – it's rhetoric.'

'Being spied on . . .' she goes on.

'Sandrine? She's just a fugitive.' I say. 'It's all in her research. She seeks, but not a thing you'd find.'

'You have to find the thread. Then, the direction. Not fighting, though,' Varya says. 'There's other things. You could be postmaster. Design more stamps. Publish the letters of the dead.'

'Letters are too ponderous,' I say. 'They're like the universe. What for? you ask.'

'If you don't want stamps,' she says, exasperated, 'then drum. Like Africa. The silent drums, the vibes, that fill the everything, that everybody uses now.'

I think, 'There's no job, no pay in that,' I say. 'I'd want a place where I can be a communist. I don't trust the others. It's my personal lullaby. I hope no one else will try it. A monkey trick. The highest stage of a low animal.'

'Oh,' says Varya. 'Where you might go is full of Old Believers!' and she laughs.

'That's it!' I say. 'Belief's a false guide. The more you experience a thing, have it before you twinkling, the more it seems to start by accident. It has, right at the start, an accident, not chance: a crunch. A collision. Two elements that meet, and then explode.'

'It all begins that way,' she says, 'the dialectic makes the universe. Then comes what you don't want, a space that moves indifferent to you and everything, inexorable. Pointless growth.'

'Oh,' I say, 'I'm reconciled. Wanting it or not – it doesn't change. What I'd like to hear is why? If you know that, all the consequence becomes banal, just rivers of those digits without hands.'

'Well,' she says, 'no one knows why. The question's naff. Decide. Sign up, put on your kettle, start to steam open orders, despatches, steal the cheques. That's the normal.'

It's a mistake. Varya pulls me in, into the labyrinth. I tell all this to Gaspard. I say, 'She knows it all. I worked it out myself, and probably I made mistakes. Why we're all here and what I should do in life.'

'Nonsense!' says Gaspard. 'She gets it off TV. The *putes* watch it all the time. They think men are all Africans, and precarious. Of course they'd say that. And the TV doesn't tell you everything. It does repeats – but things move on.'

'What do you get from it all, Gaspard?' I ask. 'All your invention. Not for cash. Recognition, a pat, a stroke?'

'I'm outside the human touch,' he says. 'Your people – what have they left? Fascism and the pizza. Here – Piaf and the guillotine. It's starts and stops, like a motor running out of gas.'

'You're right again, Gaspard,' I say. 'If you're right, you don't suffer. Not so much, at least. I'm not journeying, you know. I don't want to change myself. I know the answers about the universe – those that might affect me. I know all the ways you can put it down – on vinyl, on air, on nothing. I want to make designs – and then see what the picture's of . . .'

'Oh,' Gaspard says, 'self portraits! who cares?'

'Not necessarily, Gaspard. The picture – could be a battle – or a map. A circuit. A holy book. Tower of the winds. A Charenton . . .' I say.

'An automobile, gassed up,' he says. 'You could rough out a continent, scumble some clouds or woods. Not getting caught, for anything, and no remorse. Doing a picture – means you don't have those risks.'

*

'You're naughty!' Varya says. 'Don't believe that Gaspard! You need adventure, taking control . . . Not latching on to things that are, that mooch around the fields, that skitter into forests dark and all-encompassing.'

'It's true,' I say. 'Maybe the time has come . . .'

'For us – time always does. Maybe there was a time before there was a time . . . But now, that's all gone by,' she says.

We think about that for a while: then she says, 'My friends – we're here in France, *la douce, la belle*. But maybe America – there's hot and cold there, wet and dry . . . Everyone is foreign there. You speak the language as you please, you eat the food you brought from home . . . You, my dear – fascism and pizza, yes, you'll find those over there . . . But you're a visionary. Maybe you'll mistake the continent, and think you've gone to India . . . China . . . who can tell?'

'Yes,' I say. 'I'm an explorer, navigator, poet and philosopher. But – I need to get a global fix. On where I am. China, India – wherever it may be, to leave my mark.'

'Exactly so!' says Varya. 'You've got there by yourself. I knew it! I just start you off, and on you go, straight . . . or, rather, curved. You get to Cuba – but Colombo – that's off India. Your mistakes are poetry, prevision. Epiphanies.'

'So, Varya,' I say. 'The offer?'

'You go to Russia,' Varya says. 'You'll be the front guy, representative. The president of global corp – if that's what blows you up – a title. But – you'll have the power . . .'

'I'm not so sure,' I say. 'It seems I'd drift, rather, while you, your friends, have all the fun and do the work . . .'

'That is our sacrifice,' she says. 'Go on the high wire – and you see the roofs of the whole world. But if the wind blows . . .'

'As it does . . .' I say. 'Yes – I'll go. I'll be your representative. That is democracy. We two . . .'

'Oh no!' she says. 'In this, you are alone. You'll keep my soul, identity. My body – takes the plane: America! My spirit stays with you.'

The bargain isn't good. I think of Russian tales – the bear that lost its paw . . . bundles of souls . . .

But – Gaspard says – 'She's right! You'll keep her spirit, while her body does check-in. The question is – I'll go with you. A court needs its musician. Yet – the forests there – are full of songs and symphonies. Maybe a grassland suits? Potatoes in the loam . . .'

'No offices,' says Varya. 'You'll be in the field. A true explorer.'

'We'll meet again?' I ask.

'A real explorer returns,' she says. 'Always. Or else – how'd we know? It may seem absurd – you go in order to return. You seek to find. You risk – after, others know the way and bag the slaves. But – at least you're pure.'

So – here we are, Gaspard and I. In the field. It is immense – far off, a horde of cows huddled and sad. You'd expect some crows around, to pick among the crap.

'It's orderly', Gaspard says. 'Birds in trees. Cows unequivocal in fields – still present, even if you look away. Realism abounds, even if it isn't socialist.'

Varya instructed me. 'There, law is the ultimate punishment given to apprehended criminals. Cannibalism, incest – that's the least. Avoid the law, avoid marching crowds. Anyway, you're already in the crowd

– don't go outside. In Paris, you protest against some power or other. Where you're going, power has won its position. Respect it, and its methods too.'

'Varya is a true reactionary,' Gaspard says. 'I told you – watch TV, become a *pute*, wherever you are. I shall do exactly what I want, even if no one notices.'

'Supermarkets!' I say. 'I don't see myself at home there. It was sweeter when there was all penury.'

'It's my fantasy,' says Gaspard. 'The beautiful machines, standing in wait, not knowing what they might bring forth. The colours . . . Put them together – a show immense, a ticking – throwing out a human sound without a body, a throb that isn't life and yet . . . maybe it could become . . . If that is what you want.'

'You, Gaspard – what is it that you want?' I ask.

I think I'm taking on responsibilities for things I haven't guessed.

'Oh,' says Gaspard, 'I'm tired of broken humanisms. They remind me of those cows. Voice lessons, the casting couch . . . Careers – they nauseate, all that throat and lip and belly. It's hit and miss and tantrums, crying, dressed up in feathers, mobbed in the wings. The sounds that humans make . . . oh no.'

'What will those machines play, Gaspard?' I ask.

'They used to produce. Now, they're just engineering. Clockwork more precise than human strumming. Furnaces, kettles, pans and silos. A lower creation, but perfect in its way.'

'I see all that, Gaspard,' I say. 'It's nearly all been done before. The colours . . .?'

'Grey. Lots of it. Red fire.'

He's happy.

The police here in Russia are different from the ones I knew in France. Shorter, wider. I fear investigation. Or expulsion. With retribution. Complicity and guilt. Cannibalism, and incest – all the people round me who have disappeared, rejected my talk of love as 'inappropriate' . . .

I've no defence to anything. What is illegal? Animals for the hunt –
maybe that ought to be, but it gives a chance to everyone, and makes
some bucks. Hiding identities? Not knowing all the crimes I'm
covering . . . not really caring.

'Yes,' Gaspard says, 'your innocence is the exasperating and
unlikely thing.'

Can we fight, is that the good response? Against the world? Punches
on the nose exchanged?

'My work's expressive,' Gaspard says, boxing the air. 'Your crimes
are empty, without signature or authorship. My silences are fruiting.
You think there's nothing in them, they are voids. It may be so.' He
makes a sad face. He goes on, 'Maybe you should do a tract, talk up
some rights. But what lies underneath all that? Just that, the thing
itself. My work is profound. If there's no end, no bottom to the well –
that is the answer! That's what void, oblivion is for – the final answer.
Your stuff – has no question. So – from the start, there is no answer.'

'But Gaspard,' I say, annoyed, 'you talk about my stuff – I have no
stuff.'

'We all have stuff,' says Gaspard, 'and we go on collecting – more
and more, bringing it out and polishing, and screaming with frustration
. . . It's inaudible . . . Just as it's meant to be.'

'The something is the nothing, then,' I say, 'and contrariwise.'

'Oh,' he shouts, 'it's not as easy as all that. You have to do the
exercises, to show they're not for you. You should know – the nothing
brings you suffering. The something – that as well.'

Standing in the field, in the old factories – we look poor and
suspicious. In an office – there, you feel free . . .

I see the first lions, peeping from the birch trees. There's impala,
vaulting the cows as if they're horses in gymnasia. 'Mind the pythons,
Gaspard,' I shout to him. There's a wallow here – a hippo scouting . . .

I wonder if it's legal. Maybe this is the tip for notables – and then . . .
the rest? . . . What is their destiny?

'Gaspard,' I say, 'when can we leave? When's your concert due . . .?'

He fools around, being Laocoon, twisting some snakes around his neck. 'Oh, I could go on, found a conservatoire,' he says. 'They've nothing on me. I don't crawl to publishers. No insults in my work. No criticism, and no discords – that is still the rule. It's easy to comply . . .' and so it is.

There's a pile of vibrant boxes – marked 'leaf-cutter', 'fire', 'soldier'. There's a hardware store of worms and borers, jackals, hyenas, inedible and maybe edible . . . Bacteria, viruses, 'fatal', 'nearly fatal'. Trees and termites, sticks for sticking, poison for arrows, nets and spades for traps.

'Hervé's a literalist,' I say. 'Is this the idea? Come, guys with guns, and pin it on the wall? The continent exported?'

'Orders are orders,' Gaspard says. 'If they ordered Africa, this they get.'

The head cop says, 'No one minds being eaten by a tiger. It's a man thing. But chewed up by some clown ants . . . No one pays for that.'

'Those are the conditions,' I say. 'It's the new realism. The ants taste better than tiger. You can have them live in your house.'

'It's a political thing,' he says. 'People pay to be winners, not to die.'

I ask if he knows Marianne. 'La France?' he says. 'I know La France. *Belle.*'

It's too painful.

'Your principals,' he says, 'they know about contacts, for sure. But knowing is a way of hiding. You know – others don't. You,' he says, pinching my arm, 'you have the look of a goat on a tether. Are you a sacrifice? Are you waiting for the tiger?'

'I know about forests,' I say, 'and what they can hide. Just let me run in – there's all my friends . . .'

That's a mistake. Gaspard would have stopped me. He's still engaged – the pythons, big beasts, all over him. His art's the antithesis of serpentine, and he's wildly trying to find their top and tail, slithering up and down their length.

'I don't have friends,' I say. 'Be clear on that. I have this artist, Gaspard, who'd give you entertainment . . . spectacular.'

I think of Gaspard's critics, their poison, their embrace. The snake pit. And I laugh. It's a mistake.

The cop takes it all in, and makes it pure, like Apollinaire would.

'If you're responsible for them . . . the animals,' he begins, 'or if you leave. Or if we shoot some, leave the rest to sting and bore . . .' he pauses. 'Every question's interesting. But – you're the only part of the debate that we could put in jail. For sure, that way there's consequences that do damage – simply hunting them, pinning their fluffy suits in trophy rooms, do not.'

People, animals – fellows and comrades: how we should love them all.

Right and wrong, snakes and ladders, consequences and charades – we consider all the angles. Then, 'The trouble is,' he says, 'if there is something big, you're much too small for it, and if it's small, the same, but it's no matter.'

'Leave me aside,' I say, 'the boxes and the life will come, in profusion, just the same. My boss won't know how many beasts you've killed. He'll have an algorithm – he'll suck up felines, ship them on . . .'

We both have the idea. 'We'll make another Africa,' he says. 'Planted here. It's long been my project, my design. A forest, then a jungle . . . a refuge here, and then, new men all, we'll out! and cross the bridge . . . America again, and Asia – all round, a better kind of guy, with warmer blood and hotter heart . . .'

We're complicit, we could be partners.

'New Soviet Man,' he says, the dream bright in his eyes. 'Rebirth. Homo – this time – Sapientissimus!'

'Suppose there's snow this year, like last . . .' I say. 'The *taiga* lives that way. Who would survive?'

'No problem,' says the cop. 'There's icy mountains in the Rift, the Congo. We must all adapt!'

'Adaptation – that will come,' I say. 'Wanted or not. But – what about the rest? All the other Russians, and their friends? Will they all be reborn, and follow us? And – might it seem colonial, this surging from the forests?'

'I suspect,' the cop says, thinking like a feline, 'we might not tell the rest. Or – better still – we'll start an enclave. There's arms in abundance here. It'll take ages for anyone to come – and what's the change? It's like Spain's empire – on us, the sun will never set. As for the colonialism – it's our example wins. If we're the best – the others follow.'

'No hunting, then,' I say. 'Let it all grow. Let each eat who they please – the best come out on top, the vital ones chew rotten wood.'

'If we don't hunt, though,' he says, 'we shall not be the best.'

'If you hunt,' I say, 'you'll upset the balance. You won't leave for Africa. You'll be stuck, on termite stew. You'll be hunters, that is all.'

'Not hunting, then. We'll be like all the other profs. Culling here and there, crying, measuring the rain, poking the nests. Like everywhere. It doesn't need advanced republics to do that,' he says, 'And fail.'

'The cages?' I ask.

'Keep them coming,' says the cop. 'Till we decide. Always we can dump them. As for you – I see no use for you. I'd let you go. Your friends had cast you as the goat . . .'

'And me?' asks Gaspard. 'Where do I fit in?'

'Your spectacles – bring out the numinous, and freeze it, Gaspard,' I say.

'That's what the schoolbooks say,' he says. 'I want to get away from that.'

'The scene here will be unique,' I say. 'It's absolute originality, but full of numen, that's for sure. You can set off with us, the first new men . . .'

'Oh,' he says. 'The jungle – that's enough for me. The old machines will play their part. Tick tock, like beetles.'

'Right!' I say. 'I'm off. Free!'

'It would be a great mistake,' says Gaspard. 'This is your place. The forest full of animals, real, begging for your understanding. An enclave, that you've so desired – it can be yours. The cops – you always seek their friendship, poor deluded worm. Here, you're in their midst. Back? you think. How trite! Marcel and his friends, blue stockings and blue beards. Back to your Varya, your Russians, who set you up, betrayed you? Back to your poverty, incompetence – a falling leaf, disoriented, negligible?'

'You're convincing me,' I say. 'But the promise is of death.'

'You set more store by fripperies than me,' Gaspard says. 'Suffering, for instance: yourself, and others that you witnessed, and did nothing. But suffering, when the cause is great, magnificent . . .! You want to spend your life waiting for some racist guy to treat you at the bar? The *shef* – maybe he exaggerates, but there's an insight, intuition there . . .'

'Oh yes,' I say. 'I am convinced. We understand our destiny. That is what counts.'

The chief says, '*Kolbasa*, vodka, our good black bread. The primal diet.'

At night, the sentries sometimes take a pop at shadowy beasts about their work. 'When we go, we can't leave the jungle animals behind,' I say.

'Oh no,' says Vsevolod, chief cop. 'I've stacked the crates and boxes here. So's not to slow us down, we'll pack them up. Nothing, no one will be left.'

'There is no gas,' I say. 'We'll have to walk.'

'Of course!' he says. 'That's how it's done. The boxes carried on the head.'

The chief, our Vsevolod, inspires us all. 'And has he told the people where they're due to go?' asks Gaspard. 'I must do my spectacle before you leave,' and he pours oil over rusting cogs.

'When the time comes,' says Vsevolod, 'they'll know. Like they
had known before, but only as a fabulous tale. See – walking and
running makes you tall. It's in your bones. And then – it's true, the
Russian soul is pure. You come from Italy,' he says, joshing with me.
'There's evil there, in every one . . .'

'Yes, but there's all sorts there,' I say, 'Greeks, Albanians, French.
and Austrians.'

'A prison-house of nations,' says Vsevolod. 'As you know, I
believe in instinct – like the animals have. They never read a book, or
saw a movie – but they last out millennia. Our learning comes from
books – often they're wrong. I recommend – the Bible, the Qur'an.
Marx's philosophical manuscripts of 1844. The Bible has those
genealogies – each one correct. I've checked on each. Already we
behave as the Qur'an says we should. As regards God and gods – when
we arrive in Congo, or the Rift – we'll have to start again inventing
what is good for us. The journey's the most pressing thing. See . . .'
and he stands up tall, his pants reach to his knees, his stubby arms have
elongated, and – yes, his face is darker now, the skull expands, his cap
won't fit . . . 'I am responding to the call!'

The barber left, went north. We all have dreadlocks. We put no faith
in the Selassie, though. 'Suppose the Americans bomb us,' Gaspard
says. 'They'll do a deal, someone else hits somewhere else . . . Then,
they'll send those stinging creatures . . .'

'We'll be in the forest,' says Vsevolod. 'The Russians – they won't
bomb. We are them – at least for now.'

It is a happy scene – the folk live off their plots, at dusk the roads
are full of happy singing, and at night we dance. Or take refuge among
the trees.

'It will not last,' says Gaspard, greasing a locomotive. There are no
tracks.

'It must not last,' Vsevolod says to me. 'If they can't all come, you
and I can make it. Just us two.'

'I know Madagascar,' I say. 'But we're two males . . . new Soviet woman should be specified.'

'Forget Madagascar,' says Vsevolod. 'We're walking, remember. Did they send us yaks and camels? No! We'll ditch what can't adjust as we go onward. Same goes for my lads. There's a risk. But look back – your friends, all the screwed up lives, the 'situations', the 'psychology' . . . Your Marcel spreadeagled in his room, Dana blown to pieces . . .'

'My friends,' says Gaspard. 'If you escape the politics, the geography will do for you.'

'Who gives a fuck!' shouts Vsevolod, laughing hugely. 'We'll be dead long before that matters! Let the survivors take the rap, newly make a mess of things. We'll be long gone, our blood brown in a bog, our bones pointing the way to somewhere in the desert,' and he gives me courage, slapping my back with his long arms.

Say we leave tomorrow. Two of us, a posse. Who knows the way to travel? Shall we come back for the animals? Gaspard can ship us – what, a disc? a movie? – of his performance. Bland, derivative, over-inflated, politically amorphous – that's what the cops will say about it.

Those mysteries – La France, Sandrine, the others. The mystery is theirs, inside, inscrutable: not mine.

'It's not for you,' Gaspard says. 'Stay with your own fantasy. Don't hitch on to someone else's.'

It's true. It's not for me. Too bad! We train. Desert, mountain, walk and run, hide, sequester. In circles and in desperation. 'There!' says Vsevolod. 'The people here – a ragbag of all peoples everywhere . . . we could make them into Russians, then all Russians into something else.'

I see him in the fields, tall as a stork, standing on one leg, eyeing the cows – the beads and feathers in his cap give him a scarecrow look. If only our adventure was not historic: knowing the profs'll come long after, look for bones and beads, maybe get our gender wrong. But we'll be celebrated. 'Into Africa again . . .' The higher level everybody seeks.

No one bothers us. We don't secede. In our heads – we're a republic independent. No one cares. Vsevolod is the cop he's always been – with irreproachable results.

Me? Inspired? In and out the forest. I have no gun. I can leave with Vsevolod, become an archaeology, a history. Or stay. Or – the choice is mine – back to Varya, and her gang.

'The *taiga*, the old *taiga*, is no more,' says Vsevolod. 'It got hot: we killed the animals. Then the new way came, so we could train for Africa.'

'He's just a cop,' says Gaspard. 'A stereotype who thinks in stereotypes.'

'Some guys he treats well, others bad. Being right – it's not the point,' I say. Maybe it shouldn't be like that. We know – the predators attract. But – they go for the weak. Nothing can protect the weak.

'Insatiability,' says Vsevold. 'That's how you survive here. You eat all that you can, living or dead. That way, you skimp a life. Sometimes nothing, sometimes far too much.'

Gaspard says to me, 'The way you're going – it's death, fascism, a dead end. Maybe it doesn't involve you, all that – death is coming anyway, and besides, you shake the bag – it all gets better, all gets worse.'

'I understand,' I say. Gaspard has my destiny in mind.

'If you go back to Varya,' says Vsevolod, 'Her bleak life . . . If she was still here, I'd put her straight in jail, with all her friends. The thing is – have no doubt,' and again he buffets me – 'Being unsure doesn't make you come out right.'

*

I ask Gaspard, 'Your show – what will it mean to people here? The metal they once polished, gave them to eat – position, satisfaction – now gone to tick-tock. Will they bow down before the memory?'

'The words are trite,' he says. 'It's the emotions. They won't see the time that's passed, it's rusted out, gummed up and brittle. It's remembrance. Infinity, they think, eternity. Mothers and fathers, nurses, playing in the grass . . . It's not the past for them – it's what lives on in their heads, that makes it seem immortal. Them – immortal too.'

'If it's all there, waiting,' I say. 'Just needs to be evoked: whether they see your spectacle or not – it's quite irrelevant. Everything's inside them – so they think, and they'll end well.'

'It's true,' says Gaspard, 'there's some sleight of hand. You must make it live, your show. Of course, it doesn't live. But then again – it doesn't die, even if no one's ever seen it. It's like the bear – although the axe took off its paw – no one believes it's real, or suffers. If you don't add something to the brew, they'll think you're conning them.'

'The bear talks,' I say. 'The more qualities it has, the less it lives.'

We watch the forest, as we drink our *kir*. 'You could come too, Gaspard,' I say. 'Try a real trip.'

'Oh,' he says, 'my work is dangerous enough. When you've left, who knows what vengeance comes?'

'We'll cross the frontier, Gaspard,' I say, 'then we'll see. Desert and grassland. The birds will give a sign.'

'It's too late then,' Gaspard says. 'The big beasts – they'll come down from Moscow, looking for Vsevolod. Complicity with Varya – what a web!'

'The hunting isn't about animals, Gaspard,' I say. 'Those are the weak ones,' and I spread my fingers out, an elk's horns, to show. 'The competition's between the men. The animals get shot with rifles – between the guys, it's pistols – just like Lermontov . . .'

'You don't know anything,' says Gaspard. 'Forests and blue birds. That's your tale. For sure, Vsevolod's done awful things – they all do that. It's his fear of being caught that makes him run, aspire . . .'

'They've found another earth,' says Vsevolod, as we pack our bundles, hook them on our sticks. 'Maybe they've reached a further stage. Post-men,' he says, and laughs. 'All writing letters, tramping the earth, delivering them in person . . .'

I'll miss the faded blue and grey of shacks, the cockerel, grannies shaking rugs . . . You could be happy here, for half an hour, and wish it would go on and on, but now, an hour – you're bored . . .

Gaspard's show – the last rehearsal. The metal whirrs like wings.

'It's a mistake, you lucky guy,' says Gaspard. 'What a wonder! – you survive, and err again, doing no penance, learning no lesson. And I'm stuck here, doing my difficult show, that no one understands, because it's them. A mirror. They want something else – a panorama, an enchanted wood. There isn't one.'

Vsevolod and I set off amidst the whizz and clunk, past the few lads on bicycles . . . into the grass . . . Oh no! I had forgot the blackfly, how they sting! – our faces swell like footballs, our nostrils disappear, ears occluded like a seal's, the eyes intelligent dots, quite saurian . . . 'They'll take our faces off, when we get there,' I barely hear Vsevolod, his mouth invisible, locked in his flesh. 'All part of the plan. There's no new man without a face to match.'

'Our photos, Vsevolod!' I say. 'Passports!'

'We get by on vodka,' says the chief. We pass the guards, the frontier – the vodka works its miracle. We hand it round, our bundles empty now. The road turns into sand. It's night. Gaspard's rockets far away leap towards the stars, the distant Earths.

'We should have brought a mule,' says Vsevolod. 'Those you can eat when they break down, run out of gas.'

Even if we'd food, our heads are too swollen to let us eat.

'Of course,' says Vsevolod, mumbling. 'To our good Kazakh friends here, we're just *gadjé* or suchlike. They won't tell on us, our past, the little paradise we leave: there's republics all over – Altai, Bashkortostan. All sorts live among the marches – it's biodiversity. Only wolves want to live all together in a pack. There used to be many of them . . . They made a mistake, and the wrong enemies.'

He whispers through invisible lips, 'Listen. Don't acquire the wrong idea, the hopes. Blackfly will never rule the world. Guys like us – we always will. And those like you – tack on to us. Will you enlighten us? Or use us for vendetta? Forget it! We understand your sufferings. We weep with you, even as we hand out punishment. It's what the scorpion says as the fox bears him across the stream; what the lion says as he eats his cubs. It's nature.'

'They could be someone else's cubs,' I say: if my eyes could, they'd weep. I'm not moved by the tale – I'm poisoned by the flies.

'Mine's all information,' says Vsevolod. 'Learn by experience – that's my message. Not that I'm a bad guy. If you can't keep up, I'll abandon you. That's what explorers do. And – don't scratch your face. It will come off.'

'I might abandon you,' I'd like to say.

'It won't happen,' he would say.

Marianne wouldn't abandon me. Maybe she did. I can get a new face from Varya. Maybe it wouldn't fit.

'The women wouldn't save you,' I think Vsevolod says. 'Their nurturing nipple is withdrawn and gone to porn. The comfort's up to you, your female side.'

'It's only so's to be put back on the road,' I'd say. 'Meet up with some figure from my past . . .' He strides ahead.

'If you abandon me,' I say, ' the fault will go to you.'

'Oh no,' he says. 'I'd say I looked for help. You'd lie here – exactly as it happens when we first leave Africa. When I next looked, you'd gone. Disappeared. No great loss.'

'You'd be no hero, Vsevolod,' I say.

'Your story – passes to me, becomes mine,' he says. 'Like Varya gave you hers. I'm a hero if I end the trek. The epic will be mine, all in my name. That's how it goes – people, real or made up – you survive, so, you take them over, totally. Their spirits go back into nature, but their voices, the projects, the endearments, insults, the rustling of the clothes they drop, the squeak of boots and shoes . . . all yours!'

*

I know great things will come from Inner Asia. They always have. Only men and women came from those forests deep in Africa. Oh, and timber, and apes.

We walk on, silently. Our faces thin, then thin on to the bone. Our sweat is thick and yellow.

'Your head is shot,' Vesvolod says. It lolls. 'I love you,' he says, taking out his pistol. 'You knew: only one – at most – will make it to the goal. Epics are like that. Two at the finish – it would be a comedy.'

'It doesn't end like this,' I say. 'There's everything suspended – the doors aren't locked, there's people waiting to spring out and say their piece.'

'That's always so,' says Vsevolod. 'Imagine! Suspects! My cases. All left luggage . . .'

'Maybe so,' I say. 'But – I don't have the gun.'

'I do only kindness,' says Vsevolod.

'No kindnesses,' I say.

We go our ways. Vsevolod tramps on, with confidence, it seems. His purplish cap fits, down to his purplish ears.

*

'Well,' Varya says, 'someone's paid for something. When the money stops . . . the animals – will be shot, or not. All over, it happens so: those Slovak pigs, hunted down in Tuscany . . . There's nothing for you, though. You're finished. Just take a rest, and – wear my face.'

We drink our *kir*. 'You're shaken up,' she says. 'No one can live in Paris without a face. Except me. I'm still in hiding.'

'Maybe I missed my chance,' I say. 'Following the cop: adventure. Judgement by the world. All would have come.'

'Yes,' she says, 'you missed it. Though cops have friends who're cops all over. They know everything we don't. We're their neanderthals. We all miss out: I sang and danced, on stage . . . Behind this vulgar guy who shouted out. The sound – a tide, a mountain . . . I forgot to block my ears, my drums blew out. I don't hear anything. I love the concerts still – silent, concentrated, the guys waft to and fro, the crowd, their arms red blue and green like branches in a forest waving inconclusively . . .'

'You read my lips?' I ask.

'Yours don't seem to be saying anything,' she says.

'How's Hervé?' I ask.

'He weeps,' she says. 'Most stuff that's shipped is crap. He, instead, ships riches. It's their eyes . . . thousands of them, all over him. Seeking protection, love – hope, from the butcher. He won't outlast the trade. Liliane – maybe his shield.'

'You could dance, Varya,' I say. 'Even if you're a criminal . . .'

'It doesn't work like that,' she says. 'Not the dancing. Somewhere there must be sound, even if no one hears. You should have gone with Vsevolod, then claimed the prize.'

'Set me free, Varya,' I say. She's already turned away.

'Set me free,' she says. 'If I can't have what I want, let me be free. Take what you want. My ears have gone. You can't wear my face if I've been freed. You think you don't need anything of mine. Don't take my eyes. Everything else. All the others, friends, are free; in their bound, branded way. I can't hear the key, if it turns. You must tell me. I'm forever in your prison.'

'I must be on my way, Varya,' I say. 'You can't ask so much of me. Taking from you, exposing, disfiguring, transfiguring. I'm not your captor, grasping your quiddity.'

'Then curse you,' she says. 'Go knocking on doors with your false limbs. Starve.'

'I'm nothing, Varya,' I say, anxious to be away. 'I'm just a poor man.'

*

'This is your room,' the lady says. 'Don't go near the *Bois*.'

'Oh,' I say, 'I won't. I know Paris well.'

'Only God knows Paris well,' she says. 'These Jews, Muslims, all the rest, all gathered here. What does God plan?'

'He probably likes a rough and tumble,' I say. 'It's sterile. It's digging up the burial ground.'

'You must live clean,' she says.

'Oh, I do,' I say. 'I don't have clutter.'

'Where you come from, there's those wars down there,' she says.

'No!' I say. 'The wars are far away. I only left because there was nothing I could do.'

'Don't lose the key. You'll not be able to get in or out – depending.'

*

Finding a way out. Finding work? Daring: jumping from high building to next door, slightly higher. On stage, singing cocky, suicidal; risking your drums. A private eye, at the keyhole.

'You won't find anything, frowsting here,' says the lady. 'You must submit to the guy who questions you, that's how you get work. Find your rich father, soak him.'

'It costs you more to find work than they pay you back,' I say. She smiles.

'I do a favour,' she says. 'Fitting out bad guys and girls. Migrants. Bringing them here, setting them up. Finding them friends. Holding a *salon*. Stylish.'

Might it be a step upward from animals? 'Suppose they turn on us?'
I say.

'They're bad, real bad,' she says. 'They wouldn't bother you.
They're so bad, they're running. They've suffered terribly. We cuddle
them and hear their tales. They've told their story – a thousand times
plus one.'

'That sounds quite humanistic, what you do,' I say. 'Whatever
they've done, or want to do? Protection, for everyone?'

'Of course, if you know everything,' she says, 'you might
discriminate. But – who are you to do anything?' She appraises me,
with a cold boiled eye. 'Would you say I'd been the object of desire?
That rocked the earth?'

It's a hard one, that.

'Well,' she says, 'while you ponder. I am. Right now; I am that
object. Guys lie and steal and kill for me. If I was a country, millions
would die for me. Both sides.'

'This city's safe,' I say. 'Politicals are never sent away.'

'Safe?' she says. 'That's a box you put your cash in when you're
afraid of thieves. Remember your aspect: always *en fleurs*. Your
innocence must be contagious.'

We work. There's too many to be good or bad. Trying to come in,
trying not to be thrown out. Bemused. A Raft of the *Medusa*. We
protect everyone, they're all good.

'You have to make a wood, a forest, round them,' says the lady.
'Somewhere they'll feel safe, although they're not. Some get eaten the
first day, others live for ever there. They must pay us – they expect it,
without the cash, it isn't genuine. Without the cash, we wouldn't think
of doing it.'

We don't look into their eyes. It's not like hiding Varya: these guys
don't look at you.

'It's history,' the lady says. 'These people have walked out of
Africa. And India. All over. Think of them as planning civilizations –
that's what we can help them do.'

I think of Vsevolod – he'll be in the desert, in Iran. Burned, converted. Probably he's changed his name. His uniform. He'll dream of trees. Walking a straight line.

I hear from Gaspard. 'I've a new idea,' he says. 'These tribal people Where do they all come from? – their hidden roots, I'll bring them out. Remember – Medina! Trekking to places inhospitable, and whittling emblems, *tamghas*, on their spears. And you! – stop trying to change the world. Be like me, and understand it!'

'A true reactionary, your friend,' the lady, Louise, remarks. 'Here's a puzzle for you – the people we're protecting – if they're here, they must be French. And yet the French don't want them here.'

'I bet you have a design, an end, for everything,' I say. 'Please – don't tell me what it is.'

It might mean walking . . . Berbers against the Visigoths, long marches in the sun, Cities of Peace, a garden where the rivers meet. Who knows?

The people we deal with are in bad shape. Who can tell when they recover, where they'll arrive? Paradise or purgatory? A cluster round a bedside, survivors watching the death of friends?

. . . Marcel, his ambience, comes into my mind, is pushed back out. Long time dead. Or – will they endure dull and rackety lives, stoned among the projects . . .

'You're a trafficker, my friend,' says Louise. 'Don't write it in your passport.'

'I don't see it,' I say.

'You must get your motives, your convictions straight,' she says. 'Money comes in, but it's not enough for the risk.'

'We make life easier,' I say vaguely.

'La France!' shouts Louise, 'Doesn't think so.'

'Good people agree with us,' I say. 'Plant those trees! Cover, don't banish.'

'I go deeper,' Louise says. 'You have your easy answer. I've been shut up here all my life. I see further, even if it's not beautiful. If you can't be a prophet, you must be a general – keep the right distance, don't mix with people. Say you love them, and have done with it.'

*

She calls to me, Louise. 'I got a beating,' she says.

'Yes, you did,' I say. 'Don't die on me.'

'You should leave now,' she says, 'before the cops or someone comes.'

'How did it happen?' I ask. 'We're so careful, so precise.'

'I crossed a line,' she says. 'Remember – the straight path lost . . .'

'They did poetry in school,' I say. 'But you – we – were on the right road. Even if the wild wood we're in is rough, resilient . . .'

'No,' she says, 'I always do the right thing, take the right road. It's not that. It's an accident. No sin involved. We don't know what can happen . . .'

'Well,' I say, 'you're right again. We don't know what is next. For you – it's probably your death. I guess I'll leave. If you're sure someone will come.'

'Oh yes,' she says. 'They'll come.'

'That isn't what I meant,' I say. 'Someone to take care.'

'I know exactly what you mean,' she says. 'Run.'

*

. . . There is a refuge. Things go better if you think of every place a refuge – where you are; whatever's happening, it's stencilled in, and circumscribed. It's up to you, the outcome, and the dialog. The woman and her suitcase here – certainly, she's Bosniac or Kurd, some identity that's branded into her, but others see as cloudlike. I may have helped her run another day, a week. And quite indifferent, each to the other.

She says, 'You need know someone, to keep the pace. Big, but not grotesque with it.'

'Well,' I say, 'I'm sure a president will come and bring his tent and shoot my animals. All the Russias – those must count. And here – they talk about "the people", but they pin you down, they chase you out . . . The revolution: just the usual cookie-cutter, in the end.'

'I know all that,' she says. 'It's quite banal – all that you say. You need a cop, a criminal – someone who'll take you in. Us two – it's not for sex, so don't think that . . .'

'I know,' I say. 'We've found this room. It's like a parcel round us; I'm a gift for someone, waiting to be found . . .'

'I don't think so,' she says. 'Spare us that.'

'I could be a diamond bow,' I say. 'A piece of gristle for your dog. Someone to remember . . .'

'They say it was the cops, did for Louise,' she says.

'She overdid the scruple,' I say. 'Wanted everyone to come, start things off. She talked of rebirth, not of making more French guys. But – what if everything turned bad?'

'Louise wanted too much for the cash,' she says. 'Wrong trade for troubled spirits. For me, yesterday was average bad. But she was interested in tomorrow. Like me – it's my obsession.'

When I wake, she's gone. She's left the key.

*

I go back, to where I came from: start again to leave again.

*

It's a wondrous life – moving like a god, like Apollo being dropped in His balloon on to Galataea, this taking the train, crossing the frontiers, going down South . . . a meagre document's enough, and all those guys outside, waiting to go North – impotent, invidious . . . walking through fire and continents, bearing their origins, the towns and villages like crowns upon their heads.

The forest has burned, but springs again. Each tree has refuse round it – it's called fly-tipping, here come the flies. There is no Sandrine – maybe she burned. Maybe she became a bride.

Someone says, 'It was the Africans, burnt it down. They camped here in the forest.'

'No,' says someone else. 'That way it's cleared for building on.'

Without the forest, there is nothing here. No birds, no anything.

Life was full, outside: quite inconclusive. It's time to have more, fill the barrel. Move on.

There's a new bar here: 'Eyes'. 'It means look, don't touch,' says the barman. 'The eyes see involuntarily,' he says, 'Everything. They're greedy, but – nothing enters, assuages. Your eyes – let you drink and eat forever, but hungry you remain – expire.'

'There's Arabs run it,' says a drinker. 'It means "IS": the state of Islam. Eternal peace.'

'No,' says his mate. 'It's true they're Arabs, but it's "I's". You can be anything, anyone, you want in here, so long as you pay.'

'I really don't care,' I say. 'No matter how much you drink, the rest still goes on.'

Do I recognise this guy? Looks like his grandfather. 'Hey, old friend,' he says, 'I burnt the forest. And I dug some foxholes too. You don't need guns – just foxy holes for entertaining foxy ladies. We only have to serve our time. We don't know how it ends. No one alive, fighting, praying, wearing white coats – can have the least idea how it all puzzles out. We set the riddles. Will it be volcanoes and the dark? Or burning up and light? Or floods? New prophets, maybe? Or the old ones back and hitting with their sticks? The human project is futility. Time's much longer than our arms, our longest bones . . . Everything we do encounters a reaction cancelling it out, and equal to the effort we've put in . . .'

'You've had enough, my friend,' I say.

'Oh yes,' he says, 'I have. There's only fine-tuned words to come. In the beginning was the end – the last word. Sandrine . . .'

'Whatever happened to Sandrine?' I ask.

'I buried her,' he says. 'Her blue bird got away – scorched by the fire, flamingo-pink.'

'Unrecognisable,' I say. 'You've mixed it up. Work, sex, music, destiny. And the fighting. You've made soup of them.'

'Sandrine was a pile of ash,' he says, 'even when she lived.'

'I can't stay here,' I say. 'It all burns down too quick.'

I run from Eyes. You turn the corner – and you're gone, invisible . . . I hear the drunk guy shout,

'You must look up! Here, we looked down . . . a grassy spot to put our feet . . .'

'You stopped too soon!' I shout. 'You should have gone to the end, like in France. Lived with everything you can't resolve, don't want to. Your feet – they're charred. Pinocchio's.'

I'm not staying!

I take the slow train back to France. Maybe they're looking for me. I'm still looking for La France. There's a guy opposite, quizzical, devious. Spy or turncoat? Warrior, deserter? Cop or refugee?

'I remember!' I say. 'You had the secret, before the forest burnt. You were selling secrets, door to door, right at the start. You, your mate, in black coats . . . I remember!

'I still have the coat,' he says. He eats a large *porchetta* roll. 'Pig's not so bad,' he says. 'Don't believe what the books say.'

'I've no money,' I say. 'You'll need gift me that secret of the universe.'

'I don't need sell any more,' he says. 'I'm on the slow train because my accountant lives right on the border, like Voltaire. But don't think in the world there's only sell or give. There's lots more. The secrets change, and you'd never know.'

'Where's your partner?' I ask.

'Gone where yours have gone,' he says. 'Where do you expect they go – "Camps. Ruined cities. The squatted hi-rise. The bush. The forest.

The great Iranian desert"? You want to read about all that, somewhere when you're safe?'

'I don't know where I'm safe,' I say. 'I don't read much.'

He doesn't care: he says, 'Maybe you think I'll say something crass, about how much it costs – the secrecy, and is it legal?'

'I'm amazed,' I say. 'You wear a trilby. Recognisable – no need to describe you any further.'

'Look at those glaciers,' he says, pointing at the scummy grey. 'As they recede, you find palaces and barracks.'

'I bet there's caves and friezes too,' I say, trying to lighten. 'Frozen friezes.'

'It melts,' he says. 'The soldiers come out. All alive. It's called cryptogenics. If you're a civilian, it costs an arm and leg. Military is free. First come the Nazis, then – the People's Army. Myself I find it all appealing – those wasted troopers, tumbling down Mount Elbrus. I've a soft spot for the rebels – though it's not romance – not in Donetsk. Not in Damascus either . . . that magnificent mosque . . .' and he rubs mist off our window. 'In the end,' he says, 'it's soldiers hold it all together. The Greeks called arming up their guys "democracy".'

'I know,' I say. 'They're always telling us. Me – I'd say fuck them, if they voted for me to put on that hat and shield.'

He laughs, too long and loud. 'They couldn't find you – you move ahead of that pink postcard,' he says. 'The one that tells you where your regiment is.'

In the meadow, the frozen stiffs are standing up and forming fours. Some form threes – some fives.

'That stuff is all passé,' he says. 'Now – everyone wants to crack the secret – and keep the answer secret – the cancer, comets, the big, the tiny. It's all gone commonplace, though there's still enough who talk of mystery and wonder, and so they ask me in – coffee, gin, I don't much care.'

'The line follows the frontier all the way,' I say. There's guys running up and down the train, and leaping off – cross-stitching, one side to the other of the border, cross-rhyming to the tracks.

'And – you're wrong,' I tell him. 'Wrong about everything. What holds it all together is people just like me.'

He stares. 'You might be partly right. It's true – the French can't handle all this modern stuff. They've no idea. It's way beyond them. The Germans – well, who'd go on a ramp with them? After all that? The photos, names, and everything? The pits, mass graves? Modernity – if that is what it is, they don't have it on their map. The French have wrinkled brains – it rules them out. Americans – brains smooth as skidpans. They're the only ones who plod on through the showers – the sizzling rain, the rocks – without umbrellas: shaven heads . . . onward, though the heavens fall . . .'

'It's stereotype,' I say.

'You know,' he says, 'we're here to eat inferior creatures. If we stop – it is the end. The end! It's a great fallacy, that there is more to things than that. Astronomers talk big about the acid stones and boiling seas unearthed. Why don't they ask "What's there to eat up there?" "Is there cannibals?" "Incest after?" No – it's as if there's laboratories, a billion of them, circling in the sky like mobiles in the nursery . . .'

'If you've a scheme,' I say, 'it's time to cut me in.'

'All mine I've passed you so far – they're only little secrets. All of them are true,' he says. 'You've learnt – if people that you've known don't stay around – maybe they're dead. You're lucky – some die inadvertently, shielding you. Some just – get in the way. And on you go.'

The guys run through the fields – looking for their better life.

'What if it's a fallacy?' he asks. 'If they're deluded? Shall we stop the train, and tell them – "There is no better, and no good." And if we joined them? Wandered?'

'I don't think they'd mind,' I say. 'Or care. For them it works – the better life. I don't get your point, in shaking their desires. And – the enchanted wanderer stuff. I've done that, read it, been on the steppe alone.'

'Hmmmm,' he says, poking the unfinished roll into his breast pocket. 'That's rather what I thought. Starting to run is rational: not knowing where you'll end . . . probably is not. So, what does that leave for you to do? Philanthropy? Engineering? Saving a lover?'

'Offer me something you can guarantee,' I say.

'How far will you go?' he asks.

'It's you! You are the chancer, the beguiler! How long can you pretend?' I ask. 'You've no secret. They're all present, all revealed. Those institutes have fused – Advanced study of rationality – and of irrationality: they're one. The Theory of the Lot, it must contain them both: it's like the Bomb, the game, its players, the binary, all with two elements, two players . . .'

'That still leaves you: the problem. You, the humanistic nut,' he says. 'You're small time. Often inexplicable and masked, a connoisseur of locks, of boxy rooms once full, now voids. You're a bluebeard, opening every cage: the birds have flown. That leaves you – nothing, quite exactly. I saw you at the start, now – I guess, you're somewhere in the between.' He spreads out his legs, grows confident. 'Before, in our little history of men, they looked for simple explanations. The big, the simplest one: monotheism. One cause, one destiny: one straight path. Then, scarcely more complex – the equation, the kids' computer. What we need,' and he scowls at the spread of pork grease on his suit, 'is you, the pattern, your architecture. Your person singular. You, your context. Everything that's been: from your first flight to the forest, to your grand schemes, your irritating gyres, petty fiddles, grand re-orderings . . . Something beyond information, power . . . those are chimeras. What we need is something that accounts for you, your interaction with all else, your muddled understanding of it all . . .'

'It isn't flattering,' I say. 'How you judge me. Though it is true – my story . . . yes, it must figure in an explanation of what is . . . But really, what interests me, is what comes next. Don't predict! If you're right – it's luck. If not – you lose your credibility. Leave it to me, what I do next.'

My architecture! My singularity – how could it be immortalised? A machine? Stood in the corner and wired up? A creature . . . would be best. With russet fur, a *Heldentenor's* voice . . .

'Now, now!' he shouts. 'I know that glitter of speculation round your head. No doubling up! No extra *fusis* hung up like Mister Punch's worn-out suits. You and the Thing are one: you are you and only you.'

'How much will this cost?' I ask. 'This picture without canvas, without frame?'

'Depends,' he says. 'How much are you carrying?'

'All in forints,' I say.

Populations move from one country to another: we see them hop across our tracks.

'Kitsch,' he says gloomily. 'There can be no other outcome. Hybrids from hybrids. Now: think of yourself – the spirit, eternal, when your grubby body dies. Machine! Ghost! Quite excessive, and misleading. Your afflatus still hangs like marsh gas, where you conquered your women and discarded them, some even post-coital . . . You're unforgettable, I promise.'

'I love kitsch,' I say. 'I haven't suffered, I'm the fox – hunted, I feel excitement, fear. The suffering comes at the end. Not spiritual. You trust your speed, the twist unencumbered. Your brush is for your masterpieces.'

'There's the difference between us,' he says. 'I'm a scientist. You're an artist. All you have in your head is secondhand. Hybrid: producing the Thing you hope expresses hope. Or anything. The wandering, just like these guys.' We're surrounded by them.

'Wrong again,' I say. 'People I know have been in the artist world. It's not finicky like science. But me – I'm quite original, no artist. No one foretold me, and when I'm dead, I want commemoration in true kitsch.'

Soldiers pour off the melting glaciers – cross-gartered, with pompoms on the knee, in black and yellow stripes, with ostrich feathers, coal-scuttle helmets, Mona Lisa moustaches – there, a swarm dressed as drab green aphids – makes you think of roses; here, tall blue mutilated spears, delphiniums, waiting for you to give them your seat in tram or bus . . .

The tracks are blocked with angry guys, the engine stops. The countryless, their cultures bundled into swags, sprawl out upon the metals. I jump down, tumble on the grass. The preacherman, my friend, looks down at me. 'Don't forget,' he shouts, 'it isn't finished, isn't done. I haven't told you what to do to be remembered. Or what they have to do to you . . . Take my blessing . . .'

I love the poor, they're all around me. I'm not poor – that's the first blessing.

My friend – he didn't tell me what to say, or where to go. My culture, though – it would scarce fit into a suitcase, two of you sitting on the lid. You can go round the world with such a case – it's big as the world, like it's supposed to be.

Aeroplanes are coming off the ice. Maybe they'll take me to Paris. Here's one, 'The spirit of Maeterlinck', it says. A papery biplane. 'I need dropping off at Sèvres-Babylone,' I say.

Here we are. I have my ticket, thanks. Babylon and the china factory, all dropped, shards, all that weeping . . . take the train, the métro –

Off at Madeleine. Proust! That's why everyone chuckles, as they ride the Métro. That's *echt* culture. Of course, we think of Marcel. And his friends – like mine, some dead, some half-dead – those you don't know what's become of them, maybe there's some hope left, some muscle tone, their skulls shelved, 'anon', in an ossuary down in Naples, their bodies free to wander somewhere else. Like the pilot of my plane, just his body, well attuned, landing in the traffic, off again, the machine a dragonfly, a newborn lustre on the wings . . .

The iron tower is hidden by the new tall buildings, thickets of them. Here's a table, a café, at the foot of a dull structure, a mountain you are dared to climb, glassy ice-clad, no snow. Offices, no caves. Who has the nerve, the pomp, the boots, to climb?

'Turk coffee,' I say when the waiter offers French.

'A connoisseur,' says a guy, complicit, laced in tight, with a woman who approves my choice as well. Chancers? A con, or public intellectuals? 'Poor Marcel would agree,' the slender woman says.

'Don't be dismayed,' says the guy. 'These big buildings . . . Don't think Rome, Cambodia – their ignoble end, their purposes so inflated, their creators reaching for the stars, the moon, a footprint in the sky, a peephole from up high. These are offices. But – think! – the form migrates, the shapes pass from life to dust and mud. Once, elephants and lions. Those were the biggest things, the living structures, imposing, risky . . . Tranquillity, determination, power. Now – these buildings – scrape no skies. They are inert, impotent . . .'

I interrupt, 'Oh, I know all about the animals, the feelings they inspire . . . Their size . . . how they walk past, like ducks in shooting galleries . . .'

'We knew at once you were a sensitive, adventurous guy,' he says. 'Our story's this. We wait here, Nadia and I – I'm Albéric – until some gullible but active guy turns up. It could be you. Then we initiate the scam.'

'The last one in's the fish?' I ask. 'The *pollo*, mark, the falling guy?'

'No, no,' says Albéric. 'It's true that Nadia and I – we're not last ins. But the scam is not for us. It can be for anyone. We're quite selective. Ovidians and symbolists are OUT!' suddenly he shouts, his perilous triangle of beard leaps up and down.

Nadia nods, 'It's good,' she says, 'to be deceived. It shows an open spirit and a superficial mind.'

'I fear that actress, beautiful La France, may not exist. I may have read her credit wrong . . .' I say. The thought is chilling. Into the glacier I fall.

'That, we shall find out too,' says Albéric. 'Perhaps. But – no one of us is left in penury, however things turn out. Our good faith lies in these . . .' and he hands me a chinky bag. 'These pavement chalks will be your guarantee, your tools of trade, survival, if the rest should falter, die. These, and a cup, a piece of Sèvres to hold the cash will do, or a vase from Babylon – abundant here – they'll start you off on fortune's trail.' He laughs, and Nadia laughs, maybe at different scenes.

'It's true,' I say. 'I understand why guys do awful things when they are ordered to. Fear and the lure of projects grandiose – combine to make one abject and obedient. What I don't grasp – is passion. Excess of action, fired by unselfish sentiment. Can you give me, show me, that?'

I think of Vsevolod, of Liliane, of Sandrine, Varya – driven by devotions I don't have, a force I lack, possess in spurts at best . . .

'Oh, passion,' Nadia says, quite brightly now, smoothing her fatigues, and finishing off her *kir*:

'We're fuelled by that. The element of chance, of random, in our choosing you, and now our scheme – means we are in the line of those last passionate guys: our bonzes! *Surreal!* Surrealists! Us! Before the plodders took the stage; the tinkerers, uncertain and illusionless . . . Rivers of blindness. Saliva. Spittle in the eyes that glues them shut. Our inspiration: surrealists! Here they come, in suits and beards – after the guys who sold their daubs at last, and screwed their models – then abandoned them and went to live in Nice . . .' She grabs my ears, holds my head up high, like a prize athletics vase – 'What holds this place together is not military – it is us. The imagination, the imaginary.'

'Your ancestors,' I say. 'The inspiration. I see it all. But – those were a calculating lot as well . . .'

'Oh, absolutely so,' says Albéric. 'They thought the game was just a game. They switched it on and off.'

'They didn't calculate the prize for winning, or bother what happened to the loser,' Nadia says.

'It's all rules and orders. You must pass through the glacier to live. Or through the fire to reach the forest. And you may stay burnt or frozen all the same. There's nothing direct, spontaneous, nothing is yours,' I say. The tenderness, the pathos – it makes me weep.

'Don't start to cry,' says Nadia, 'There'll be time enough. You've said it all: whatever's yours – it's an expression first, spontaneous: then it becomes a property. Possession. Not really ever yours, but something round and yellow, circulating, clipped and weighed. Your actions, thoughts and passions – down they go, into the balance. You are found wanting. Or you're too ebullient. So, you get sheared, or put into the crucible, then ladled out, and minted fresh as something else. Someone else's head and shield stamped on.'

'Maybe you're a fox,' says Albéric. 'It's all laid down inside you. Everything is you – nothing at all is yours.'

'Anyway,' says Nadia, 'we don't go looking for lost people. We don't take on regiments. Everything is up to you. If you can't get what you want, you'll end up fleeced.'

'I don't want anything,' I say. 'It's the game. I want to play.' They look briefly at one another. I go on, 'The idea of buildings, structures, being lions. Or elephants. It brings them up to size.'

'Yes,' says Albéric, 'but there's a host of animals they might be – or there was.'

'You haven't got the point,' says Nadia, offering drinks. 'I know you don't like this brandy, but it's good for you. It's no use saying you want nothing, nothing but the game. The "game" is what you want – to do, to know, to have. And so, like any game, you start with rules. And context – can you cheat, do you have a board . . .'

'A board, Nadia?' I ask. 'You mean made of card, with dice? Or plywood? Stood against, then pinned with knives?'

She ignores me. 'To do, to see – everyone thinks those are far apart. But they are equally perilous. Carry the same penalty.'

'Maybe the idea is to reduce a danger?' I say. 'That rather draws the sting.'

'That isn't possible,' says Nadia. 'What someone does, then you want to see it close – it can all end "pouf", at once, for both of you.' We drink.

I'm on this mattress. Nadia says, 'We have to see just what you're carrying.'

Albéric – I don't see him. Nadia says, 'Those shoes . . . guys often put their gold in them, make the soles, the heels of gold. The walking's really heavy . . . Relax your fucking feet . . .' she screams at me.

'Nadia,' I say, though I can't move. 'This is cheap.'

She's laughing as she tries to wrestle me, my inertia, then she cries, and kisses me. If these are rites – this is the good part, the kiss of peace, and then beyond.

'Albéric?' I ask.

'Albéric's an idiot,' she says. 'Not a useful one either.'

She's naked, Nadia is. I'm wrapped in my flesh like a tight-rolled cigar in its box. A match must come.

'What do you think this means?' she asks.

There's a flypast – national 'planes – from this angle, they're pilchards.

'When my grandfather went on the streets,' she says. 'The General brought the tanks out. It's your turn now. Make a comment, at least. Don't pretend you're happy.'

'It's not easy to speak,' I say. It surely isn't.

'It's this way,' Nadia says. 'All three on the Métro. Albéric plays the fool – reads poems or the newspaper, everybody stares. I am the dip. I take the stuff while they're enchanted. Pass it to you, and you get off.'

'I'm amazed,' I say. 'I'd something in mind much less direct, and more reflective. Good and evil, rights and duties – that kind. With hope of being redeemed some time . . .'

'Oh, it's all of that,' she says. 'The stuff is classy – Char, Breton, Jacob. You'll love his Apollinaire – "In a mass grave like a bear, Each morning I walk there . . ."'

'I know a different class of bear,' I say. 'And a different Apollinaire.'

'We have to start with this, so's we can eat, and buy you drink,' she says.

'Suppose I go straight down, on to the sidewalk with the chalk,' I say. 'The problem is – I can't draw, not anything.'

Nadia says, 'If you're afraid – there is a store that sells the stencils. You just choose your subject, then you scribble – out will come your scene. A virgin or a sunset, animals or stars – even La France, if she exists.'

We get on at Stalingrad, or Jean Jaurès, and at day's end, finish at Anatole France. I'm not satisfied. It seems the job's the highest we can do, there's no promotion, the future's down.

Albéric declaims, '. . . the wind blows over the world's solitude, so I recall those dear beings, frail desolations . . .' It makes me cry.

'Just think,' says Nadia, 'we're entertainment. If we didn't lift some cash, our clients would buy a bronze, an installation, of no intrinsic worth . . .'

Life in the tunnels wears us down. Our nails grow long and curved, like we were dead. 'I look younger than I am,' says Nadia. 'They'd let me go. Whoever caught me.'

'That isn't so,' says Albéric. 'Nadia – you're still a dwarf, but you have aged. When we have cash enough, we'll set it down – a tract, a tractatus – that covers all we wish we were, the people trudging off to work or idleness, the predators down here . . .'

'Why don't we cross the line,' I say, 'from stealing: Albéric can do his act. We'll just collect. From stealing – we can go to beg.'

That is what we do. Nadia and I – we are the foxes, but quite tame. Holding out our paws for scraps. Albéric stands, recites: a flightless crane. 'We should have music, since we can't have a machine,' he says. 'That sends out sparks, or says how far off are the stars, or looks into your soul and turns it black.'

We can't have music either – other guys do that.

Albéric says, 'I rescued Nadia from her dragon. She was so young – he nearly killed her with his jealousy. Remember in the *Nibelungen* – the dragon breathing fire and worked by steam?'

'I don't remember,' I say.

Nadia burrows deep into her tale.

'I was in Rome. We'd tramped the world. This fireater guy – the smell!' she says. 'I would have killed him with my jealousy. But there was Albéric. He came to rescue me. What a figure! That fine rust-coloured suit he wears. His long thin legs, a skeleton quite unique. A talent for something, a quixotic throb, like pus waiting to become a pustule . . .'

We can beg all day. Albéric's ambition is so strong, the poetry is inexhaustible . . . thieving, though, you must rest up for days in case they recognise you.

'It's like the painters,' Albéric says. 'Their fate, to be avoided. They waited generations for their recognition, and they were dead and museums got all the cash. That's why I must invent; you get a *brevet*, and maybe that protects.'

'The dragon with the boiler – that was Siegfried's,' Nadia says. 'Forget the treasure, Albéric: ours is plated. I have my Siegfried,' and she pinches my nose. 'Maybe he'll get fired up. This time the dragon shouldn't stink of kerosene.'

'You have to think of inventing something quite precise, Albéric,' I say. 'It's not like painting or a poem.'

'Oh, I'm not so sure,' he says. 'There's plastic. Steel. Wire. And wood. They're quite general.'

Nadia turns away: her mood has shifted. 'I loved my dragon, the bastard. He shouldn't have been slain. Now, all the rest is shadow.'

'There's danger down here too,' says Albéric. 'You must defend yourself, and do the good. Look out for trains. For people.'

We sleep down here. Albéric asks everyone he sees to make suggestions for inventions. I can't help him – I've my own thoughts. People, and plans – blown away like ash.

'We can't have fire down here,' Nadia persists. 'And where'd we get the wood? Or see the seasons?'

I miss the forest too, though anyway – it burned.

'We don't need three of us,' says Albéric. 'It's costly. We need a new idea, not an ageing appetite.'

'Maybe you'd like to fall on your sword, dear Siegfried,' Nadia says.

It's all much harder than I'd thought. Even underground, you don't feel safe. There's cops and regulations everywhere – and then there's your brothers, your lookalikes, all swallowing swords or standing still, painted up and deathly: your competitors. No one reviews, or recognises you. You want to grab and shake them, but they'd fight you back.

'We'll keep an eye on you,' says Nadia. 'When you're outside, and in the rain. You understand – your chalks won't take upon these tiles. You'll have to find another pitch.'

She moves away – I can't hear what Albéric mouths. He could have left the dragon safe in Italy, safe in its forest, being prudent so as not to burn it down.

I see Nadia, small, waiflike, trying to con the crowd, pestering with her cup, her tiny face tough with contempt and déjà vu.

*

I must have a hard rock floor, even a wall, to do my act.

~ Happy ~

~ Sheep ~

It was long ago. I soon left that country. There seemed no choice but to go down the mine. Most people do. Starting a band – you need other people. I won someone's girl, gaming in a bar. She never spoke – resentful, strange . . .

They keep a goat in the garage. It roams free, but isn't fed. It's for Eid. They're supposed to give some to the poor. I'm poor, I never get any. I'm glad. I don't approve. It's too domestic. Religion – they do what they want, but killing people in the house . . . It's a delicate beast, it thinks maybe I can help. What do we know of destiny? In the goat's case – chance isn't part of it. Now, if it were a sheep . . . The same end, better publicity. No hope. A martyred guru? Another festival? There's a debate about it, that way maybe chance starts to take a hand. 'The sum of choices' – that's life, they say, with no chance. It's not at all convincing. Sometimes, there's no choice at all.

No one can hate this awful country. I do. It's a hole in the ground. They've sold the topsoil, poisoned the Indians. Dig enough, you find the other country underneath. Richer, but still brown, yellow, anthracite. Not that it matters to me, except as themes. Symphonies, perhaps. Nature gone crotchety. Never explicit, never speaking. It's not like Cancer Ward, telling you how they hid the tumours. The Captive, *La prisonnière* – all first person, so you can avoid writing in the wars and stock exchange. Memory – even less pondered than a history. Raskolnikov, and 'his duty towards humanity'. There's a lot of talk about it here. Those are my three books. A course – what in, I never grasped. It didn't lead on. Mostly they don't. They end up pinned in a frame.

The goats, eating natural grass, brought in to show the ground is healthy, the tar spun off. It doesn't fit: the picture of the jolly farmer's wife, cutting out the meaty ones.

I love roasted goat. I can do without – it's not a great sacrifice.

You take an exam to get here. Do you take another, to get out? Or just step outside, not come back in.

The war against the cows. Hard to say who's winning. They've made a movie – *Le sang des bêtes*. There's casualties. Hung up in the cold. Then you breed more and more and when they're at their best – you eat them. I love steak – but it costs. I can easily do without. It's not about eating. Nor about the animals: there's a world order. It's about the order, and its balance. Some species leave a hole, if they disappear. Bees, for sure. Humans – even more for sure, maybe. Cows and goats . . . there's times and rites, and every species has them. The fleshy ones, they do all right, although they cost – the cows do.

There's no cruelty, it's not about that. If someone is in minerals, digging them, they'll find oil is the new thing, and paid better. It's all work, though, that gets harder, longer.

The cows should have got together with the goats. Solidarity. But there wasn't much of that.

'They don't like you here,' says my friend. 'Walking about, not unbuttoning your head.'

'I can't step away,' I say. 'Even my science comes out in first person. I'm not a liberal – but that's the way it is. I know no one made it all for me – invisible stars, rocks slung off . . . vandals and viruses.'

'Don't dissimulate,' he, Frank, says. 'Talking doesn't absolve. For certain, you did wrong. Leave quick, before you're made to pay.'

'Those books,' I say. '"Moral responsibility", that was their theme. If you can't do anything about where you are – maybe you've no responsibility. The prison camp you're in . . . Then Proust – there's no responsibility – just sex, no guilt; just swap the attributes around. A *pédé* and a peeper. The lady prisoner . . . Those quadrilles . . . "The dimension of Time", the ever-rolling stream, stands in for everything. And – punishment – the dark bird that will get you. You're not responsible, however much you fear the wings, the beak.'

'You don't need prison, nor a punishment, to discharge responsibility,' he says. 'To accept it, or deny.'

'That's what they say,' I say.

'I'm not sure you understand what you say,' says Frank. 'It's not your job, after all.'

'Words?' I ask. 'What words?'

'Moral. Responsibility,' he says.

'You're right, Frank,' I say. 'My friend. Well-named. Frank.'

'Be a beacon,' Frank says. 'If you can't be something else. Or have a job that makes clear what you say.'

Good advice, even if you don't understand it. He continues, 'This society – we're all a tiny bit responsible for what goes on.'

'Bees,' I say, 'they must each feel totally in charge.'

'Well,' he says, 'we're not. We vote. That shares it round. Then, those that do the thing, they shift away. They're just appointed.'

'"Responsible" I understand,' I say. 'It's "moral" – if it clings more, or less to other words.'

'Whoever made you read those books,' says Frank, 'should have been clear. Maybe you should go where it's not an issue.'

'Yes,' I say, 'but I expect I'll always remember you.'

'The thing is, you're exasperating. You ask questions not knowing the answer. And that stops people doing their job,' he says.

'Those questions might have been my job,' I say. 'But it seems it wasn't to be.'

'It's that responsibility,' says Frank. 'It clings, though you don't want it. Maybe it could be moral too. That's what you seek. Good luck – maybe someone will give you them . . .'

No, I don't want that at all. I say, 'I want to do propaganda. And hope it turns out real and true.'

'Then you want the opposite of what you want,' says Frank.

'That's clear,' I say. 'Though I don't see why you should understand.'

'Or want to,' Frank says.

Leaving this country's easy. It's one of its best qualities. Walk through that door – adventure! The sky! Then, a mass of poor guys, wanting to recruit you with their story.

*

You're at the helm. Wear a chauffeur's cap, no one will ever ask you for your licence. I drove this guy, a fuzzball like some weeds give off. Two tiny legs, the abdomen, a face round and unkempt. We often go to Switzerland, but live no place in particular. He has a Rolls, a Cadillac. 'Which is best?' he asks. Origins and destiny – uncertain, for this Rufus Borzhoi.

'The Rolls is hard,' I say. 'It's the Cadillac that rolls. Rigor or plump.'

'I choose the soft,' he says. 'Bring your girl along.'

When I leave, I'll sell the Rolls. The cash will smooth my journey. My girl – she didn't say goodbye. She waved. Her trade is choosing *now*, not luck – she's learnt. The proud call it betrayal, an offence.

When you drive a guy, you get time to read the books – those with the tricks, those with the panorama. On the road – you see the banks, the bodies. The 'little friends', boys and girls, the deadeye guys pushing deals. And you see – 'oh! the seasons, and the castles'. The great disappointment – Mongolia, with permanent constructions. On the road, it's all ephemeral, and jigging round the jams. How it should be. I grow – leaves, boughs, fruit: my three books, infinitely repeated, reproduced. 'Power lives to betray . . . humans blow away like cotton fluff, some get in your eye and throat . . . don't do the dirty job unless you're sure you walk away, unharmed, unburdened.' All the rest – air in the tires.

Brown tracks, black roads. Poles, stalls, and pumps. Back to how it started, the digs, the tailings, yellow clouds. In the beginning – the digging. Brought forth – roads. Roads where you go anywhere and everywhere. Black strips – the view. The poles, the lights – useless, will go. We need the pumps, the stalls – the eats. There's guys – twenty-four hours beneath their arms, flagging you down to do a deal. The *filles de joie* in their culottes, the chicken pieces on the stalls. What interrupts? Passages of sheep and goats. On we go, to Troy, to Herat, on to Harbin. All graded, flattened. On we go – Borzhoi in back, spitting the sunflower seeds, a spiky parrot. 'On, on: don't stop.'

'You're bad seed,' says Rufus. 'There's never a change in register, no other point of view. It's always yours. The poet, staring ahead, avoiding the dogs, the crash, the ditch. Unnatural. What do I think? Your girl – leaf-tossed, a double blank. You've no idea. Straight ahead, on, on . . .'

'It's so,' I say. 'It's the way we're built, and the work I have. It's more secure than other kinds of sitting down. Ahead, ahead, on and on. Avoiding the calamity. Avoid the other people in their motors, cruising, speeding, broken down. You're going down the funnel, you're sand in the glass, going from narrows into broads, the trees – reeds in the flow, the poles, the palaces, on and on, the world a steppe, the Cadillac our shoe that steps . . .'

'Exactly,' Rufus says. 'You choose to be the driver. All decisions are yours, and every accident, all the arrivals – due to you, in silence and in fasting. All yours.'

'These guys here,' I say. 'Been driven from their houses. My idea – would be to put them underground. So – they're invisible. No danger – everything beneath – they eat the mushrooms and the beanshoots, their cows no longer crazy with the sun and wind. Tiny brown chapels – no domes, no squinch to give them airs. No one to come and drive them out, and knock down everything . . .'

Have them live down there . . . they're safe, the tanks and boots – unsighted, trampling upstairs.

'Hmmmm,' he says. 'It may be you just want a panorama – with no features, just a plain, a planet horizontal – so you can drive without a person, wolf or sheep – that springs from roadside, drops from tree . . . It's all your interest that's in play,' he says. 'You want the flat. But –

the messages! They'll all be traced! No matter if you're in your chapel underground . . . Someone will hear – your prayer, your curse . . . and dig you out, or bomb you in . . . No, no, the answer is elsewhere. The brain! You can't send guys to live on Mars or Venus – cutting off their language root, experience, eyes and ears – the bleats, the singsongs and the dance . . . The brain's the gewgaw you must work on . . .'

'I hadn't thought,' I say.

'This awful body,' Rufus says, holding it up so I can see him, a blob, sea-urchin, oblonged in my mirror. 'I want rid of it . . . Instead, a brain that travels anywhere, without the pains and stimuli, the search for food and dictionaries, the sex, the soap, the waffles, calvados – and all the rest that body craves, insists on. Until that brain – that travels into space, or roams among the daffodils of yesteryear – is plastered in, Oh! driving man up front! Feel my frustration, longing, anger. The struggle! Brain and body, screwed together in unending strife . . . It's prison, friend. You walk with it, you cut its hair and nails. No crime, and no release.' Bobbing up and down – now you see his moustache, sealion or walrus – now the wavering beard.

'Well,' I say, 'that's all incurable. What I propose – instead of driving into nothingness for ever – maybe I could be the helmsman? A voyage. Steering. Not letting on the purpose, or the goal, the destination . . . "Going home" they call it. Though there is no home. There is oblivion. Dust. Maybe they dig you up and stain you brown. That's it. But . . . helmsman. Yes – it has a ring, sonority. It's got a crust . . .' I'm fascinated.

'Stop swerving, you idiot,' shouts Rufus. 'Just because you've found your crack in existence, your sunlit wall, your calling as a cold and supple lizard, – keep to the straight!'

'It's the joy,' I say. 'I'm sure it passes. I don't need you, Rufus, nor anyone behind me . . .'

He doesn't challenge me. 'Oh,' he says, 'I'm just a cuckoo. I tramp the world, I leave my eggs in other's nests, throw out their spotty little kids, in shell or skin . . . I take them over: my projects are so big, enormous . . . Invasive. "Cuckoo" they cry. And everybody tilts their ear, "Aha! I know that theme," they shout, and run to see . . . But – you never see the bird. It's flown,' and he laughs, long, too long, too loud.

Hiphop in Mongolia, fire alarms in Bangladesh – the schemes catch on, replete with plausibility.

'My fortune,' Rufus says, 'comes from intelligence. Poker. This noble lady – maybe the deck was lightly stacked. She loved me, wanted me to be her prince, but all I got was . . . her liquidity. Her French – had Russian endings. That's real class.'

We motor on, in silence. People all over – driven out: camps hidden in the hills. Their offence – passivity. Born wrong. In wrong places. 'This goddam tar, the tarmac. Filling up with gas . . .' I say. 'It all goes back to drills and mines and pipes and pumps. Holes in the ground – gold, cobalt, oil: it's all the same. My miserable origins . . .'

'Here is the sea!' shouts Rufus. 'Thalassa! Bars. Smokes. Hands off the wheel, and let some guy take . . . his wheel. Then off again. I know it's purgatory – but what comes next is worse.'

The sea – infinitely sad: jungle invisible. Bells ring with no human hands – fog, scored for unseen horns. There are no sheep, no cows – no church – attached.

'Your pain will cease,' says Rufus. 'A machine will drive the motor. Guys who thought they'd see my face, decide if it was honest – they'll scrutinise me on a screen. Your work, its pain, will cease. Remember – unemployment is secure. No interviews, anxiety, humiliation. On and on . . . Me? I'll be fine – capitalism rides hard those electric tigers it invents.'

'Rufus,' I ask, dismayed. 'I'll be a helmsman still?'

'Oh yes,' he says. 'You won't drive. But "helmsman" – all you guys, you warriors, you guides – yes, all of you will keep that honour . . . your destiny, your own, alone . . .'

Rufus sits up front with me – it doesn't make us equal. The road's a line, you follow it, then crossing it there's lines with cops – the frontiers. There's a good line too – the sheep that intersect, that you can count, and think of sleeping with their warmth – a stall . . .

'Take it from me, my friend,' he says, 'there is no promised land. No promise. And no land.'

'Should we load some women in the back?' he asks.

'Your hands are free,' I say. 'They might damp down the springs. Those waves, the rolling – it brings nausea.'

The driver. Without the motor, you are still a helmsman. You don't need, won't have, a ship. Those don't belong to you in any case – there's a Rufus somewhere, with the document. 'Reward the followers', 'administer the people', 'hail the victory, death to the faithless and backsliders' . . . You drive – that's it. Guys and gals in the back? Who cares. You steer the ship? The problem's with the storm, not the passengers. What keeps the sheep in line? The shepherd ahead, the dogs behind? Or simply being sheep, going after grass. No promise. No land. That's the secret everybody knows. You're the helmsman, doctor, wolf and saint. On, and on: onward, the soldiers, the faithful patients, the guy with the sandwich box full of dough . . .

'There's a layby,' Rufus says. 'We'll doss down here.'

*

The guys who come to rob us, to steal the motor – come from the camp that's out of sight.

It's what I'd do. We're the same species. Rufus doesn't ask for help. It's not my job – and I can run so fast! – maybe I'm blessed; a providence, a faith. Or that he's slow. You know he has the cash. He needs to justify his wealth, even – an apology. They try to start the Cadillac – it's way, way beyond them, so they stamp on Rufus. That's what I would do.

At his memorial, we sing 'The Enchanted Wanderer'. We weep. I read from *La Prisonnière*: the corpse 'a stone which encloses the salt of immemorial oceans', thinking of our voyages, and my pay packets .

. . 'the sealed envelope of a person who inwardly reached to infinity'. I don't mention running hands over Albertine. Rufus is dead, his sex as immaterial as his brain, his body. He wanted to be rid of one, or both. There was nothing in him you could know. Like Albertine – maybe he wasn't real. Or bits of real people, and so unreal. His capital lives on. His associates are in the room, all singing like a hatch of frogs.

I sell his Rolls – it's my new life, the cash. It's the least I could have done.

We mill – we mull – around the absent cadaver.

'Chantal!' I say. 'The name is beautiful. You're the thing of beauty Rufus left, I'm sure. In life, one's all you are allowed. You know – the motors – those he left to me . . .'

She's not so great – rather, it's her scent. And clothes. Take them away, and . . . 'Here is some cash,' I say. 'There was no will. I'm sure you were the one, despite the lack . . .'

'Oh,' she says, 'I'm in the *Palais froid*. The castoffs, castaways end there. But they get paid, and into the mausoleum they go too, when the emperor decides to go to paradise.'

'That's poetry,' I say. 'How did you cleave to him?'

'No cleaving, dear,' she says. 'I organise the coursing of the hare. My castle grounds . . .'

'How does it work?' I ask.

'The hares are freed, they make the run through the long grass, and clients shoot them. It's their fun,' she says.

'I never saw him, Chantal, with a gun. We were all innocents, up there,' I say.

Chantal folds my notes away, the serenade is done. Farewell.

'I am the hare that gets away and makes the massacre a sport,' I say.

'That's trite,' she says. 'You say you're an escapee. Everybody says you are the heir, with Rufus's cash and all his tastes.'

'I know the universe was not created for my contemplation – though when I die, it all will disappear. Rufus didn't leave me money – maybe, sitting behind, staring at my head, the patterns, the designs, priorities carpentered in his brain . . . he passed them on. Someone did for sure. I didn't invent them all myself – the colours, tastes, the duties and the punishments. And yet – they ended up inside,' I say.

'Sometimes imposed, sometimes inborn,' she says. 'That's the dirty trick. How to sort them out?'

'Oh,' I say, 'it's not because there's animals, along with us. Everybody gets a weapon, like the gladiators – a twisty wing, a claw. Never the right combination so you'd always win – the armour's holed, the sword's an edge but not a point. Everyone is equal, as you never have the right accoutrements. It's not that. You can't object to it. What I strive for – it's being not imposed upon. Speaking as if the language is your own. Escaping.'

'That's what the guys did who stamped on Rufus,' Chantal says.

'I escaped my destiny,' I say. 'I'll go on doing it. That's all, the best, that you can do. Then – you get caught, cornered. That's too bad.'

'You should be good,' says Chantal. 'Then nothing matters more.'

'I told you, Chantal,' I say. 'Escaping is the best there is.'

'Then what? Do it again?' she asks.

'Leave no trace,' I say. 'That is immortality. Curiosity – the only quality. No heritage, no lesson. No amusements as a legacy.'

'Well,' she says. 'I do the opposite of all that.'

'Maybe not the exact opposite,' I say, wanting to be pleasant. Or because I didn't know.

'I absolutely have to leave,' she says. and so she does.

I think those animals, the hares, the sheep – know everything they have to know, to do. What they don't know is humans, their motive. And that, it's quite irrelevant for them to know.

The sheep is good, are good. It's the shepherd we know we can't be sure about. He or she is good and bad. It doesn't matter to the sheep. Me? I can't be a sheep – but I needn't be a shepherd. Because . . . we know . . . Without a tribunal to investigate . . . we know all about being human, everything we need to know. And all about those shepherds too.

'Keeping shtum about the cash? I envy you – that's all pleasure,' and here's another – a Diana – after me, after the good life. This one – maybe in from the street, 'I'm Britney. A relative.' A good cry for Rufus. A lake of tears, some kind of race – a treasure hunt.

'Oh no,' I say. 'All these people. Hunters – a hunter isn't quite a predator, but here are predators. Bend down – you see their legs, it's like a spinney, birch and oak.'

'We're all here because we're sad. We've all lost . . .' she says. She doesn't bend.

'It's like the guys in France, romancing,' I say. 'Partying, making a fuss about the boys and girls they hunted, and the size of those big cheeses who'd take tea with them. Writing it all down, seeing themselves as master of the dance.'

'There's no tea here,' says Britney. 'This scotch is real. The hunt is harsher too. The spirit is elusive. Rufus – no body, now no soul that we can catch . . .'

'You're right,' I say. 'The hide and seek is rough. It ends, quite sensibly, in other deaths. For Rufus – oblivion: he left no record of the banks his wealth was in.'

He clutched that sandwich box. Could it have fitted all in there, the cash, and disappeared?

'They'd find a wood, and trap the stag inside. The huntsmen were all round – they couldn't see each other, so they talked with horns. The different calls. Muster. Gone away. Each move was musicked. Then the dogs went in,' I say.

And there is Rufus, a red-brown envelope, transparent – leaping out, his antlers bright with myth and gold . . . Away, away, down the hill – that's the instant you forget the numbers of the bank accounts, you're pure and poor, your carnal self is disinherited. Off, down the hill – use the stream to throw the dogs . . . the elfin fanfares fainter now, a silver horn plucks at the silver air . . .

The mist, the frost, turns us all into an ancient silver print . . .

'Everything has changed,' I say. 'These people here, looking for his memory – they are not friends, whose intimacies become my tales. Not my friends, not his. Now, they're after *me*. If they can't kill the absent Rufus, quarter him – they'll go after me . . .'

'Your eyes,' says Britney, 'brim with fear. I love it, your humble humanity.'

'Ah yes. The gift of fear . . . Where I came from, there was work,' I say. 'Once, too, I'd have begged to be a servant for Chantal.'

'So?' Britney asks, 'what is your point?'

'I thought it was quite clear,' I say. 'Joining some class. Dying for yourself, your cause. I preferred to drive . . .'

'Where Rufus said,' she says.

'Rufus was no messenger,' I say. 'I chose the road. You saw – I'm not a slave. Chantal took my cash . . .'

'An error,' Britney says. 'Or else you stole it from his corpse. And so – it weighs.'

'Oh no,' I say. 'It's feathers. It's lighter even than the work you do today, and there it is tomorrow, just the same, always starting over, like the tide. Or sometimes not. Cash – it's always there. You don't feel a weight.'

They cluster round me – a rally of animals, a-sniff. What's the driver – sex? Food? An excitement that can end in both?

'I suffocate,' I say. 'You bear me down.'

'Oh – really?' says Britney. 'I'm the dependable type. A Buick, built heavy.'

'To me,' I say. 'You're more a samoyed. They give you lustre in the city, pulling them along, reluctant on their string. But in the wild – omnivorous and bossy.'

I'd recognise these people in the street. Each one has a dignity, an exclusiveness. A different shape, a timbre, gait, a set of tastes and smells. That's good for them. I look around the group: here, tales abound. I'm not like them, I don't gather anecdotes, and I don't hunt.

Then – a moment of epiphany: once, you'd have said, of revolutionary consciousness.

'Rufus – the best shepherd you could have,' I say to Britney, Chantal who has turned her ear . . . 'He was so quiet and satisfied, sat back there, wherever I felt like taking him, and doing all the work.'

And now, I'll safely graze on what his motor car has realised. Sheep aren't so stupid, though they may be limited. The inspiration – it alights. The company's alert:

'Why,' I shout, 'you're nothing but a pack of dogs!'

New life! It flares up like a star.

~ Always ~

The gauge always shows full. It's most convincing when it means – I'm empty. Up and up, the path made of shifting stones in mud. Stacked pines, amputees beside the track; others, survivors, tall pensive ones, heads in the clouds. Up through the mist, the space. It seems there's no top, no top to anything. No view, no depth to fear, driving into white swirl, concentrating like you're in an arcade game. At last, a clearing, opaque . . . the wiper arms, metal stumps, the rubbers stolen, have carved uneven tracks upon the glass.

Here's a shack, a restaurant. There's black continents of sodden wood mapped through the ancient whitewash; an entrance through an outhouse door.

'Here you are, at last!' shouts out the guy, the boss, the chief, white shirt a little stained. 'Now, I'll make the best meal you've ever had.' There's no one else: I've never been here, never seen him.

He has a rifle, maybe he hunts. A gun with hammers, no bolt.

'No, no,' I say, drawn in, falling in his trap, his pot. Don't kill for me, to show off . . . 'Don't bother, I'm not hungry, not at all . . .'

He's prone. He aims. Down in a clearing, some guys, maybe they're foresters, swigging something, perched on their stumps. 'One shot,' he says. 'The war will start.'

'No, no,' I say. 'Those are my brothers.' A trick of speech, but still . . .

'Idiot,' he shouts. 'They're not your brothers. They're more likely to be mine.'

A potshot? From a master cook?

Strong patriotism. It must be that. A fratricide, cannibalism, or – just straight hatred? A love of country, even one quite shabby and corrupt, attracts, when it appears. Maybe it ought not. I've known, admired so many Russians, proud of what's been done and not . . . but – this guy is too excited, we are not in Russia . . . and he has this wart

119

stuck on his nose – pink, with a tip, brown, waggling as he rants. Not a Napoleon, a Caesar. They were smooth.

Slowly, the guys below go back to work and out of sight. He waves the muzzle where one woodsman was . . . stands up, uncocks the gun.

'Now!' he says. 'I'll show you how it's done. My special food.'

There's cheese that tastes of bitumen. Red turnips – I'm used to them much better cooked. The milk – sour; or 'full of health', he says, the tingling taste, the lumps . . . maybe just strange. The bread – tough grains, black, brown and ivory, hard as a marble floor.

'Are you charging this huge sum?' I ask, when all is done.

'I told you, it's a special meal,' he says. The bill is written out in full, a purple stamp on top.

Months later, there is war. I'm far away by then.

1

I know how to be happy. It's what everyone wants. I have it, the trick, so there's no need to do it all at once. If you're happy when you die, there's no reason it shouldn't go on for ever. It's really not what I want, though; not to have it as my accomplishment in life. It's trivial, after all.

There's a broth of people here – naturally, that's unsettling – the different paths pursued, most in silence, all those beliefs that boil down. You feel for yourself, your security, not knowing what direction something that happens might come from. You move close to people you know, even if they're not the cream.

In Europe, in a market, you don't need distinguish any country in particular. You're on a continent. Hassled and on the move.

Toni: might call him a parasite – steals things from you, when you move in or out, slips into the house, the apartment, and takes something. Violence is a failure, but he has a Stanley knife, cuts your face – blood and fluid from your eye; while you check, he's gone. 'How'd you get in here?' someone asked him. 'I used my imagination,' he says, and they laugh. That's the best line in movies, though it sounds better there, a swift cut – you're in!

His friend Adnan: moves in the poorer parts, writes letters for you, finds a doctor, a lawyer. Often he has to cheat, but not for much. Doesn't steal, unless it's new, homeless stuff, undeliverable . . . He has a memory of his good book, that helps him strive. 'You should do French philosophy,' he says, 'but not live like French people, in hypocrisy – they're not especially free, certainly not equal, and not fraternal, especially if you get a syntax wrong.'

'I love this market,' Adnan says. 'Here's a white porcelain bowl, too small to hold anything at all. Now, if it were genuine . . .'

'Remember the bombers!' a small guy's shouting. 'Remember where and why you bombed.' No one reacts. 'Some are planes, and some are people. They'll always get through,' he says.

'This obsession with conflict,' Toni says. 'I don't even feel angry.'

'It's all about winning,' Adnan says. 'Your good book, Toni. The Prince. Fancy explanations. Nonsense. Win – that's the start and finish. Look – there's a copy of my book,' pointing to a mauve, unjacketed thing, *How to Cheat at Poker*.

'Not your book,' Toni says.

'Of course, I didn't write it. It's beneath me. It was my book, like "my coat", "my girl". My property, like your theft.' They spar around, comfortably.

'This isn't the Italian quarter,' Adnan goes on. 'They're swarthy, but they don't speak the language. None of them. They just don't speak.'

'I'm swarthy,' Toni says, 'but not like them. In Italy, there's light and dark. That doesn't make a point.'

'I see you in a picture, Toni,' Adnan says, 'covered all over in black silk, like it was your religion. Medium height, some education, slippery.'

'Like a warrior,' Toni says.

'The birdman. Hawks return, sit, crap on you, that structure, all in black,' says Adnan, and he laughs. 'That's what you stand for. Getting taken over. That will to win – you're not the only one who has commitment. It's a word not often used, not nowadays. It's all about yourself, the winning. You're not so smart, you lose: you're taken over.'

'Dark forces, dark forces, Adnan,' Toni says. 'Sure, they're there, for and against you. Hope? They call it insanity – doing the same thing over and over, each time expecting the same result.'

I sit near them on the bench – they don't talk to me, and I don't intervene. They've had this conversation over and over. It's reassuring. On the wood, I see tiny red spiders, maybe growing their own food, each with a tiny brain, or maybe part of one big one, believing in something.

'I saw this movie,' Adnan says. 'Remember how keen they were, the Vietnamese, and all the guys here – that they should win their war? It was a movie – about what they eat! A carpet of chicks, cute and rounded like lemons, cheeping their song, each one. Then – a swarm, a company, hoisted in a bag, dropped in a boiling cauldron. Silence. Instantly.'

'I know,' says Toni. 'They feed the cadavers to the snakes. What's new? To each his taste, snakes too.'

'It was the silence. All boiled alive. What was that supposed to teach?'

'Everyone wanted them to win,' says Toni.

'Is that winning? The silence? Futile,' Adnan says.

'Better than going live into the snake,' says Toni.

Adnan says, 'Is that the lesson, then? Better dead than something else?'

There's a silence. Then Toni says, 'It's a terrible way to live, I know. I can't live any other way.'

'People live bad,' says Adnan, 'And I am one of them. I share it, all of it.'

'Where'll we go?' Toni asks. It's a game.

'Not France. They've those long sticks to beat you,' Adnan says. 'Rome – they're pretty rough, but it's the indifference that wears you. And you can't call an Italian stupid. It's the worst insult. The truth is always the direst word.'

'You think I'm stupid? Fuck you, then,' says Toni. 'Berlin. That's the best. They treat you like porcelain, in case you break and haunt them.'

'Somewhere colourful,' says Adnan, ' Not painted on. Not Berlin, then. A market, full of busy people.'

'Kashgar,' says Toni, and they both relax. It's their pleasure, a trip that always ends in the same place.

'You know,' says Adnan, 'the people I go to – they don't want to know about their cancer, or their deportation. They want me to help their psyche.'

'No one does psychoanalysis now,' says Toni. 'They want capitulation. No doctors. What we do isn't pleasant. What's pleasure? Little routine things. Better look for something larger.'

'Pleasure's quite out. No one wants sex with you, Toni,' Adnan says. 'And I didn't say "analysis". I said "psyche". They want to know if they have one, and if it'll help them. Death is the proof, of course, whether you have one – the next best thing, if you can't get sex.'

'I'm looking for something solid,' Toni says. 'In my line. I know you disapprove.'

'Be careful, Toni,' Adnan says. 'There's no room for you, not to be free, and not to go deep in, serving some racket, working for some guys. They'll dump you, if you don't get caught.'

I sit, not looking at them. They know me, know I'm there. They don't care, it's their game. You can't be serious all day. The trees here – they drop stickiness in our hair: they must be limes.

'You can't get a passport, Adnan', Toni says. 'It's called restraint. This here's all the room you'll ever get.'

'If you can't steal, you must beg,' says Adnan.

'That's a proverb.' I interrupt.

'Beautiful and lifeless, worthy of the teacher, Jacko,' Toni says, kidding, maybe.

'I'm not a monkey, Toni,' I say.

'"Mimic and repeat", that's what monkeys do,' says Toni. 'All monkeys are called Jacko. They break the beauty with their paws.'

'Where my people were, that's the place for proverbs,' Adnan says.

'You don't have a place, Adnan,' Toni says.

'Everyone has a country, tucked somewhere in their head, where they can stride around,' says Adnan.

'That's a laugh,' says Toni.

'Laugh. That's a good one,' I say. 'I'm always looking for good couples: beg and steal, laugh and cry. Laugh. I'm glad I don't need to teach them how to spell. These refugees I teach the language to – how they resist! They don't believe a word!'

We're better friends than I would like. '*Il y a toi sans doute que je connais pas*': is it here the voyage comes to term? I. The eye, the one of three, always thinking he knows best, better, seeing more. Quite pineal. Journey's end – may be good, or bad, but it's the end, alas. There's always someone there, along the way, we never knew, we won't be remembered by: no doubt.

'Hey,' says Toni across to me. 'You! Listening in, like we were on air.'

'My crew got drowned, jumped ship, married mermaids. I'm the captain of the raft. I get to tell the tale. The history's all mine, also the favours owed me by variegated gods and other spirits of the deeps,' I say.

They're satisfied with this. I'm the familiar void. Another stranger, stories of massacres and battles, fortunes lost and women won, dragons decapitated, jade discovered by the ton . . . They've all been washed up here, the same shipwrecked tales, the poor and frightened lot, all scrabbling. Don't get hung up on the thorns of their experience.

'Just think,' says Toni. 'If we were good. What havoc we would cause.'

'Think – if we were rich – what havoc!' Adnan says. 'As it is – we're just the grease that makes the whole thing hum and shake, and have a form. To change ourselves – what shall we do? The first step sets the direction, points the boat. The hardest, the decisive one.'

'Behind you, to start you off – there must be the pretext,' Toni says. 'You must see your shadow safe behind you, try to outrun it. That's the deal.'

'Adnan and I – we exploit ignorance,' I say. 'Toni – their forgetfulness. It's not so terrible.'

'The thing to do,' says Toni. 'Is follow climate. Something doesn't fruit or flower. Pine-nuts, for instance. The kitchen begs for them – there are none, save in some museum. So – that's the market you must corner. Some insect's eaten all the dates. You're in!'

'Informing,' Adnan says. 'That's what the three of us can do. Work for the cops. It's clean and easy.'

*

'What do you think of me joining with Da'esh?' asks the lad.

'Since it's me you ask, I think you won't,' I say. 'It isn't you. I'm here to teach the language, so you'd function anywhere. Religion? Fighting – that's imponderable, I guess. The religion bit, at least. That doesn't involve winning or losing. But winning – that's imponderable too.'

'So,' he insists, 'ponderable and imponderable. That's a couple. Of opposites?'

'Yes and no,' I say.

'It's the reasoning I'm interested in,' the lad says. 'Not the doing.'

'Yes,' I say. 'Maybe *those* are opposites. Reasoning and doing. History and having no beliefs. Fighting for a home, and having none. Taking someone else's. Being modern, being less ancient than someone else. Your modern being ancient too. Being cruel, being evil, so's later you can be merciful, show you're good.'

'Hey!' says the lad, 'you're mixing up. I don't want to go, but I'm free to go. That's the upside, the proof I'm well off . . .'

'Paradox is a cruel master,' I say.

'Napoleon said, "*On s'engage et puis on voit.*" He was a great slaughterer. He won. He lost in one of the many ways. You could have bet on that,' he says.

'There's no casino where every customer always wins,' I say. 'An altruistic customer might wish for one. Or if they're trying to get your winnings so's they can play with them.'

'Love makes you do gross things, and yet it makes the world go round.' He peers at me.

'There's more grown-up explanations for rotation,' I say.

'Well,' he says, 'if it's not belief and obedience, maybe it's duty does it.'

'That's a slippery fish,' I say. 'Your ought, indifferent to the is? A sacrifice, a suicide? Exiting the game.'

'Or,' he says, playing me along, 'there's making a new home.'

'A house is just the start,' I say. 'A decent place costs lots, takes years.'

'You're not teaching me anything,' he says. 'You don't know the arguments either.' I say,

'Bad causes, lost causes – they're always causes. when things go wrong, you need something to tie the ends. Don't freedom and sacrifice stand for anything?'

'They seem to stand only once and for all. You either have it, freedom, or you don't; and if there's sacrifice, you're dead, out of the game,' he says. 'Most don't want that.'

'Then you're in the wrong game,' I say. 'An older one, a newer one. Tying everything together when if flies apart – and doing something that changes it all. A glue.'

'Or you could let it fly apart – just to see where the pieces fall,' he says.

'Yes,' I say. 'That attracts me too. Are you sure you need these language lessons?'

'Oh,' he says, 'I'm missing nothing. I don't have cash to pay you. I'm the teacher anyway, as much as you. More, it seems.'

'That attracts me too,' I say. 'I gain, whoever does the teaching. But remember: beg or steal. No use begging from you – and I'm not sure you have anything to steal.'

'I don't believe in decorations,' he says. 'Those naff posters and stuff.'

'If you don't have them, people who come to rob you find nothing, beat up on you instead,' I say. 'I'm protected,' he says. 'I'm too young to be a target. That's a temporary gain – it doesn't mean you'll never die.'

*

'It was provocative,' I tell Adnan. 'I like that. I saw a book in his room. *The Veda Made Simple.* I guess that's provocative too.'

'Well,' says Adnan. 'Don't mix him in with us. That would be strange.'

'Strained,' I say. 'He's our age. It's just that he's behind with language. He's not interested in this religion, or another. Or who rules which piece of land. It's what holds it all together, and makes our intention give it meaning. The cosmos. Our ritual: that's our intention.'

'It's gesture,' Adnan says. 'What holds it all together, makes the moon rise, the snow fall – is language. The ritual of language. Or – the language of ritual.'

'No no,' I say, 'that's just the fallacy. The snow that falls, the sand that's blown: and then, our gesture – you can't have one without the other. It's not all one thing, mashed into speech. It all must interdepend, dear Adnan.'

'I never heard a thing that's so banal,' he says. 'The observer makes nothing. Nothing happens when you observe. Happening – the cosmos happens, but it takes a ritual to make it so . . .'

I wonder if he has got where he had meant to go.

'This person,' I say, 'I'm supposed to instruct him. In some ways, he's far ahead. He finds my questions childish. But – his vocabulary lags.'

'How does he live?' asks Adnan. 'I bet he begs, one way or another. Selling his brain, keeping his language hidden somewhere. Not marching off to war – that is for sure.'

'Young guys,' I say, 'younger than us – they think a war will set them up, pre-empt the real big one everybody says is coming soon. They think – "warriors, women dealt out, and living right and good". A man's life, that.'

'They say we should feel guilty for the massacres. Really, it means we should be feeling guilty for our debts. Paying them back to some guy, so's he can lend some more,' says Adnan.

'That's normal,' I say. 'Lend, get paid back, lend again. Normal, though to me – it's mad! Why not just spend it? It's clear – I don't understand normal.'

'As usual, it's all about us,' Toni says, dropping in to end the talk. 'Us, the solution that's the problem. I'm out, I fold. That's my solution. You guys – just carry on. If what I do is hurtful, you'll get over it. Then you can all go on and deal out hurts to everyone, yourselves the most.' We ignore him; I say,

'This guy, my pupil, Alp he's called – maybe he wants to clamp some Veda on me?'

'Or he's an astrophysicist,' says Adnan. 'A starman, like I always say.'

'He wants to dissent,' I say. 'But you need a special country to do that in. Here, you've to do something so unpalatable, you get arrested, and no one's all that interested. Wild things here – they come in concerts, ticketed on a stage.'

'We're supposed to like simple people, sympathise with their ideas, however reactionary they are,' says Toni. 'You don't like him. He isn't simple. He doesn't think there's anything better than what he's got. So, he's immobile. He doesn't enquire – "who makes me happy?" If he wondered, maybe he'd be sad.'

'He's happy,' Adnan says. 'It's his responsibility. Like when he's sad.'

'Don't you have a female student?' Toni asks me. 'Change the music. No opposites. Sits in a corner painting her head, so's you can't see who's inside. "That's my idea of fun," she says.'

'That's long ago, Toni,' Adnan says. 'It's too late. Punk's gone by. That's what you want, because it's dead. Women want what men used to want. Things change – you haven't.'

Despite what they do – they don't dance or sing. Free, here, they learn nothing. If they do a little time, for commerce on the side – they'll come out rapping, with some new dance. Make a name. They're strong, and they'll get stronger.

They're my best friends, my mates, my *potes*. We understand, we grasp, we know each other – strands in a rope.

I have to get away from them. I doubt they'll miss me. Away, away!

My disease was love; my new companion – solitude. There! There's the reasons. Or – trying something new? At the bus station – there's a bus, leaving for Kishinau.

Alp helps to load the stuff, the travellers. 'Do they pay you?' I ask.

'Some say "thanks". You know, you can always get off along the way,' he says. 'You pass where those delicate poets live – the scent of nutmeg, sound of rutting stags – in through the study window.'

'In the bus, there's little nature, Alp,' I say, as though he doesn't know. 'Sometimes a wasp . . . and then there's commotion, a massacre, then everybody's friends. Leaves, buds, night . . . they're all the same. Roads. A stop to pee, a stop to pick up never-speaking friends. It's delicate too, you see. It makes you think, "Is this a copy of another trip? where did I finish up? Why did I want to leave? Where do I want to go?" On the bus, there is no crime, no deals, no compromise. You go where it says up front.'

'There!' says Alp. 'Now you know it all.'

In Switzerland, there's sea acquaria. Those blobby balloons, bemused and gawping. Couscous in France. Is the journey driven to escape the horrors? Running to find the start, the home, where the pitcher will throw the last, the fatal ball. Off with your head . . .

'Here comes the prof,' shouts Alp. 'He knows all what you don't, and all what you might want to know.' He bangs on pans that's fallen from a bundle.

The guys inside make lots of space. No one sits near. That's rather good. Maybe I don't want to go with them, my crew? The smugglers, the expelled, those with a false identity, and those with none. Maybe a guardian, close beside? Maybe a lost princess who's cast a shoe?

I hear the talk:

'They gave him a new heart, but they forgot to put the nurse inside. That's what costs. You need someone within, to prod it all along. Or else it stops again.' They're good people, the passengers. I'm as happy getting on the bus as now – I'm getting off. Maybe I'll never see Moldova, but there's many other countries – they're being made up all the time – and I've so many years to come . . . I'm off the bus. Alp shouts, 'Here comes the Prof. A prof off, not off!' And to me, 'Your princess? Somewhere along the road to Kishinau? Your honour? And your lust?'

'The story of the love betrayed?' I say. 'Let's leave it far behind. A pact of silence. Let's say it was in Istanbul, or Troy, and not be sure. That story's over. We're all free – let's not confuse that, insisting with revenge, nostalgia, chasing old flames that come and go above the bogs. Now, shed our skins, tattoos and scars, and grow a newer, scalier one.'

'So,' says Alp. 'I don't get to sing your song. Nor row your ship.'

'Honour and love,' I say, 'have shrunk. They're spandrels in the brain. They live in stories, and in songs. That's all.'

'I'll get a refund for your fare,' says Alp. He seems disappointed. 'Those Greeks,' he says, 'believed in honour wars. Women and gods, they're all mixed in. The soldiers – on cold Thracian hills . . . those crowded tents, comrades in arms, each others, that's for sure . . . Both ways, or any way, was good.'

'Keep the refund, Alp,' I say. 'Now, you can pay me what you owe.'

'No,' he says, 'let's invest.'

Toni and Adnan have a stall. Piled with stuff found and robbed – they're tired of being chased.

'We're now legit,' says Adnan. 'It's all collectable. We put stuff on the stall, and tell the cops who stole it first.'

I collect. I get the rush. Objects. Make it clear, the subject's you. You are the pharaoh, but you don't die, you collect grave goods all your life, and then.

'You didn't follow her,' says Adnan. 'That Russian, stole your girl, and took her off, over the plains, fiddling his entrancing trills, a devil, bigger than you'll find round here . . .'

'He wouldn't stop in Kishinau,' I say. 'Deeper and deeper, past the guns, hop over black fields, black mines and blackened folk – on, on – the silvery trees, enamelled snows . . . My girl, tucked underneath his arm, as on they go, deep into Russia, through those huge cities no one knows and no one leaves. There, on the border, there's Mongolia – there, you're safe. No targets for the bombs. Everybody fears a Genghiz; when you're exhausted . . . then, out ride the soldiers. Despatch who's left.'

No one listens. Already, they are frightened.

'We specialise,' says Toni. 'Time capsules. The bourgeoisie is crazy for them. They're buried bones. We dig them up. The stuff is rare. It's bought, and buried, then we dig it up again.'

It's so. The stall is full of tubes, stories banal of trivial lives . . . true history. Choc bars and comix, a paper with the sport.

'Your girl,' says Alp. 'Your honour. You won't follow either . . .'

'They're ghosts,' I say. 'They're in the depths of Russia. Those two are there for ever, refuge sought; and now anonymous, a nuisance. Dragging out a life, perhaps. But – ghosts. I know where they are, if ever I should want. They're mine . . . They've only me to haunt.'

'Adnan and Toni, they collect the capsules so's there won't be future. No one to dig, nothing to be dug,' says Alp.

'Or maybe they don't want someone to be left, when they are not,' I say. 'We're all time capsules, but mostly we don't get found. Or even buried. Remember the song, "The soft wind wakes the buds, the naked trees put on their green – but you, my love, are bleached and gone, stolen by the frost and ice . . .'"

'I don't get it,' says Alp, indifferent.

'It's not that hard,' I say. 'But it's your loss. I've had mine.'

'If you don't work for someone,' Toni says. 'It means you're worthless. Not worth a tuppenny twizzle.'

'We all work for something, but it's not tat, not like this,' says Alp, knocking stuff to the ground.

'It's all a cover, Alp,' says Adnan. 'But you're not worth it being told.'

'There's no qualities in us,' says Toni. 'That's lacking. No one in the news has more than we have.'

'Boarding for Kyzyl,' the dispatcher shouts. It's tempting. I don't move. 'Ceuta, Batman . . .'

'Don't you guys tire of antwork?' Alp asks. 'Picking sticks so's you can sit and pick your nose and pay some rent? Waiting for the cops, the envelope . . . the tumour, the demand . . . Even being in the wrong's a bore. Things move along, fall off the edge. Things don't ask where you were and did – only you do that. The future? Where is that? Who invented it, and who'd be in or out? And do you need a passport?'

Then – he's gone. Dark smoke, a roar, some bundles abandoned, scattered. Like whales, the buses leave. 'Everyone must come through here,' says Toni. 'Gawping and mute. We never knew young Alp that well. Can he have gone to war, decided how many years he'd want to live, do bad things, be forgotten, turn, from subject into object?'

'There's a couple, Toni,' I say. 'I never taught him that. Subject, object. Which you might want to be, and if the choice is permanent.'

'Oh, for sure it's irreversible,' says Adnan. 'But there's more to war than that. The most guys do is make the soup, censor the mail, bury cadavers, chivvy the prisoners. It's dull.'

'Alp doesn't want to fight,' I say. 'What's he to do here? Mind your stall? Clear attics? Maybe he wants to find another history. You've no suggestions, Toni, Adnan.'

'I can tell you,' Toni says. 'Exactly how it falls. Adnan's poker book just makes you enemies. Mine – shows you anyone can be a Prince, and how to stay one. People's the start: the world – that's the only place you're able to liberate the souls. The cards say that: Astarte, Plato . . . Winning's not survival, it's the soaring up, away from traitors and bad women. That's what you must do – or rather, what one of us may do. People disappear. The easy way is thinking they are dead. But maybe they've migrated, their soul like folded wings, borne off. Alp's too bright to be a soldier – that path is slippery and short.'

'Bad women, Toni?' Adnan says. 'You've been with them, hidden it from us?'

'The devil keeps a stall,' says Toni. 'That way you see his breasts, not the forked penis dangling in the crate . . . Bananas! That's on every box. Don't believe it. He watches as you pass, decide not to buy. It's rubbish – but someone sees a glister, pauses. Is sucked in. Then you hear his violin. Maybe you're the fool; or plump and in his castle . . . It's a test, a trial. Maybe your soul will flutter down, the powdered wings transparent, useless . . . Like you, Adnan. You think it's all revealed. "Obey" – the happiness will come, if you repeat the mantra. Instructions on the carton: follow them, and be content.'

'No, Toni,' Adnan says. 'The mantra is a rite. Get it out the way, an itch five times is scratched – and then the time's your own . . . You are the chief.'

'It's not enough,' says Toni. 'One brief life. One bounded context. Everything stored in a banana box. One chance, one group that understands, one wave to surf . . . It's clearly not enough. Even a golem can't make its way – they're all pitched in against. Immortality – already, that has its monopolists. I don't ask that – just time, lots of it, stretching out.'

'I could float along with you,' I say. 'I guess. But that makes me a patsy. "All for the cause, respect for comrades, agree to disagree . . . the imperative of shedding blood not mine . . ." – then, you get stuck! Sat in the getaway car, the cops all round: and you are all alone.'

'Well,' Toni says, 'I've no intention of sitting there with you. That is the point. You see decline. Only that. Adnan thinks the bad will pass him by, if he just tends his goats. It's not at all like that. The present will explode – and I'll be there, right in the frame, installed upon my rock. My rocket.'

'He means,' says Adnan, 'what you are now, what you think, what you have . . . when the flames go up, it doesn't matter. No money, no trades. Away with the charm, the smarm. No one will have anything. You start again – maybe you won't.'

'Fire!' shouts Toni. 'I'm the salamander. They pay guys to imagine – what they call catastrophes. Because most don't come about – they think that's the end of it. But – I'll be there, the salamander, pitterpat through the flames.'

'Salamanca,' the dispatcher says. 'El Andalus.'

'Yes,' says Adnan, 'that would be my place.'

'Do you see the flames, Jacko?' Toni asks me.

'Of course,' I say. 'And I'm not your monkey, Toni. You don't respect what I have done.'

'What you've seen, not done,' says Toni. 'That's what you mean.'

The flames plait together to make a crest. At the base, there's green and yellow, little dancing sprites, then they grow up, wavering, become adult. Why this orange, then the red? Why the transformation, earth and two-by-twos, into such beauty? Purple and violet . . . you see those too. The rocks go white and dusty.

I don't feel the heat.

'Your boat,' says Toni, 'lodged in the canal at Corinth – the walls on fire, the iron bridge scrumples like a taffy, the stone burns, spurtles out, going up, smells like a hedge of thyme . . . your ship, papery, veined like a pea-pod, the harpies on the bow – my! how they scream. Will you get through? Will you hell!'

'And you're the helmsman, Toni?' asks Adnan.

'Not me!' says Toni, 'I'm the bugger with the torch, running ahead, sending it all up!'

'It's your fantasy, Toni,' Adnan says. 'Like my goats.'

'Well,' Toni says, 'I'm not one of your runts, thrown squealing in the hopper.'

'There's a guy I know, proposing a thing,' I say. 'Could suit us all.'

'Really?' Adnan says, 'a boys' thing? Like *Star Wars*? All boffing together? With our light-sticks? No, no: I'm not in.'

'Proposals aren't all into space,' says Toni. 'There's the hanged man too, upside down by one leg, an anomalous crucifixion. But – it's true: the stall is doing well.'

'The array is good,' I say. 'But nothing's sold.'

'It has to be good to look at,' Adnan says, 'or there's no hope. Investors work that way.'

I know what Toni's thinking, at any moment, and what he returns to. More than I know about myself. The uncertainty of happenstance – it breaks the lines . . . Adnan – he wants some certainty. Well, he won't have that, not ever.

'Everything makes a difference,' Toni says. 'But nothing of that is interesting. Not to me. People believing, changing their minds, where they live: even the mountain top that overlooks – blowing itself off . . . it's all changed, but it isn't what I want, it can all be painted in, it's all within the edges of the canvas.'

'What more is there?' Adnan asks. 'People present their projects – and it's all about people, in the end, and they're not loyal, not predictable.'

'That's so,' says Toni. 'In the end, it comes down to clothes. I loved them – the red, the yellow, the vinyl; umbrellas with a tiny frost of strass. The things here on this stall – each one has my respect. I want each to leave, find the new vocation – stretched out naked and needy now. Find the gift.'

'They are the gift, surely,' I say. I don't understand.

'Oh well,' Toni says, 'I'd find some women, really down, no cash. Maybe a need. I make an introduction – I'm some guy with cash, a need . . . Then – the girls'd maybe take the poison. Couldn't stop. I tried to be a high-class seller. It was the clothes, in the end attracted them, and me: quite wild!'

He can't be believed. But it's true, things that rest on people, can't be trusted, can't be secure.

'Pimping,' Toni says. 'It doesn't suit. It's like a hospital. They have to get a fix – then it's out the bed, and off.'

'It seems an easy job,' Adnan says. 'Stand around and take the cash.'

'It wasn't cowardice,' says Toni, 'that turned me off. It's not something you take a risk with, like being shot at dawn. It was empty.'

'But not the clothes,' says Adnan. 'Those are full, then they get sold, on someone's stall.'

'Some to museums,' Toni says, quite glum. 'But people gawp at anything, even if it's not for sale. Old pictures, shoes, stone heads. You put some venerable date, an impossible price – there's lines of *polli* round the block. It seems it's all the peepshow crowd.'

'Everyone wants to be like you, Toni,' Adnan says. 'No shame, and no originality.'

Sure, Toni's a fetishist – it means he should prize his ancestors. But – there's his talk, relentless, maybe false. And Adnan – I see the tree, a family tree – the prophets and the patriarchs are always at the top, descendants the branches, upside down . . . a tree of which he is a twig, silent and nodding . . . and him? A flower? A fruit? What might arise? Where can he go?

'Well,' Adnan says. 'Tell us – what's the plan? That guy?'

'Nothing,' I say. 'It melted quite away – maybe as we spoke.'

*

I'm rid of them. And here – a vast deposit, like heaven's done a clearance . . . here's a noble hi-fi, in a cabinet. 1950s, I should guess, still plugging on, those tunes, the massacres still underground, unheard. It could be a gift, the nickel trim, its box silver and black in whorls . . . the stall!

I feel so good! Rid of them, Adnan, the silent would-be good, and Toni, would-be bad.

I ask a guy, 'How much that box of song . . .' He grabs my arm . . . 'Away, away . . . it's mafia stuff, full of *plastique* – and now our state will blow it up . . .'

A whistling sound, and we are thrown around. The Bible does disasters well – the plagues, the winds, the floods, the fires – no other faith can match . . . I put my hand up in the dangerous air – then I remember, 'the bear's paw', the bear who has to hide the stump the woodman vengeful for his principles, the axe . . . the story rambling on, its meaning sneaks away, a stoat among the trees . . .

'It's full of splinters,' says another guy. 'Your paw must go.' Here it lies out on the slab, curved like a chop, quite fresh and wholesome. My destiny has always been an amputation . . . a foot, a leg. Compensation for something – like the builder raising towers or digging holes. There must be sex behind the fear, every fear prefiguring yet another loss.

'Hey!' shouts the guy. 'Hold still.'

'I thought there was one bone in arms,' I say. 'You've found another . . .'

'No, no,' he says. 'Only cartoons have us with five bones in all, a head to crown. Arms are quite complicated,' and he saws away.

I miss the hi-fi cabinet, the gift – and now, if I do music, I can only play the brass. I might conduct – the wrong way round, it makes no difference, the band plays on and on . . . Of course, there is the fuss of reading music, though no reason that should interrupt careers, if you distinguish one tune from the next, you're all too human, waving your wand . . .

'There,' says the guy. 'It's off. An honourable wound, fighting some crime. We can even call it war. Your gift, that cabinet – it's taken off a limb. You will adjust. I'm sure your gesture was correct, although more prudence . . .'

Losing a hand – it makes no odds to happiness. You know how it's done, whether you are bland or evil, being happy is the same. I'm happy still, and always.

The guy, the butcher, white-coat, says, 'It's all your tale, unique. You won't be here, to see if was tragedy or justice. Someone will write it up, and judge. You just need think of where your parts should end.'

'I think of that,' I say. 'My heart to Xipe, naturally. The year with virgins, under the sun, *fichi d'India* on clay plates, calm, delight. No hoeing, no trekking water, no obsidian blades stuck in the face. Then – a quick surgery, your heart belongs to Him. Sure, you have to play the flutes, but little pot ones – that you can do with just one hand . . .'

'Then there's the cancer,' says the guy.

'The pale Galilean – he can have that one,' I say. 'The question is – my hand?'

'Oh,' says the guy, 'they've brought the bears back in. Like unto like, you'll finish up . . . it's right: your paw will make a snack. The nature's for TV, of course. Someone should take a shot . . .'

'I might end,' I say, 'in the arena: as beast or man . . .'

'That blast,' he says. 'It wasn't mafia, though they said. Some youth, a bomb – see, the body goes to pap, but lo! epiphany: the head comes off, and – straight up in the sky.'

And there it is, unmarked, a smile, a rictus. Someone's certainty, or dread.

'My hand?' I ask.

'A splinter, nothing more,' he says. 'I fear the cabinet – imitation nacre, a plastic wonder, still humming with those melodies, spun out before they learned to rock and screw . . . I fear your gift's for making sacrifice.'

'The blast disoriented me,' I say. 'I have this sense some limb is lost, something cut off and fed . . . it's a recurrent scene.'

'That's normal, friend,' he says. 'A hero usually limps, or needs a warrior to help him string his bow and fire the arrows.'

'Just a splinter?' I ask. 'No cause you can rightly blame? Just one of nature's bangs?'

'I'll help you,' says the guy. 'Since you seem new into this world. Everyone everywhere must do more or less the same. That way you survive – otherwise, the strong would always win, the weak get sympathy, the sceptics always beat believers.'

That's true. 'What country are you from?' the guy asks. Maybe he's not a sage.

'No country, it was London, I was there. We didn't follow the traditions. I was in New York – the same,' I say.

'A bang on the head – disorientates,' he says, not digesting anything.

'On the hand. Just a bang,' I say. 'They go on all the time.'

'Looking for work?' he asks.

'No,' I say. 'I get the kind of work you wouldn't look for.'

It's all clear: Toni's what they call a cop, Adnan's what they call a terrorist. It's all still in their thoughts, of course. For now, it's friendship binds them, the economics of the stall.

'No!' shouts the guy. 'Hold still some more! I'm curing you! Forget the cops and robbers – fantasy! Your splinter – those bombs have many causes, the effects are even more unsure. Ordered time is spooling out – then bang! as if you prick the tape, joggle the kaleidoscope, shuffle the pack . . . who knows where it all ends? They're let off in hope and ignorance, those bangs, and in despair. You waggle the machine, the ball goes crazy, and you win the pot, or else it's TILT, game done. We're all tensed up, we think things may end differently from what we thought . . . Each spurt, each belly wind, each methane blast – it seems a portent . . . as though a ghostly wind reminds us there's some ancient god reviving narcissistic plans . . .'

My hand – is like it was. I ask the butcher, healer:

'How do you stand them – the banal, the repetitious? Putting things back, just like they were. Always better, always cured.'

'At times I cut things off,' he says.

'My friend' – I mean Alp – said, 'Stop! Wipe it! Stop the past, and start again. It happens all the time. You break up with a lover – here comes another: everything is new, what was is only aberration. No influence.'

'Alp,' I said. 'Stop saying stop, on with the new – do you think the new may cancel out the old? You can't be so naive. The crude way is a restoration – a time way back, now forgotten – you cancel out what came before, and all the twisty paths mistaken persons followed since. It's new. And – it's old – but mainly it is old, a travesty of what it may have been.'

He said, 'Mine's just the best conclusion. Don't pretend what's gone is somewhere . . .' Here he is again, Alp.

'Where were you?' I ask.

'Up the road,' he says. 'There's just one road, now.'

'That's sentimental, Alp,' I say. 'That's what happens when you learn just part of some new language. If you'd stayed, I'd have taught you the whole thing, the words and the machinery. Then you could put everything in place.'

'It's not like trains,' he says. 'The bus goes everywhere. And everywhere there's law. It's terrible. Those drunk guys, freaks of all dimensions, sitting on their bench, cutting off your head. We're supposed to like it, law the impersonal, the taking no account. The lie there's justice at the end, or at the start it comes from some loving will, big face, some graven stones . . . Oh no – it's locks and keys, taking your cash, nailing you to some crap family . . . It gives you boots and badges, then it blows you up.'

'I know,' I say. 'I've just had trouble with a hand. Maybe there was law, some law I hadn't learnt, behind that too.'

'The only thing that matters,' Alp goes on, 'the law does not concern, and it's what matters, the only thing. People – who're no longer there, who go, and don't return, are disappeared. Gender's not in it – men, women, young, effusive, old and taciturn – they go. No explanation, irrevocable, and not a tear. It's all you have to care about.

Those who are gone, without a sign. And there it is. Not covered by the code.'

'Not covered by anything, I fear,' I say. 'You want to live in anarchy, or in a book – where there's always everything and everyone, unfettered, scripted. Fine writing by the inch. Hungry guys, all roaming round.'

'That's meagre!' says Alp, much cast down. 'Maybe if I don't want the trivial things that you can offer me – it's quite impossible, what I want. Impossible's a condition in the smallest and the largest things. What can you do to help? More lessons?'

'"Impossible things",' I say. 'That's a study that can take you all your life – and mine. Two lives – bottled in the same space of time.'

I'm pleased with my little paradox. 'You get your puzzles from a book,' I say. 'I bet you found it on the stall.'

'Oh,' says Alp, 'I'm far beyond all that. The bus did a comfort stop in Italy. Florence, I think it was – one gents is much the same as all the rest. The ceiling said the evil and the non-believers went to hell. The judges saw to that. There seemed no point in going further as I'd planned. That's the universe, in egg and oil. All had been said there. It seemed we'd shrugged that off. Who doesn't want a paradise? . . . But no. I told you – law is punishment, and nothing more.'

'The ceiling's there to catch your gaze – you needn't think, believe, a thing,' I say.

'I could do philosophy,' says Alp, 'along with loading coaches. Or bouncing: that gets you money on the side: I wonder,' he says, trying to weight his words, 'do philosophers know what it is they write about? It's writing, with no "is".'

'Here's another couple, Alp,' I say, 'writing and saying. I'm not sure what our lessons lead to – but: don't write. Remember "beg and steal". Saying is beg, and write is steal. And stealing is the law round here.'

'Who gives you lessons, then?' he asks me. 'When you know it all, the whole machine – then comes the vision. That's what I don't want.

If you're poor, they lock you up for having visions: if you're not, or you don't want to be, it seems you get a gun, a map that's blank.'

I talk about the frustration, the poverty, the aliens rampaging up and down, insulting, the impossibles, people who boss you, hard to live with, more aliens . . . those granny's tales . . .

'Everybody knows all that,' says Alp. 'There are never shortages of causes, causes for everything. It's outcomes that are interesting. Some leave you in the ditch.'

It's true: I say, 'Your trouble, Alp, is you're a dissident. And there's no dissidence here. No one bothers. You've no authority – but your friends think you're harassing them.'

'What friends, then?' he asks. 'You need a window seat, that's all. Everywhere there's bands – the innocent, the armed. Waiting for the trip, the good life. The discipline. The end of discipline. Millions, on the move. Only me with a passport, and a ticket to go anywhere. Nowhere I want to go, everywhere I can go.'

'It's the theme, Alp. You need some variations, or else it's the game – nomads versus settlers. We can't be the only ones who like nomadism.'

'You need animals,' says Alp. 'Being one yourself – it doesn't count.'

That restaurant among the pines: the gritty cheese that pulled like gum. That was a lesson, that's for sure: 'Be sure you ask the price before you feast.'

'You could change your name, Alp,' I say. 'That would make life easier.'

'It's for the Great Seljuk,' he says. 'That shows I'm ambitious. I need do no more.'

'We're all familiar,' I say. 'Broadly. Though not everyone can place the story right.'

I don't insist. It's a small matter, shows our feet are on the planet, now, have been so for many years.

We circle round. Each other, and the places, the solutions and the horrors we might have almost countenanced, then shrank from, and ourselves as well. Not us! We're not to blame, we had no part, no active part. Quite the contrary, when the meanderings arrive at a last judgment, it's never mentioned. It's provisional and cautious.

What is between us, Alp and I, it must be friendship, for a period unspecified. It rubs the corners off what goes on around, and what we trivialise with fencing talk.

We're friends. That's that.

'Your guy?' asks Toni. 'With the new idea?'

'Oh, it was just cash,' I say, 'so for sure he's sucked it out. It's over. Too late.'

'Well,' he says, 'we – me and Adnan – we've found a city. Just dig it up. It's gold! And maybe gold is there – but that belongs to someone else, it always does, without them using spades. But for the rest – it can be ours.'

'I had to leave,' I say. 'This city – is it real and hidden, or just some guy jumped out on you, bearing a parchment?'

How I wish – I could be rid of all of them, start the real life . . .

2

They show the picture: the city – of the good, the poor, the pure – is ankle high. All terra cotta. Squares, no bigger than jail cells. 'Even the doors and roofs were made of earth,' says Adnan. 'Not a tree was harmed, no hole was dug. So, when came the flood – it washed away.'

There's movement: a woman, picking stuff from broken stuff. Crabapples? 'Those are the heads,' says Toni. 'What is left. They were the doorknobs, more resistant than the rest. You see – the city was a place for the tormented. For torturers, for guys who liked to peep, and journalists as well, I bet,' he laughs. 'The city of the pure . . . Each time you turned the knob, going in or going out, you twisted hard that knobbly head. Made you remember where you were. Your brother – gone today, and you tomorrow.'

'So,' I say, 'we don't know where it is. You made an offer. There's just little squares of mud, and all is ankle deep.'

'They did the graving on the floor,' says Alp. 'That's where they slept and did their trades. Faces down, faith not more than calf or ankle high.'

'There surely were *favelas* where the guys did drugs, were proud, and played some kind of football. Painted themselves upon the walls,' I say.

'All was low down,' says Toni. 'No towers. No monotheism, no tall windows, all that pagan stuff. Leaping up to God – no, they would slink, lie on their backs and watch the spirits writhe above, each small divinity with a list of punishments prepared, inflicted. And I guess – they'd no insurance, but the taxes were immense. There were bosses. They liked seeing their people tormented.'

'It's going cheap, the site,' says Alp. 'There is no gold, no statues. Bones, and scratchings.'

'People will come,' says Adnan, 'wander about, and buy a ticket. Some will have epiphany, for sure.'

'The trades,' I say, 'used stuff reused, the brothels, markets for labour and for scythes and birthday cakes . . .'

'Yes,' says Toni, 'birthdays were quite significant. Electricity wasn't invented, naturally – but there was hemp and nails, you can surmise. Of course – there was no drama and no stage. No rock. Just clay, and no loud noise.'

'Many cities will leave less,' says Alp. 'Think of the dumps, that all rot down, and everything is sold and used and sold until it disappears.'

'Those markets,' Adnan says. 'Those fields of junk that flower and fruit and millions are sustained – the walls collapse. Then what is left is concrete squares of roof. Or rust.'

'Remember, I saw everything. Not as a scientist,' Alp says, 'but I'd my food, my music. Jellyrolls. I bring it back, mapped, as a scape. But not with sharp edges, not wet tears.'

'Jellyrolls,' says Toni, admiring. 'Yes, Alp, you're our original. You know how it all sticks and chimes. Your eyes and ears – they're clearly all your own.'

'This site,' I say. 'It trashed itself. All gone, the bosses too. We must invent, to make it palatable and new. Adnan, Alp – forget your lingering thoughts about the past, and how it harboured truth.'

'No, no,' says Adnan. 'It's all gone. Each day a better truth arrives – who knows how it can end?'

'*May* end, dear Adnan, It's not through truth it ends or carries on beyond our sight. All that is left to us is to invent: not truth, not faith, not treaties, and not common sense,' says Alp. 'The animals have none of these – but some of them go on for centuries, eyes on the ground and round their backs.'

'Hey there, young Alp,' says Toni, riled. 'You think you're part of this, this archaeology? It's me and Adnan. Only this guy here,' and he prods at me. 'This storyteller, has some claim to invention. Maybe a crumb will fall his way . . .'

'We need hands!' says Adnan.

*

'You need me,' Adnan goes on. 'I've been everywhere, seen all the peoples of the earth, shuffling along in ragtime, gospel rock, groaning the blues and allelujah. I'm indispensable. I go with the beat . . .' and on he talks, at times he croons, and waves his skeleton.

I'd like to get away, forget them all. Forget the furrows and the mounds where bones lie mixed with dragon's teeth. I don't seem to have the fare . . .

'The music of time? What's the line-up?' Alp asks, provoking.

'The drums,' says Adnan. 'The full kit. And the Brazilian jungle – boxes, sticks and gourds. Rattles too – you hardly hear. The beat goes on. Just the one. Riffs from a sax. Voices – dolphins or mermaids? Or the lost loves? The big surge – why, the good old Wurlitzer. Set it on automatic . . .'

'Nothing classic?' asks Toni. 'No melodrama?'

'That all stopped when the ladies left their spears and went to AK 47s,' Adnan says. 'And when the anguish over breach of promise, ruination, stopped.'

'We can pipe it in,' says Alp.

'I saw myself quite live for ever, at the console,' I say.

'Animals!' says Adnan. 'How about them?'

'Long live the animals!' Alp shouts. 'There's few I saw from the bus, taking their ease.'

'Lizards,' I say. 'Blue, green and yellow. No flags, but coloured animals – there's ants. Red, white and blue. Or black.'

'Colours?' Toni asks. 'We must have them.'

'When we sprang from the earth, we were all red,' Adnan says. 'A healthy glow. The animals are the colours of all standards, every palette. The sun, the moon – they are on flags, it's true, but their routes are mapped. The animals will move about, like frontiers.'

'What'll the animals eat?' asks Alp, as if he's created worlds before. 'They can't all open cans.'

'I'm against the foliage,' Toni says. 'It blows about, there's leaves to sweep. And if the creatures eat each other, we'll have nothing left.'

'That's the point of lizards, stupid,' I tell Toni. 'Lizards can survive, millions of years. The ants eat mushrooms underground.'

'And us?' asks Adnan.

'We shall eat the ants,' I say. 'Just like our fathers and their fathers too.'

'No arguments,' says Toni. 'Alp wanted animals, so he'll look to them.'

'No, no,' says Adnan. 'We're all responsible for everything. The places with a single Maker, or a set of rules for all the universe, its different rocks and plants and liquid poisons – those are all a mess. Everyone among us must look after everything. In Sinnersville.'

'Maybe the site was an original, a city of the plain,' I say.

'No literature,' says Alp. 'That way we end in Disneyland or Proust.'

'I want bees and dragonflies,' says Toni. 'I like some honey on my bread, a shimmer on my stream.'

'Then we should have animals who're colourless,' says Adnan. 'Owls and bulbuls. No colour, as they make their noise when we are all asleep.'

'If that's the plan,' says Alp, 'then we should have some dodos, buffaloes and such – extinct, but you don't see them anyway.'

'*Dajé*!' Toni shouts. 'Give over! Dead city – lets us give up thieving and be philosophers. Don't fill it up with imaginary beasts!'

'Not imaginary,' Adnan says. 'Imagined and real. Invisible, that's sure. Depending for appearance – on the time, the beat.'

'Here it comes,' says Alp. 'Back in the minor. Once – overlooking Persepolis with Coltrane in my ears. Now – mud and progressive jazz.'

'Transform!' says Adnan. 'It won't come fresh and clean through wires. What you see and hear – you make it up. It's always different – only the labels and the maps persist.'

'We're not romancers like you, Alp, not patricians,' says Toni. 'Fortunately uncool. But if you're in commerce like me, you become an expert in the banal. You must get used to deserts of it: always back, back to the minor: fallout. Remember – everything started as a bomb. And everything thereafter is an anticlimax. Climax – then shards. Nothing. Is something on the cards? Something out of nothing, the inscrutable quiet, the space – real space – not really there, like everything else. Wait for it! and wonder . . .! Bang! There it is: "something". The Bomb. Then after. The smell of cordite, the big inedible mushroom – then at the last, we're on stage! – waiting for the god who ends the tale, resolves the harmony. Bombs, my friends – but not the little ones that scare you. No! The big one – that will never come again. Whose hand dropped it? We can't be sure. Terrorist or defender. Then, nothing to hope for – nothing to fear.'

'God, Toni?' Adnan asks. 'I use the term loose,' Toni says. 'As it always is. It refers to all the things unknown that may not come. Someone like me must be around to take the universe quite personally.'

'What I must do now,' Adnan says, not much interested, 'is find the cash to buy the site. We won't know where it is, for if we knew, the price would go right up . . .'

'Or down,' says Alp.

'There'll always be a stall,' says Toni, happily. 'Always you need a souvenir. That's me.'

'For sure, Toni, they'll remember you,' I say. 'But – beware! Guys sell off the good stuff and the stones – then sell the site "as is". Divinity: it's bled from all the little gods, and put on sale. Aesthetics – blatant idealism, Toni. It's like horses – when you buy a good one, someone'll have taken out its speed, and left you with a crock.'

'I bet some power dammed the river, so it washed away those guys,' says Alp. 'The art – it went downstream. And all the prayers and chanting floated off. The bosses – they were losers. All the torments – just shouting in the dark . . . "you lose" – the game is ended. No win.'

'Now what?' I ask, wishing to dominate, but not be seen involved.

'I'll run the stall,' says Alp. 'Adnan can ride the buses. I'll have a word . . . the drivers love me . . . Toni – looks for stock, it's all he can ever do.'

'Everything is souvenirs,' says Toni. 'That's the good and bad. Accumulate – it's all a memory. But not everybody wants to pay to have their souvenirs rubbing against their brain. As for a city no one knows where or when it is . . . there's few souvenirs around from that.'

'What do I do?' I ask. 'Hmmm,' says Alp. 'You hold the money Adnan finds. Then – add class and style. The high, the low, the quick the slow. Remember – give it all your beat!'

'This money Adnan's off to get,' I say. 'We've capitalism, my friends. Call it "late" – if that can cheer you up. The cash flows back into banks; it isn't lying by the road.'

'That isn't so,' says Alp. 'There's people moving round, and armies flattening out the folds and wrinkles in the map. Something . . . must be on the move.'

'No, no,' says Toni. 'People and armies! People's just small change, not worth a blink. What lasts – is cops. Intelligence. A water barrel, and some wires. Uncooked flesh. It doesn't cost: it sinks right in, deters. Who isn't frightened off – is game. To hunt.'

'I know what I shall see,' says Adnan. 'Guys following the flags. They ought to know, these poor exploited guys, or those that think themselves to be – those flags are marsh gas. On they go; the shells, the sabres, swish and whistle: bravely on, or pushed: there's hope behind vainglory. Vain hope. It's most attractive – who wouldn't cheer them on? Hope. And all around there's wasted sites, like ours. Smashed by the storms, the years, the generals – and yet we poke around, breathe in some exhalation, maybe it exalts: more time will pass. It's all philosophy . . .'

We stare at him. There's even tears behind his eyes.

'Look, Adnan,' Toni says. 'There's always devastation. Find this bit, and hope it brings us bread.'

'Adnan's right,' says Alp, shuffling time capsules on the stall. 'It's like the women that we say we suffer for. Or men. Or anything. There is desire – then, maybe, climax. Then desire again – nostalgia's how it's called. It's not. It is desire again. First subject first, then second. It's all about desire – not suffering. The rest – the sex, the infidelity, harmonics fiddled – it's all fine writing. A tickle in the head. We should enjoy the hope, the wanting – followed by . . . the wanting, the desire for what has gone, quite immaterial. That is what there is. Is all there is.'

'Yes, Alp,' says Toni. 'That, we know. But in your case – the Layla that you seek lacks the one thing you need to make your picture move: desire. Desire for you, dear Alp.'

'Hey, guys,' I say, as every mystery's revealed. 'We're veering into metaphysics. For that we need some figures. Female ones preferred.'

'They always have an animal attached,' says Alp, being younger, knowing more. 'An Afghan. Not a panther – those come with the meths.'

'A cat,' says Toni. 'I know the one. We can compete for her. Desire lasts long enough to cover procreation. Then it's on to the next.'

'Women don't need cats,' says Adnan. 'They're hard. Tough. They have to deal with kids. They don't need cleave a skull. Don't trust the cat. They're soft outside, within – there's a twisted cable.'

'This machismo men don't have,' says Toni, 'you're right. Men are hysterics. They march up and down – then it's blood and tears, and "oh forgive me", and do it all again. Just think of the great thieves – Chingiz, Temur, Napoleon – all that gold, sewn on to pyjamas and chaises longues. What taste! and their admins – the simplicity. Killing machines. It's the fallacy of Lenin's cook: of course government is simple if you make it so: but watch out! It comes with a club and bone-presses.'

'Maybe the site we're looking for is one of theirs,' says Alp. 'And the graving on the floor. What can it be? Accounts? A map that's like a fallen wall? The colour of earth, with earth's inconsequence? Roots dried out, strands wreathing out without a leaf?'

Toni ignores him. 'Adnan and I were communists, you know, I mean good communists. How we suffered. Then – the epiphany, the change of life, from sacrifice to indulgence. Slipping in to the dark side. Not for always, not necessarily. It's more full of life, more bacterial. Really good communists we were.'

Adnan nods and smiles, waits for him to finish, to come down.

'Things have to collapse,' he says. 'Or there would be nowhere flat enough to build.'

'Nonsense!' Toni shouts. 'Get on the bus! You're not out there to build. We mustn't build, you idiot! We're to live on the destruction. That's our bread. Like the real great ones do.'

'You quite disgust me, Toni,' says the girl with the kitten, not joking.

'Got your jelly rolls, Adnan?' Alp asks, pushing him on the bus. Adnan peers inside the bag and counts.

I think, 'The Lady with the little cat' . . . what'll she do for me? Desire, then spent: a memory, and claws.

I pull Adnan off the bus. He's crushed the jelly rolls. I tug the music from his ears. Jazz Messengers – that'll drown out anything. 'Colonialist!' he croaks. 'No one will give you cash. A flat to you sounds like a sharp: the site . . . its flatness will not seize, not captivate . . .'

There's the driver prostrate – it must be evening prayer. His socks have holes. I hope, from pressing pedals, not from penury. The lady – she'll be there, if I come back When we trekked out of Africa, the ladies wanted to be white: they'd no time for skin or soul that's dark. Remember the song, 'I am black, but Oh! my soul is white . . . I am black, as if bereav'd of light.' And vice versa. That's me, for sure.

Alp gives the sign: so, where's the bus destined for? 'The Place', it says. 'All aboard', and here we go, the other warriors, escaping their Penelopes, off to find a piece of Helen: with a stroke from Afrodite, if she's on their side . . . As we leave, only the kitten seems interested. I have the photo of our flattened site. Adnan's still lying in the road, as if a wheel went over him. Toni's arguing, Alp's thinking of metaphysics, slipping maybe into physics. The driver shouts to us passengers, 'You guys – you've had what they call a sensory war. In the books and on the screens. Time to reflect and be prepared, and take a side, or maybe two or more. Where we go now – it is quite natural. So don't be scared. There's camps and fields, and guys who try to get on board. Just look – or if you're really scared, or sensitive – don't look. You'll see it all – the arms and legs, the places where you brought good governance, and where it didn't seem to stick, and where you brought your creed, or where you didn't care. Remember – there's a window here that lets you see it all – and it protects. If the guys stay on their side, you're safe. Maybe you're safe if you get off. Hospitality is everywhere, of course. Now *schtum!* – for I must steer the craft.'

We all sit back, relax. There could be seas to cross, and frontiers too. The drumming in my ears proceeds. Adnan gets up. I knew he would.

In the aisle seat beside, a lady sits, hoping I'll give up my window.

'My name's Rosine,' she says.

'It's a music-hall name,' I tell her. 'Short for Rosinette.'

'I know,' she says. 'You won't move, I guess? Away from the view?'

'Oh,' I say. 'Sit tight. The aisle. You've earned the good seat.'

'There's powerful guys aboard,' she says. 'All off to Cythera, I think. All looking for a site. Or something harder – the Winged Victory's head, for one.'

'I'm powerful too,' I say. 'But I've no cash. A site, and cash. That is my trip.'

'These guys up front – they choose a place, a site: a state – and put their money in. Then they rent the people who'll work there.'

Oh no, I think: I say, 'You're not one of these freaks – the anti-cap, the anti-state?'

'Oh no,' she says, 'I think the system's great. They don't buy slaves, if that is what you mean – they rent.'

Still, we have suspicions of each other – the more we might agree, the deeper go the arguments.

'That drumming,' Rosine says. 'It irks. Don't you have Coltrane? Or Monk?'

'I don't do jazz. I'd hate to improvise. It's just the sound, how something can go on, become another. It could be anything – it's all air. They say the cool's about Persepolis,' I say.

'We won't go there,' Rosine says. 'And you're wrong. Nothing becomes something else. It's all variations. Nothing changes much.'

'There must be start and finish, Rosine. We can be sure of that. That means there's change,' I say.

'Why waste time on me,' she asks, aggressively. 'It's clear I haven't caught your thread.'

I peer at her: she's wearing wraps – stuff for the aisle seat. I think. 'Put on your red shoes,' and I see she has: I can't say, 'Let's dance.' Maybe she's an addict. Guys get on and off, with plastic bags of cash. They spot a site – crumbles of walls, some guys with stalls, kids with snot all over, others with a dirty pullover . . . I muse along. We talk of cosmos. 'How sad,' I say. 'Monotheism was simple, but the complexity before – every stone and stream a shrine, lair for some demon or a sylph . . .'

'The complexity as unavailing as the simple,' Rosine says. 'Where are your notes?'

'Oh yes,' I say. 'That.' Adnan wasn't counting out his jellyrolls – it was the cash.

'Here,' she says. 'Have some of mine.'

The notes are rose, eye-blue – you see the flecks of mulberry budding from the linen . . . 'The Lost Boys Bank', they say.

'Are they good?' I ask.

'As good as anything round here,' she says. 'Now, the head of the Winged Victory. Maybe we'll find it – what's the sign? A smirk? A tear? Grimace?'

'I think they made it with no head,' I say. 'Couldn't think how it should look.'

'Nah!' she shouts, the guys look round: some stop their poker, others fuel their samovars or count their worry beads. 'Nah!' she says. 'The Greeks don't do irony, awareness. It's win to win for them.'

That's what Toni says. Those heavy broken wings, the stony lump, not going anywhere . . .

'This must be Anatolia,' Rosine says. 'Where the Italians came from. Before they thought of Troy and being refugees.'

'What's behind you, Rosine?' I ask. 'Who's the backers . . .?'

'Same as you,' she says. 'Winning. Finding a devastated spot that earns us cash. What else?'

'Are you coming back?' I ask. 'When it's done?'

'What an odd question,' she says. 'You know, these rolls of notes – there's a miracle and they turn into jellyrolls.'

'Those kids are selling Turkish pie,' I say. 'Thrusting through the bars on our windows. A delight! Forget the rolls.'

She laughs a little, 'You can never have too much security. That's the paradox. The window bars that protect, attract. You're always insecure. Especially with other people. The bus has "The Place" written on the roof. It's for the drones. Does it attract them? We may never know.'

If it wasn't so dark in here, I could try a line: 'I love you': 'Everyone knows what they want, the problem is finding them once you've let them go . . .' No, too baroque. Besides, it all comes from movies that I've seen. It's the streetcar they name desire – it's not that desire's expressed in it . . . desire I don't feel. Rosine in the dark – I see she's wearing lots of clothes. It's freezing here. Desire. You get it in the aisle seats, there, you can get up without excuses.

Guys are finding cities all around, getting off the bus: you can't tell if they're cities being built, or falling down. We see the gangs, exploding rocks and carving them, standing them on end, on one another. I could do all that. I'd rather boss the others, though.

'I'm feeling sick,' I say.

Rosine says, 'You can't. You're empty. And you smell.'

'It all seems tragedy . . .' I say. 'Outside. My friends I want to leave behind. The crossroads here – hang a right – India, Africa. Arabia too. Ahead there's China; to the left – Siberia.'

There's plywood shacks around, and holes . . . I guess they're digs.

'The workers now,' Rosine says. 'No odd ideas about them. They don't want you, and you won't get paid.'

'Rosine,' I say. 'Don't be a monster. I know it's how it starts with monsters – a friendly body, then the scaly tail, the fire . . .'

'If you get off,' she says, ignoring this, 'you'll need to pay the driver.'

He does the five-a-day. That way, we don't have accidents.

'When you've the cash,' I ask. 'How'd you make it work?'

'You find some friends,' she says. 'Even politicals. If you like them, and it's mutual – you give them cash. What's left goes into tourism. Archaeology as well. Building up the past.'

'If no one likes you? If they've odd ideas?' I ask.

'It's to do with friendship, not ideas,' she says. 'Geography as well. If they don't like you, you must give them much much more. Or much much less. You'll maybe need to stand ages by the road, and wait for another bus. Put on a helmet and a sword.'

'It sounds good,' I say. 'Better than I've had.'

'Oh,' she says, 'you should go back to your friends. They're all you've got.'

'That's a rubbish argument,' I say.

'It's not an argument,' she says. 'It's what'll happen.'

'My friend Alp,' I say. 'He's a Seljuk. They rampaged here. My site – what can be written on the floors?'

'Your language,' says Rosine. 'It's all wrong. No one writes on floors. It's an illusion. Your friend – he just took the name. These Seljuks – they been long effaced. A layer, no more.'

'These villages,' I say. 'Botched together – hard-working people, building as it comes. Like where I was born. It helps if you all think the same.'

'Is this conversation?' she asks. 'Or is it sentiment you're looking for? That's not at all what it's about.'

'It's silent, all around,' I say. 'Except for the motor, and the guys, dealing the cards.'

She makes her silence, lots of it: it comes out like raw wool.

'Those are my bushes,' she says. 'I hope you know the language. There are several.' She gets off. She's left three rolls of 'Lost Boys' notes.

I get off, in a little while. I pay the driver with a roll: he says, 'I'll take the rest when I come back for you.'

Here's a guy: I show the picture. 'Are these old?' I ask. 'The foundations?'

'Who knows?' he says.

'I can pay,' I say.

He says, 'Now you're talking.'

'Whose property?' I ask.

'Who knows?' he says.

'And I need some food,' I say.

'Now you're talking,' he says. There's chick peas in a bowl, with butter sauce.

'It's called "drawn butter",' I say. 'I wonder why?'

'Who knows?' he says.

'If they're shacks knocked down,' I say. 'I could build up.'

'Now you're talking,' he says, and takes another roll in payment. Chick peas are expensive here.

'Who knows what's written on the floors,' I say.

'Yes, who knows,' he says. He takes the last roll of Lost Boys. 'What do these mean?' he asks. 'That you'll come and rampage here, make friends and enemies, sell us guns, and charge me interest?'

'Oh well,' I say. 'That's quite inevitable. I'm sure protection comes in too.'

'And you'll bring people here to view this stuff, and pay?' he asks.

'If you dig around, it comes out like this photograph, I'm sure,' I say. I tell him about Alp, and Adnan – Toni I keep for when we're intimate.

'It doesn't reassure me, friend,' he says. 'Scum's scum whatever are their names.'

'I know these ruins are not yours,' I say. 'You're not responsible. But – people from afar will come, to get amusement from them . . .'

'Things move around,' he says. 'The happiness goes with them. It isn't cash. Those peoples, staring at our stones, inventing tales and sentiments – those stones, they are ephemeral, the people too. The centre moves – over that hill, there's China. Everywhere you guys had rampaged, here, and places where you came from when you were black – that's where the centre goes. Those piles of rocks you're keen to gawp at – think of them as flat. As ankle-high at most. No inspiration there.'

'"Look on my works . . ." the song comes into mind,' I say. 'Maybe you're right. Once, we were into variations: now, it's ragtime.'

Here's Rosine, high up on a ridge. 'Hey,' she shouts. 'You found your stones? Now you need protection. I could sell you some.'

'I'll need to borrow from you, Rosine – my cash has momentarily gone . . .' I say. 'And – artistic touring . . . maybe it has had its day . . .'

'No, no,' she says, descending, kicking at my stones. 'Revival. That's the thing. Make dance floors. Black Bottoms, Charlestons. Havana smokes and drinks . . . Theme it away, and frolic on!'

'That's not me at all.' I say. 'I have ambitions. Need to make new friends.'

'There's no friend better than the one you owe,' she says. 'I'll lend to you, and hug you close, you bet!'

Rosine wears a foulard, but she has the clothes of a banker – the long FBI overcoat, the breasts pushed toward but covered – or maybe, the costume of the bag lady. Everything ends cast-off. And I see her face – some spots of glitter, a fire-red mouth. Not like on the bus at all.

'Rosine,' I ask. 'Who are you?'

'Oh,' she says. 'I'm looking for investment. The chances. You can say I'm one of the goddesses – half in your world, half in an other, immortal one; with servants.'

'I'm thinking,' I say, 'maybe this place is not just scrub – it could be dangerous. At home, there's ruins. We already have a stall.'

'Faintheart,' she says. 'You have no home. Others run your stall. You could be a warrior. Fight for something – or at least dress for it.'

'The fighting,' I say. 'It's an illusion. It's like love – the desire for risk, the losing of oneself, the hope you will survive . . . taking the step that makes it probable you won't . . .'

'Oh,' says Rosine, seeing I'm provoking her. 'Don't get excited. I'm not buying you. It's him I'm aiming for,' and she points to the guy I'm talking to.

'This travelling around,' I go on, making contrasts so she'll be drawn out, so's I can explore. 'Staring at some culture different from yours – it's all a sickness. Just dissatisfaction with oneself. Or ignorance – not knowing what is yours, and shopping round. Trying to pick up what goes on elsewhere, and maybe breaking what you see.'

'I'm not travelling,' says Rosine. 'I'm coming home. It's you who's on the lam. I know about things here, who's on the up, who's the bigot, who makes peace – all the strategies to be a big man in this scrub.'

'*Heimkehr*,' I say. 'Coming home. That's not so bold.'

'Oh, I'm bold enough,' she says. 'You'll find it's so.'

Why impress this . . . this garish woman? I guess, if you must impress, you must start somewhere, with someone.

'The only puzzle is,' I say, 'the writing on the floor. My site . . .'

'Forget the writing,' Rosine says. 'That won't get you anywhere. Look in the cellars. Maybe you hadn't thought?'

'No,' I say. 'I'm one for open air.'

'You must be born to it,' she says. 'To everything. You – maybe you weren't born. Must I guide you to your destiny? A fate so nondescript. And on your knees?'

'I smell the conflict here,' I say. 'It's like a carpet on the loom, without a knot, the colours bold. Garish and running.' I hum. 'This is our last, decisive battle . . . the human race will arise . . . "The Internationale". Of course, it turned out just a song.'

'Songs are good too,' says Rosine. 'Before the fire, the wheel, guys took over song from blackbirds and canaries.'

'Some guys here don't sing at all,' I say. 'Not like they used back there, before they had those little telephones.'

'Oh well,' she says. 'Not doing stuff just draws attention to it.'

'Toni and Adnan – they sang like boatmen, when they were setting up their stall,' I say.

'Your friends will have forgotten you,' she says. 'Here, we make history. The kind too complex and too brash to put in books. The only room for you back there – is as a humble servant. Otherwise called – a slave. Alp's a student of antiques. Toni will do what he has done. And Adnan – he's your joker, the wild card.'

'How do you know all this?' I ask.

'I'm an investor. I know everything,' she says. 'Besides, for days you told me all your epic, in your sleep. It's best to glue your mouth up when you are in bed. I tie my knees together too.'

'If there's cellars,' I say, 'there won't be cash.'

'Freud was wrong,' she says. 'Cash is not about excreting. It's living and dying it's about. No one keeps shit in their pocket. Nor in the cellar. It's not about humans, the underground. It's the digging, and the carving. Not capitalism – that's a puff, a cloud, flash in the pan. There's maybe seeds and roots. Animals. Living ones, timid and boastful, just like you.'

'Those floors,' I say, 'maybe they warn. Maybe beneath there's like the Dunhuang caves – the guys will smash and burn.'

'Oh well,' she says, 'you cover up the angels' faces, but have to make their wings still longer. I told you, what isn't there – that makes the impact. Your friends sang about the Soviet Man. Here comes the Arab Warrior, and friends. What will he make of his history, here between Russia, China, and with those dark birds overhead? Of course, there's other places hereabouts – but what we can't make fit – we'll pretend it isn't there. What will become? Another empire, like the Seljuks? A presence – like the Qara Khitai, that no one knows . . . who they were, or if. The black Chinese! . . . unwashed nomads, with the Kingdoms at their feet? You need to take some risk, my friend. It's only money, after all. It's invented so there's always more and more. It's yours to gamble for.' She holds my arm tight, her musky breath goes in and out my unkempt ears . . . 'Is it the living, or the dead you care about? Someone should care about the dead – but there's so many, so anonymous. Those dynasties . . . best to be the elder son, or end up bad. Someone should care about the living too – so many, so anonymous. It takes your life to care, and you, my friend – are so, so anonymous.'

'You care about the living, till they're dead,' I say.

'Spoken like an idiot,' she says, pulling away. 'A true one. Like the rest. Not living, not quite dead.'

'Come on, Rosine,' I say. 'Help me navigate, negotiate. The site . . . What's to happen to us all, to everything?'

'Now,' she says, hugging me, 'that's asking! Good for you!'

She has business eyes: they seldom pause on me. I go down, down to the cellar, the cave. Just as I thought – over there, under the pile of epics, there's the scrolls . . . on the walls the dancing rootlike men with tails – my! how they dance, they thumb a nose, they wave their pricks, they're cream and blue and green, the gods are there, decked out with skulls – and there's a youth, Hellenic, catamite, he bows and sidles, missing a nose, a lower leg – there's a row of priests with hats like sugarloaves and capes of human skin, there's ladders where the gods contest, they jostle, fall, and seem to curse, there's bodies everywhere of minor gods, here's three or four, a tongue, a pizzle, a poker pleasuring a sylph – or maybe . . . no, it's one of them, and here there's writing on the wall, some letters dangle from a line, others are cubes like kiddies' blocks, and some wreathe on like candle smoke . . . albino rats roam in and out, there's colonies of grassy tails and webs that gape and writhe, there's squeaking, rustling, things that's only teeth and eyes, and over there a sacrifice, some guy's been taken and they draw him out – a beige spaghetto of a tongue, the guts reel out like rosy silk, pop go his eyes – and on he chants, throat music – he's immortal, immortal in his suffering, but there are others more immortal still that he invokes . . .

How they go at it, on each other – the khan, khakan, maharaja, the strategos, the tsar, the malk, the Son of Heaven – not sex, superfoetation . . .

'Did you go down?' asks Rosine. 'Go down into your cave?'

'Oh absolutely not,' I say. 'I'm not into personals, the deities who think they have a line on you, you pray and waste the time that they allow . . . the bosses, the campaigns, the strutting up and down, and bowing left and right and singing feisty hymns . . . no, no: I ask the question, as you know, and no one answers back, and that is good and quiet, and tranquil too. For me, they should destroy the caves, and all the stuff. Something pure, in monosyllables, repeated oft, and commonplace is what I want. Just statements, like you'd like to have upon your wall in frames, or in your business too. And I'd sit here, outside my shack, a glass of tea, a dog for company . . .'

'Good, good,' Rosine says. 'You need a surface flat and plain – that holds the truth, if it should come. Just – no dog. A goat, perhaps.'

It doesn't please. 'Well,' she says, 'we went to the limit, to the edge. You know what comes then, after the edge?'

'No.'

'You'd find out, if you take the next step,' says Rosine. 'We two – we can't do much about it anyway. Let's talk about your debts.'

The site – it could have a significance: a meeting place, a frontier . . . a goal, a grove, a hermit's hut, a cage for tall white birds . . . 'If it's important,' I say, 'someone should know. Have known. Place. It's material, when all the rest have died. It's just about immortal, even if there is no sign . . .'

'You're right,' she says. 'There's nothing sham or fake about a place. It's just you need a guy to tell . . .'

'A poem. Or a song. That's what they're for,' I say.

'Hmmm,' she says. 'You've a very simple take on things. Not that there's penalty. Think what you like – you can't stop that anyway, whatever other people say.'

'When people move around in crowds,' I say, 'they're pretty rough. They need the space – especially if they've herds. But settled down – and then the bigotry begins.'

'It's cold here,' Rosine says. 'Maybe you'd bunk down with me.'

'Maybe I'd suffer for it. I made a kind of vow,' I say, embarrassed.

'Those time capsules – who'd you think would buy?' she asks. 'It's bodies that gets buried, not the time. All that matters sometimes – is a body's heat. Doesn't matter whose.' She winds some cloth around us two, so we make a bundle.

'Suppose I talk?' I say.

'Remember those romantic songs, and grasp your chastity,' she says. 'Sleep. Forget the withered rose, the lilacs with their beards expiring . . .'

So I do . . . It's still quite black. I wriggle out my knife, cut through the muslin shroud, the chrysalis. I'm free, I stand, a butterfly, and flap my wings to dry the sweat. Now, I should try to fly . . .

I had forgot the dogs. These dogs don't chase, they hunt. I run. The pack of jokers gives the tally-ho. My fear runs down, down through the bladder, pauses above the knees . . . the legs pump well, but if the lead should block the joints . . . How fortunate I'm happy, always. It's an easy thing to be.

I shout – my lips are glued. Rosine said, 'To stop you squawking out, how you're on the other side, or none.' The two black dogs, the kings, the club, the sword, are gaining fast. I think, 'You're nothing but a pack of dogs,' and laugh – but still, the run is clear, some straggly crops, a sign that maybe says there's mines – on, on: I give those dogs a name: Adnan and Toni. But for my friends – I could have been a rock star, I could have put on red shoes, been an adviser to the President: 'Grow your own coca, hide it in your poppy fields,' I'd say – 'And with one word you'd win your war against the drugs, impoverish some peoples, but not yours – so, go to!'

I could be anything: happiness means thinking that.

I must ask Rosine, 'Have you been making fun of me? The big unanswerable question posed, all the froth of doubt, enquiry . . .? The lending, and the partnership . . . smashing the horrors in the cave: have done with history and its circling round – prepare flat surfaces that hold the truth, stick to it like treacle, or like jelly rolls . . .'

I've circled round, just like the universe.

Here's Rosinette, rising like Afrodite from her muslin shell. 'Back off, you dogs,' she shouts.

I cannot speak. I'm humble. I and the animals, we pant, defeated, safe.

'Now,' says Rosine, limning her face, untying limbs. 'Ready for what comes! I've bought your site. It goes well with mine – I'm up to waist high there. You just owe me interest on the loan.'

'I can't go back like that,' I say. 'With debts.'

'It's your choice,' she says. 'The guys here – maybe they'll be smashed. Or smash each other. Perhaps they're evil – does that count? It's hard to make your way out here – there's all the rulers and the deals. It's all in quite the hardest place. In China, they thought being central worked. Hmmm. Better an island, far away. Under the coco trees, with no drive, no plan, big drinks and smokes, fish like silver roof tiles, eager to be lifted out . . .'

It's the new world, the happy end. And yet, she's so volatile . . .

'Were you, perhaps, torn to pieces by those dogs?' asks Rosine. 'People from the underworld – it happens. You can read about it. Some guys here – they don't believe in spilling blood. The dogs are not so fussy. You know nothing about business, how that goes on – with or without the dogs. You know about ingratiating.'

'Yes, Rosine,' I say, much humbled. 'I tried to sell myself all over. Some special knowledge – Moscow, or Lanzhou. But that was politics. The business that you do, Rosine, is much too slippery for me.'

'Slippery, but dull. The rules – the same all over. Beginnings, ends – uniform, all time, all people, every place,' she says, without regret.

'I do it different,' I say. 'Behind the stall, or cleaning out the stalls the horses use – then,' I say, expanding. 'With very little education, if you did maybe a year or two in school – you see your destiny. All's fluid now. Profess a faith, some benevolence, some pragmatism. Ingratiate. Be tough, be sweet. Offer yourself. Sell what you have – it's magic! Once you're sold, you're in! You show you know the game – now, you can be tough – and bluff. Or top the pile!'

I think of Adnan's book, on how to cheat. You don't have to cheat extra: the game is made for cheats. Those are the rules. I say,

'You see, Rosine, to head Republics, or a Party, you don't need to ride a camel, heft a sabre any more. You trickle, flow, spate. And there you are.'

'And that is what you want,' says Rosine. Maybe she laughs.

'No! Absolutely not!' I say. 'It is enough to know. The knowing – is the music without sound.'

'That's called composition,' Rosine says. 'And you end up behind the stall.'

'I'm not there now, Rosine,' I say. 'It's downs and ups, you don't know which is which. And – I'm happy always. Is there better?'

'I have a plan,' she says.

'No one will come here, Rosine,' I say. 'We have flat foundations, nothing more.'

'That's what I need,' she says. 'On those, we build tall palaces. People will live in them, and plot and deal. That's how new sites are raised, and then destroyed. It's history, loss and profit, metamorphosis. It starts with faith and ends with salaries.'

'I hadn't thought of that,' I say. 'Your genius . . . deserves a plinth . . .'

'We'll wait until the Chinese arrive, before all that,' she says. 'Meanwhile, the guys that come and live here – you know what they'll do?'

'I can't imagine, Rosine, but it won't flesh out their dreams,' I say.

'Stalls, my friend!' she says. 'Those are your speciality. That's how you'll pass your lives, you and your friends. Adnan and Toni. They let drop the cause. Commerce is what awaits them now.'

'Well, we're here, in at the beginning, or at the end. Commerce or construction – and we're not old, not young. We don't carry infection, we have no hopes. We'll be here, for whatever happens,' I say, jumping around.

'You're crazy!' Rosine says. 'Who knows, where we'll be, who'll come, and what they carry? Here is emptiness. Nothing above ground has any worth.'

'Can we find a crevice, put in some banknotes, and it all sprouts up?' I ask.

'Listen, Jacko,' says Rosine. 'Just because you don't understand a thing, not territory, nor paying armies, nor the true faiths – doesn't mean it all comes round the same. If it did, we wouldn't stand among the teasels here, in the flatness. There'd be titanic rocks, all stacked and glowing. When things are down – there may not be an up. If there is – you bet it's me that's done it!'

Paying armies. That's the important thing.

'There's options: tenting victims; punishing with the sword of God,' I say. 'And speculative building. There must be something more.'

'That's all there's ever been, my dear,' she says. 'And there's no speculation – it's a certain thing. And – you can always burrow in my muslin shroud. There's love. And if not love – there's *frottage* –' and she waves her hips. Billows like the ocean crossing to go home, or to Cythera . . .

'It's not enough,' I say. 'Or rather, it's not anything, and where's the people here? Still running, making a story of their exodus, I'll bet, and storing rancour up like wheat.'

'You are a silly boy!' she says, winding me tight, in her raw soft cloth. 'You can't have what you want unless you start to say it. Just wanting lacks the faith. The root. The home that someone planted in you. That is the quest. It's circular. And – it ends underground, or blowing dusty on that scrubby bush. Scattered in life, it's just you end up so: the fire, the earth – that's what there is, when you can't breathe or drink . . .'

'There's no one here,' I say, 'except that guy who wants to sell it all . . .'

'Each time they burn your house, and make you run,' she says, 'your brain expands. That's evolution. Once, people enjoyed living in bands, and everyone the same. Then, everyone who could, they had to run: they lost the taste to live alike, to be a species like the hawks, the lions. Their brains got bigger, too big to fit into their skull, be carried by those little legs. Do you think that going back – praying together, swaggering around, and being good – do you believe all that starts off again? A floor, a roof, a book – maybe a memory's enough . . . Do you believe that's all there is? For ever and for ever.'

'Oh, Rosine,' I say. 'I run. They must have burnt my house – there's nothing left, there's no address, no walls. My brain is heavy on its stalk. I roam. I don't want territory. And yet – it's like it was when we came out of Africa, no destination – looking for the green, the yellow and the black of eyes behind the tree – you throw your stone, your spear. Who cares if that's the last of them, the beasts? Tomorrow, maybe you will find a fruit, a root, a coconut . . .'

'My!' Rosine laughs. 'How you exaggerate! There must be territory, must be walls. You lose your own – then you're in business, into property. Or else – you're in the factory, you make some stuff – some guy upstairs writes down your details, another stands outside and strokes his gun . . . Which would you like to be?'

'It's clear,' Rosine,' I say. 'The stall! Of everything you show me – that must be best. And yet, and yet . . .'

'You're empty!' Rosine says, and laughs some more. 'You don't need instinct, or big names: all that drives you's gravity. You're the cheerful finch, the *Fink* – "a lovely world", it chirps, *eine schöne Welt.*'

'I didn't know you sang, Rosine,' I say.

'Oh yes,' she says. 'That was before my house was burnt.'

'That's trite,' I say.

'Your emptiness,' she says. 'You could be a great destroyer. Alexander – Iskander. Napoleon.'

'It's not all bad,' I say.

'Of course,' she says. 'It's rather enviable.'

'Or – it could be nothing. Just one of a million things a million guys could be,' I say.

'Yes,' she says. 'Quite useless – especially for the little things.'

The bus – a dusty buzz, far off in the mist . . . There's no one waiting. I don't have the fare, but maybe Alp puts in the word . . .

You imagine the horsemen coming up the ridge to have done with Rosinette. I hear nothing, though, and from the rear window, there's no sign of anyone.

3

'Well,' Adnan asks, looking displeased. 'What did you learn?'

It's just temporary, coming back.

I say, 'Oh, nothing much. I lost our site. There was Rosine – I swear, she wasn't my invention. Save for one guy – there's no one there. Just swirls of nothing that rampage. It will resolve, and people live in discontent behind new lines . . .'

'Well, that's the new, and that's the old,' says Adnan. 'Although it makes you weep . . .'

'The lady with the little cat,' says Alp. 'She's gone with Adnan.' And that's true.

'Where's the cat, Claire?' I ask. She comes down sideways, as if she's been on the swing with Fragonard. Maybe her eyes aren't put in straight.

'He got big,' she says. 'Pissed in my suitcase.'

'Anyway,' I say, 'you've got commitment. Adnan. Must take up your day.'

'Yes,' she says. 'And the gambling takes the night.'

'You need cash to lose for that,' I say.

'It's philosophical,' she says. 'If you believe in chance – what comes next? Do you believe in winning? Breaking even? Or in loss? Then, if you believe in one of those – what do you bet on?'

'It's a philosophy for sure,' I say. 'The most trying of them.'

'And the fury! The screaming at the stars. "Pop! Go pop! so's I can see you – billions, and they twinkle on! Just one expires, I'll know the principle behind it all," he shouts,' says Claire. 'There's Toni, whispering about the fire that makes him rise in feathers from the ash. And Adnan. I could accept his faith, but not his disbelief.'

'Where I was,' I say, disoriented. 'Everybody had run off, been chased and hunted – confusions of freedom and security. Like Calvin. All free and uniform, the rest go off to hell.'

'Calvin. Yes,' she says. 'I spot the name. Designs in grey. We're going into frocks. I'll run our branch that deals in rags – the high class ones, with logos. "Free, uniform" – that's a description that fits perfectly the sporty stuff that doesn't fit. I'm sure it sells.'

'I understand Adnan's fury,' I say. 'How d'you tell, if it's chance or not? And once you know – what are the laws, the principles? If it's chance – must it be all chance? Or bits – and then . . . The bag is full of questions . . .'

'It's easier with time,' she says. 'How that runs on! A train! On one stall there's history, those capsules. On mine – the cladding. The unnecessary rags we wear, obedient to time, like ragas, then cast off . . .'

'I understand,' I go on, not having a response. 'You want to start things off. We had a site completely flat. But down you go, securing the foundations – there are the demons and the khans – still at it, waving their pizzles and their axes . . .'

'Oh,' she says, 'I can take all that. I'm not quietist. I like processions, fireworks, flagellations, all that stuff. You chivvy people, peg them out under the sun and watch them scorch, and in the end, it's all revenge, reaction, people always pay, there's no one else who does. Justice, the right, they mention that. People,' she says uncertainly. 'And – it rarely happens everywhere. There's always guys up high, combing their yaks, clipping their dividends. It's like the sky. A star will pop! – there's millions more, and some explode and make another mess of boiling stones and acid ponds . . . You were in the Arab lands . . . there's always other guys to take their place. Go East. Today – the plastics factory. Tomorrow – who can tell? Now, in the midst, where the gas station stood, another continent is born. Quite indigestible.'

'Being happy, Claire,' I say. 'That's the trick. You've an eye for history. I'm not sure that helps.'

'I love it,' says Claire. 'The pyramids. All those guys, under the lash, blocks on their backs, up and down. Like the movie. You must have a favourite battle?'

'You take me by surprise,' I say. 'How about Borodino?'

'Mine's Stalingrad,' she says. 'They don't call it that now.'

'There's lots of places where I was,' I say. 'They'd been battled over lots. Hard to pick out one . . .' Rosine was Lebanese: there must be one she'd remember well. 'A favourite civilisation, then, dear Claire?' I ask.

'Mayas or Aztecs,' she says. 'They grew maize, so they'd have lots of the year to do religion in. Sacrifices. I hate crime. They had none. Just punishments.'

'I always had my eye on you,' I say. 'Claire! Talking to you now – it makes me wonder what you'd do with it. My eye . . .'

'Eyes on my top?' she says. 'It's seventies, this fake exposure deco . . .'

Later, I say to Adnan, 'Claire's a spicy taste.'

'At least, there's nothing humanist in her,' he says. 'That humanist talk – it's a disappointment always. She deals the cards quite swift – from underneath, at times. It keeps you guessing . . . Everybody takes a chance. And takes a side – sometimes three or four. The warriors push forward, the rest fall back. And in the end, you do your sum. But – settling up – that's not in the game, not part of it. The game goes into history,' he says. 'It's not like Toni says, all about winning. It's the playing. Sweeping the chips away – under the table – and playing on and on. You never do the sum. The game goes on – another room, and other guys.'

'I feel antipathy to Claire,' I say. 'I guess that's her attraction.'

'Oh yes,' says Adnan, 'she doesn't care if you agree with her or not. That's her quality. She lies lightly on you.'

'Toni's problem,' I say, 'is how you win if you're selling old clothes off a barrow.'

'That's what Claire says. It's all our problem, too. Then there's remorse. If you're winning, you don't feel it. You try to make the others feel it, and desist. So – remorse is what the losers feel. They're free to do it. But when you go to win, you do what other guys have done to you. Or those you identify with. And yet – they say that beasts know how to win, but only humans feel remorse . . .'

'That's a watery track, I'm sure, Adnan. Don't venture down those tales about the beasts. Claire's cat – was that an instinct, or an ignorance? A sign to leave? Or stay?' I ask.

'Cat? What cat?' asks Adnan. We fall silent, both of us.

'Whatever happens,' Toni says, 'you guys – you won't be satisfied. You wring your hands, you don't see there's new people everywhere. Even winning – when you're at home, even a little win is good. And Claire – if she goes in for cage-fights – there's a chance to make some cash.'

'Cage-fighting! Now, that's talking, Claire,' I say.

We'll follow her, her fame, and when she's at the top, I'll be off, off on my own, leave my soggy friends, up and away.

'Don't get no ideas, you guys,' says Claire. 'The cash I make goes in my shoe. All bets are personal, the losses too.'

'If you get hurt, my dear,' says Adnan. 'We'll be left, abandoned . . .'

'Between fights, dear Adnan, you get better, do your shopping, spend the cash. It works that way,' says Claire.

She turns to me. 'You! I know your sort. The women that you seek – "*enfants du paradis*" who dance, contort themselves and sing. I don't believe a word. You batten on to passive women, so you can act aggressive. No one is fooled. You're strange. There's nothing to be done. Why, a while ago, there was this guy – it came the time for sex. His apparatus – it was cleft! Just like the devil in those pics!'

She makes wide-eye at me. I say, 'Maybe he was punk – there's still some bands of mutilates that linger round . . . So – how'd you manage?'

'How do you think?' she asks, and laughs. 'Stupid!'

It's true, she has some muscles here and there, eye like a peregrine. No fear, at least for now.

'I know the types that come and watch,' she says. 'They're scum. Just like you lot – small crooks that hope to climb from dregs to crust.

Son of Makhno, Vlasov soldiers, SSs – all that kind. I read my screen. I'm in the dirty end – at least I *know*. You *guess*. You lost the fight, and now you trip around the world, you hope to make some friends! The other guys are into blocs, big armies for whatever is their kind, rampaging up and down, like Chinese generals, all rush about, the cymbals tinkling, pheasant feathers quivering – and you guys, over here, no longer in the game! It's over, bluffs are called, the maps are on the table, all the lines rubbed out. Any excuse is good for new guys to make a crew – your god, your colour, bits of history – and loads of cash and curious coloured dirt and rocks . . . You haven't seen it fall this way for centuries, and now you've no idea which way is up or right or left . . .'

'Is all this on your screen?' asks Toni. 'It's all quite admirable – do show!'

'Oh, that's the start,' says Claire. 'The rest is common sense.'

'You start off gentle, exhibitions, shows and interviews. A slap, a kick. Get known. Then you start the combats,' and Alp waves his fists, quite expert. 'There's talent all around – some brutes, some trained expensively. Not everyone's familiar with the rules, of which there aren't.'

'The cage constricts,' says Toni. 'But also it protects. Especially us, outside. Everything within's OK. The problem is – to find an honest guy to hold the stakes.'

'Claire puts on her show,' says Alp. 'So – where's the point?'

'It has to be a good show, Alp,' says Claire. 'The fighters each put up a bond. The judges say if it seems genuine, the fight, – or not.'

'Judges?' Toni asks. 'Where do these come from? I thought Claire was the heroine.'

'Well, my dears,' says Claire, 'I'm nobody. What do I stand for? What changes if I win or lose? It's you guys betting – that's what keeps you satisfied.'

'Satisfied, if we are rich – but not that happy . . .' Adnan says.

'Rich is out,' says Claire. 'But – this fighting show is big. It's maybe not important. Not at all. There is no territory involved, no populations – nothing at all outside the cage. But I'm fulfilled. You're entertained. Think of me as history, if you will. Decide who are your enemies – and they'll fight back. Not me – I don't have enemies.'

'Well,' says Alp, 'I'm not going where you went,' and he waves the site map at me. 'What I do, I shall do here. Behind the stall. I'm not into making new Americas.'

'It's sex, Claire,' Adnan says. 'They look for that, the guys. Not strength and blows.'

'We're in a cage,' shouts Claire, 'but we're not birds of paradise. It's idle guys that fantasise. Quite useless . . .'

'I knew paradise was part of this,' says Alp. 'Whoever does the nuptial dance.'

'Of course there's fantasy,' says Adnan. 'We live by it . . . that someone's waiting to have sex with us . . . that we're a band of brothers, sisters, all liking us, sharing our thoughts and destinies . . . that in the end we'll all live well with justice and respect for all . . .'

'It's only fantasy that keeps us all afloat, Adnan,' says Toni. 'Without that, we must sink. We look at Claire – she fights for us, her losses – just ephemeral, like her victories . . .'

'Not if you call it right,' says Alp. 'She's our ship, bearing us all away. Except – each of us should have a boat, a raft at least, to catch the wind . . . That's what they do, the heroes. They're great companions – then, battle done, each sets out separately, leaving the friends he cannot tolerate . . .'

'I'll put on a show for Adnan, for all of you, so's you can leave,' says Claire. 'When I've no fight, I'll put new labels in the frocks, make more cash for all of us. It'll never be enough.'

'How do we get away?' asks Alp. 'It's the whole circus, over and over – the Yanks and the Indians, the Guatemalans, anyone they thought was alien, that didn't fit. Over and over. The long list of smashings. Boring and hateful. You can't get away from anything.'

'Alp is settled,' Toni says. 'It means he can be settled anywhere. Or just stay here. I'll start a bar – maybe Marocco; and invite you all for drinks.'

'We'll do a show,' says Adnan. 'Bangkok, with Claire. Then she'll come back and sell those frocks.'

'First she has to earn the cash,' I say.

That's their dreams? The best? No analysis, just ebbs and flows. What a disappointment. The keys of heaven – and they're handed back, too heavy. Too rusty.

When she fights, we get to hoot and scream, like liners leaving port – like wolves, like hoopooes – if you don't, they think you've fixed the bout. It's compulsory to make the noise, of souls that's tipping over some sharp edge, on to the bayonets beneath. Our passion – never expressed like this elsewhere . . .

'Come on, you guys,' says Claire, 'I hardly hear you. Open your throats you songsters . . .!'

*

'You realise,' Alp says to me when we're alone, 'Claire's fighting. She doesn't risk – except to be a celebrity. Better to avoid it – and with the cash upon her, she won't get hurt. They never do. The thing is – she enables us. She'll own us. Her ambition trumps whatever hope we have. I know – she was mine, and then I sidled out. I passed her on. Adnan will manage her – in the professional sense, and then – maybe they'll dump each other. She'll win. She's built like a man – all shoulders.'

'I hadn't looked,' I say. 'I hadn't thought.'

'Our site,' says Alp. 'You lost it easy. Too easy.'

'I'd forgotten that,' I say.

He doesn't pause, doesn't believe, or listen . . . 'You forget,' he says. 'There's Persians. Whatever they may call themselves. They're in between – in the middle, if you like. And then – you forget as well –

there's spaces, full of Turks – and even then, before you get to China, there's who they called barbarians. You simplify. Each passage, every outcome. You're wrong.'

'I really don't do anything,' I say. 'Not to be right or wrong. I know all that you say. Claire's the one of us who sees the wormhole, the tunnel you must swim down, find the right movements to get you through the earth, the mud, out to wind, clear water.'

'It was you took the bus,' says Alp. 'Not her.'

'Claire's fighting shows the emptiness of fighting,' I say. 'But maybe that's just me.'

'She's a person generous and lively,' Alp says, 'but she's just another pinup, hopping in and out her torture, and she doesn't feel a thing. It's the adrenalin that talks. What drives, is faith in herself, her intuition for the blows. What you need is rules – not drama. People doing what they ought, and what is good for everyone. Personality – it doesn't count.'

'That brings us back,' I say. 'The rules are there for cheating them. We're back to Toni.'

'I'll keep quiet until I make my move,' Alp says.

'I know how I got there, Alp,' I say. 'The flattened site. Not what it was called. I guess the people there were terrified, or else – they'd stayed and got the hurt. Passed the wound on to the survivors. Running, being a refugee – they're options desirable, thinking of what else there's been.'

'They say it's good to have a choice,' says Alp.

We watch the fighters in the cage. Claire shouts down – 'The fucking lights! So hot, they sap your strength.'

'You have to have belief,' says Alp, 'In something. Some big souls believe in everything. More modestly – there's rules, or God, or destiny and time. Or lights. Death, or immortality. Then, there's "belief default", it's called – trust, that human nature has good aspects – you can bet on those. Adnan just wagers – there's no real risk . . . Claire takes it seriously – she takes the risk, gets her head kicked in. Adnan risks his cash. But then – he started off with nothing – and he's always got the stall.'

'That's heavy stuff,' I say, as Claire is shunted round the cage with blows of every kind. She turns, she snarls. We cheer, we howl, we dance upon the spot. She's smaller than the other – whom she lifts and throws against the bars.

*

'Well, you guys,' says Claire. 'Put on your red shoes. For you, it's dancing time. I'm battling to pay the debts that Adnan's raised. Sing the blues . . . now, I have to win each time. Or get a fix . . . My gains are set against the losses Adnan's made. Your dreams remain, my dears – just dreams. So – close your eyes, and hold your vertical.'

Anyway, I'm happy. I'd not had time to fantasise about the wealth I now shan't have.

'Claire is our mountain,' Adnan says. 'The cash flows from her, down to our Babylon. It never is enough. Who takes it, where does it run to? And – she sees double now – the kicking multiplies her vision . . . past and future . . . The present's problematic.'

'You guys,' Claire says. 'The only thing I can't quite focus on – is who's before me at the instant.'

She's a visionary, a blind seer, who doesn't tell us what she sees.

Toni leaves, deserts. There's a universe he can inhabit. It's only us who thinks he's lost.

'Hit me,' says Claire. Adnan hits her, quite hard.

'I feel it,' Claire says. 'I don't see you. Not with any of my eyes.'

He hits her again. 'Water?' asks Claire. 'Cash?'

'Blood,' Adnan says. 'No tears. Nothing more. Accept it.'

'That's it,' says Claire. 'Enough. I'm empty. Don't bother hitting me.'

'One more,' says Adnan. 'It may bring me luck.' He hits her. She doesn't move.

She can't fight. Can't even match the labels to the *haute couture*.
She's lost it, lost her aim. Lost her reputation and her fans.

'What disaster!' Adnan says. 'I couldn't pick a winner when it came
up close and kissed me.'

Claire falls back, somewhere – to the horizon where she came from.
If it were me, I'd feel some rancour – at almost everything, for sure at
all of us.

'Toni's had his success,' says Alp. 'He was keen on absolutes.
Being absolutely top. Now he's gone – and left absolutely nothing.'

'You don't like us, Alp,' I say.

'No,' he says. 'But don't mistake. You're not humankind. It's not a
general thing with me, not liking. Claire, now – she was a good sport. I
loved her – absolutely. But Adnan was the winner there. He punched
her out, but only when she couldn't see.'

'I hope she cheated, hid the cash she won,' I say. 'Or else – blind
fighters have it hard.' I think of Rosine. If she survives, she'll surely
find the new regimes give space to stand in, like the old.

'Toni had a plan,' says Alp. 'Myself, I don't believe all people
disappear some day. If there's too many, some remain. It's logical. But
Toni had his plan – when there was no one left – he'd leave a camera,
to run and run. It was a cosmological eye, you see: winning to him is
showing. His show would last, go on and on. The something filming
nothing, that was his idea.'

'It's a notion Toni read in magazines,' I say. 'It's like a piece of
music that you make it so it has no end, or no fixed shape. You think
it's immortality – or maybe purgatory – but really, music's all like that.
It's every piece interpreted – it has no start, no end. No first cause, no
finality. And sounds – are just the same. They came from somewhere,
they're always there, they dissolve in air. But they're at hand as well,
they always are . . .'

'I think you're wrong somewhere in that,' says Alp. 'Nowhere lives
by that, the materials eternally unchanging, but ready for whatever use
you want – no state, no heaven, and no caliphate exists for that.

There's come and go. Rebels and cops. Even in heaven – for sure, the music's always there, but sounds decay, new guys pop up. There's relativism all around – so, there's dinosaurs, or else there'd be no justice . . .'

And he expounds. There's nothing much that you can say.

'I'm sure there's intermediaries,' I say. 'Like bees you need to make the fruit.' He stares at me. 'Adnan ruined Claire,' he says. 'He's lucky she blames fortune, and not him.'

'Luck made them buzz and hum,' I say. 'But, Alp – you don't go in for having laughs, I fear.'

'Oh,' says Alp, 'I have my chuckle when I don't see what's coming next.'

I say, 'As for couples, Alp, remember beg and steal? There's Claire and Adnan now – they were a couple. And Toni . . .'

'Oh,' Alp interrupts, 'he'll be somewhere selling drinks – a stall set on a beach. Reading his book. Peering for the sails of beaten warriors, returning to take vengeance on their cheating wives.'

'We're close to everything,' I say. 'To everything big that happens. But not to anyone at all, a person like us or unlike.'

'Ha!' says Alp. 'Those big phenomena. It's not about impossible things people say that they believe. It's tectonic plates – on the move, islands sink or swim: volcanoes, geysers, ridges, mountains. Watching the continents edge back and forth, while waiting for the meteors that burn the trees and blow us all away.'

4

Here, there's nudes and picnics. Toni in a dishdash, sometimes arrogant, servile to the cops. Families in black. 'There's every sort that's here,' he says. 'I'm waiting for my entrance. I could be top, or toppled quick. There's people come from everywhere – to gawp, or seeking refuge – all wanting tranquil lives, warring for them if they're pressed . . .'

We watch the waves. 'We need guys in real estate, and generals,' he says. 'Rosine and Claire! How they would suit!'

'They're far away,' I say. 'We're all dispersed. Claire – chased off. An athlete blind, bobbing on the waters, weaving sightless through the tempests. Beaching on the basalt rocks. Rosine – enmeshed in business, wealthy or defunct.'

He pours something crystal from a tall pot. 'Toni, you're dead,' I say. 'It's better than being mad.'

'Oh,' he says. 'Wait! You'll see the bears on broken floes. Far, far away – they stand up tall, and then the warm currents carry them away, dissolving, gone quite under.'

'That, I believe,' I say. 'But all the rest you haven't told – is fantasy.'

'The cat,' he says, jigging up and down. 'Claire's cat. Do you look after it?'

'It's big enough,' I say, 'to take control.'

'I loved her so, poor Claire,' he says. 'But she was not for me, nor anyone. A drag, in fact. That ego . . .'

'You could winter here,' I say. 'Build a look-out. The galleys – watch them come and go. Shake off your melancholy.'

'This *is* winter, friend,' he says.

Of course! There's water for the glass.

'Be very prudent here,' I say. 'I'm sure the book says that.'

'Oh,' he says, 'I know all the book says. The people here are all from somewhere else. The locals don't live here – they're in the hills,' and he waves over to them.

'I should do something for you, Toni,' I say, meaning too 'for me', not knowing what we want, what I'm expected to perform.

'I'm the still point,' Toni says, proudly. 'I bide my time, I'm the water-clock. The rest are plastic scum, detritus on the shore, rushing forward with the tide, timidly receding. I'm the water-tower, absolutely fresh.'

It's a caricature: he chants, 'Tea, water, women and smokes!' He chinks two tiny tin cups like cymbals, on one hand.

'I could help with that,' I say. 'The merchandising.'

'You might,' he says. 'But it would shock the market. Keep off, keep well away.'

'If I fell off my world, Toni,' I persist. 'And on to yours – what then?'

'You'd land so fast,' he says. 'You'd make a bang. Explode. Like that small rock that fell on Russia, broke windows. Some guy had a heart attack. The people here . . . a boss with cash, like where we were – has no appeal. A poor guy, knowing how things work, and used to doing fruity deals, even the guys with parchments on their walls – respect.'

'Your rise,' I say, 'will be your own, alone?'

'My rise? Like a raisin in a flask of aquavit,' he says. 'The rest is dribble and chisel.'

'I came over to have a drink with you,' I say. 'That was the deal.'

'Drink up!' he says. 'No brainy fencing, not from me.'

'Time for me to go,' I say. 'What do you think?'

'It is a long way to come for a cup of water. But you're right. I don't change my objectives. I can see Adnan fallen into remorse, tramping the earth, promising redress to Claire. Who doesn't want it. Not from him. And Alp – the reserve! The only way to develop is to throw it off.

Go to one of those ephemeral places, rub some *rais* the wrong way, and get rubbed out.' He laughs, like a dog that barks.

'You find your destiny, you think, arriving at some block, some obstacle, and taking quite the opposite route?' I ask. 'Adnan destroyed. Chance obliterated by some fisticuffs. Abandoned by blind love . . .? Alp running into action for no cause except his own contrariness?'

'I'll no doubt do the same,' says Toni. 'When the locusts come, I'll not be proclaimed as their destroyer, nor be a father to my people. I'll climb my pole, out in the desert. Meditate. Dine on locust stew. This is the world, my friend. If you don't live through its contradiction, you'll be there, waiting mouth open, for the end. The judgment. Some lost brother's comment, your twin in sin. What there's written in some book they lifted you so's you could heft one down, and you illiterate and ignorant of all the rest.'

'That's heartening talk, though how to take it, act on it, I wouldn't know,' I say.

'You had your moment with Rosine. Bound in your chrysalis, you didn't up and fly. Back at the bus stop, there you were, chastened and purified. No butterfly, no wings – a worm!' He laughs again.

'Rosine?' I say. 'I wasn't keen on her.'

'That's quite irrelevant,' he says. 'Learn from the stream, the water from my pot.' He pours.

'Toni,' I say. 'That's trite.'

'Listen,' Toni says, close on me, and his breath is disconcerting – warm, hollow, odourless, 'you know who the real revolutionaries are? We discussed it often, that revolution . . . They're the ones who get no gain. No place, no honour, not a medal, not a plate of beans. They live the revolution, and they die in it, their thin feet stick from the canvas sheeting as they're tumbled into nameless graves. That's the revolution, those are the true revolutionaries.'

I want to say, 'Toni, revolution was never in your pack.' I don't. There's no 'something else' to say, no 'something other'. You call it inconclusive . . . It's not. It concludes, for sure.

'What?' shouts Toni. 'You still here? My team's awaking. They won't want you here. To ship! Away it heads! No one knows where to – all destinations are invisible from here. The captain? Lost! Hunkered in some cathouse, can't see the door for opium smoke . . . This is the East, my friend, the South! Here, tulip trees grow in a single night, your lover changes sex between the dawn and breakfast . . . Aboard, away – and don't unpack your kitbag – those aren't artichokes, my friend, they're shrivelled heads someone unknown to you has packed . . . skulls of your friends, your sages, every living thing you ever staked your money on . . .'

*

My boat's still there moored, hooting like a randy stag. There's Irina, on the rail. She shakes my hand. 'This boat goes to many places,' she says. 'At each one I see you disembark, no luggage, then you run back, a knobbly kitbag on your back.'

'Oh,' I say, 'I have short-term friends, lodged everywhere. Rolls in a paper bag. That's all I need, to keep on travelling. Even to Kashgar, the market full of Chinese things . . . My friends would envy me.'

'I see you are a traveller,' she says. 'But not so bright. You went to perilous lands – but missed the riches. Bargains. You saw defeat and panic. You should have done some deals instead – whole cities going cheap. They have to rebuild there. There's no other road, no well, no garden near. They'll be back. You'd make them pay.'

'Irina, you put on that ancient voice – it's all quite different,' I say. 'There's men there, made animals that's never seen upon the earth – made so by men who're animals, seen many times before. From Idaho. Mongolia. A scene so terrible, the cash turns to dry leaves before you reach to spend it.'

'That's as may be,' she says. 'If you travel, you must leave your mark. Or be prepared to leave your bones. Forget the animals – they're only interested in you when you're meat.'

I don't know her – so I tell her everything.

'The name is Russian,' says Irina. 'The face – Chinese.'

'My pupil, Alp,' I say. 'Curiosity got the better part. He'll go off – not to fight, he doesn't think too much of that – but to observe. Seeing, not believing. That's what he says. These states, that grow and shrink, and battle like the olden times – he wants to see quite how they work, how states are made, unmade . . .'

'It's like a ship,' Irina says. 'Maybe you've thought – they're coffin-shaped, and yet – they're full of bunks where you can sport and have your fill. First officers, then seconds – tap-tap on your door all night.'

I'm happy. Whatever happens, you know it will pass amid indifference, so if you can, you smile. If not – then happiness is still the finest deal; within, not signalled. Irina makes an invitation, that's for sure: we cuddle on her bunk. And then – 'No, no,' she shouts. 'It's too grotesque. It's too obscene!' She laughs and bats me nearly out the door.

'Irina, I swear, assure you – that's the way,' I tell her. 'It's how the humans do it, always have, almost a throwback to before we walked around upright. Culture and faith – they don't come in. There is no other way. Homo erectus . . .' I explain.

'No, no,' she laughs. 'Come back when you are serious. Even as a humanist.'

It's unavailing. Nothing I say convinces her. The passion dies, desire goes cold. But – it remains, as cold desire.

'You see,' Irina says, tidying her mussed attractions. 'My country is often misrepresented. Thieves and bullies – that's the story . . . but the trains streak like aeroplanes, the children eat and eat like foxes . . . So it must be for Alp, his hunger, his curiosity: those new guys . . . what functions? Maybe they're not so new. Are they just? Just vicious? Ignorant and bigoted, poor dolts on the make? Making states like all the rest? Digging graves and settling scores . . . in the steps of . . . Russians, Americans, Brits and Serbs? And French and Belgians . . . must I go on?'

I start to tell her . . .

'No,' she says. 'It's clear, Alp didn't think you'd got it right.'

'Irina, I want him home,' I say.

'Home?' she says.

The ship slides up and down. Sometimes, it edges forward, steering by the moon, the path it lays down, on the waves.

'You're very eloquent, Irina,' I say, at a loss.

'You mean I'm bourgeois?' she asks, mocking. 'Well, they invented doubt and certainty. What they'd been certain of, they came to doubt – and that was the end, end of long paragraphs and archives, digging it all up to put on mantelpieces. Their economics put gunpowder underneath their law. There were so many ways to make a longer story – but what they passed on was their God. Disaster!'

'Well, Irina,' I ask, dazzled. 'Are you? Bourgeois? Not that it matters much.'

'Oh,' she says, 'I'm candies in a jar. Only – there's no lid. Look on, and salivate.'

Why, I think, she could be the one. But – I am not the one . . .

'Adnan regrets his violence,' I say. 'He seeks out victims. Gives a hand.'

'He could have thought of that before,' she says. 'And saved himself from cleaning sores.'

'Having good friends,' I say. 'Makes you seem virtuous yourself.'

'Seem virtuous *to* yourself, my dear. You need be careful. The more you know, the less you can do. Study hyenas. They don't know much, but they'll be around, and longer . . .' She screws down her porthole.

'You've a future, Irina,' I say.

'That's not encouraging,' she says. 'We're all quite tired, besides.'

'The ship has lost its way, it seems,' I say. We're broadside to the swell.

'It's the captain,' says Irina. 'He didn't make it back from shore. He was happy there. Songs, a soft caress. Why should he come back to turn that wheel?'

'We too – we may be victims,' I say, alarmed. 'We may sink, undocumented. They'd search and never find the captain – he's not here. We have faces and no names . . . maybe "Irina" . . .'

'No,' Irina says. 'I've no name on anything. If you don't say where you're destined – you don't pay until you're there. My legs are used to this already. When the rest accommodates – I could stay on board. Maybe – I'll become a captain. If we drown of course – all this talk will just be pulp. Our crimes – unpunished. Our imaginations – unread fantasy. You could cry . . .!'

We run up and down – up the ladders, like two frightened snakes. 'There's no wheel!' Irina shouts. 'Nothing to steer with. Here, there's no conscience – that you need, to reach a a destination of some kind, a port.'

There's little rooms with guys who're rolling dice or shuffling cards. 'You need a conscience – alas, you haven't one,' she says to me. 'Mine – it hides, I fear, when body feels the threat . . .'

We start to argue, mind and body stuff. There are no lifeboats: Irina says, 'Big boats don't sink. They cut the lifeboats so's to make the ship so big.' The ship goes up and down – and we go down and up, trying to escape the sea, its sucking arms . . . 'The birds!' she says. 'If they were seabirds – they would scream. These, on the masts – they're green and gold – they sing . . . it's they who charmed the helmsman, led him to the rocks.' The sea is full of other boats, dark roundels in the dark.

'You sell your soul to board, and get it back if you arrive,' I say, 'but someone takes a cut.'

Irina stands inclining forward, at the prow. 'The phosphorus!' she says. 'The furrow. It is the morning star. I thought it was the moon.'

'It's phosphorescence only, Irina. Not phosphorus,' I say. 'No one has thrown it there, the light. It's from below it surges up.'

'I could make the sacrifice,' she says. 'Go in the waves.'

'No, Irina,' I say. 'It would be pointless. You wouldn't save a thing.'

'I don't,' she says, 'because I *know* I can't. It's a way I talk, that's all. And look! – our course has changed. What a relief! Although I knew it always does. There's someone down below, who's found a wheel.'

Forward, onward we go. 'You've lost your friends,' she says. 'Though you still count them friends. They're scattered. Now – towards the moon we plough . . . Until we see the city lights – I'll hold your soul, with all the rest.'

'I don't believe in that,' I say. 'Poetic stuff.'

'I am the purser on this boat,' she says, irritated. 'Until we have a destination – I'm your destiny.'

A host of frightened guys comes up the side. 'Good!' Irina says. 'We saved their souls – and ours. Now they can go below and turn the shaft.'

'I thought you were a passenger,' I say.

'That's just a choice,' she says. 'If you want to be an officer – put these gold shackles on your wrists.'

I thought they were her bangles. 'I sought a rescue,' says Irina. 'Now – I want to get off. Find a destination. With a name. Doss down. A bottle by the mattress: silver tequila. No fighting, and no prayers. Those – we had on board, there's nothing else but waves. "Save us, save us!" we cried out. No one did – but we are safe!' And she hugs me, her tears are all over me, they soak the dirty mattress, seep through the floor, bathe another mattress, there's another bottle, always more tears, a captain lying mute, out of his mind, from twisting wheels. Those gold rings heavy, as he lifts his rum, and drinks. The rooms still tilt and lilt a little, as our legs recall the deeps.

'Now,' Irina says, 'tell me all about the ruins and the caves, the smashing and the excavating. The warriors as they skitter round the craters . . . the power, the fear . . . the time that blows it all away . . .'

'You know it all,' I say. 'It's like sitting on a bus. Time always going forward. Maybe for some, somewhere, it goes backwards. For sure, it sediments, for everyone, like diamonds in the sludge: a memory. But to be happy – you watch the scenery. The bus goes forward – so does the rest, all of it . . .'

'The ship,' Irina says. 'It stopped.'

'No,' I say. 'It started going up and down. Then it went on, forward like before.'

'You haven't understood,' she says. 'I won't waste time with you. To you, it never stops. It's flux. It's ghosts; where you are, what you see, dies within the hour like a hatch of flying things.'

'Those guys who swarmed aboard,' I say. 'They were hopeful, even when they had to be our engines.'

'What do you expect?' she asks. 'Anger and suffering all the time? It comes and goes. Sometimes there's fire, and usually – it's the engines, quietly pushing forward, through the scenery.'

'Your name, your face, Irina,' I say. 'How long before there's fire there? Russia, China? Rolling on – Mexico, Detroit?'

'I shan't speculate,' she says. 'You're a renegade. One day they'll throw you off the bus and line you by the ditch. Then you'll see who's angry and who's suffering. It might be you, but you can't do anything about it.'

It's true. Is it worth pondering? Or just a thing you say, not to say something else, more measured?

'Territory. People. Everyone understands those, they're what you win with, nothing else. The rest is philosophy. And – you know where that will end, a dribble in the sand. It's what you can know about – like I do,' she says. 'But you know too where it ends. You do the voyage, and you give back the souls, and take your fee.'

'Gold rings,' I say. 'Rivers are full of them. Guarded by dwarves.'

'That's trite,' she says. 'It's pulp. That is your genre.'

'Toni's up his pole,' I say. 'Revered. Adnan is doing good, well out the way. Should we go and look for Alp? It's the thing they do. Otherwise they'll think I'm . . . phoney, like you do.'

'I don't think,' Irina says. 'I know. Thinking's the exercise. Knowing – the certainty.'

'It sounds too easy,' I say. 'Though I've no grudge.'

'Why settle for less than certainty?' Irina asks. 'Besides, it's not so hard. You're sure of what you see and hear, that's all. It's not the truth – that's something else, that doesn't bother me. I know what we all know. You think it's little – I know that it's a lot.'

'Well, Irina, if it suits, it fits,' I say. 'I fear Alp's in a city. They're too complicated. They frighten me,' I say, and feel I need to add, 'A little bit.'

'Oh,' Irina says. 'It's easy to know everything about the countryside. It's so simple; that becomes its mystery.'

'A city's like a clock,' I say. 'Someone has the key, and someone else knows what the time's supposed to mean. The spring's the thing you want to be – but that's just slog. The deal's to be a wheel.'

'No, no,' Irina says. 'The thing to be's the regulator. The rest is class and wealth.'

'The clock's indifferent to what right time might be,' I say.

'The right time's being good and doing right,' she says. 'And then you find that's quite a different thing from time.'

'Alp's an observer: that you can be anywhere. It isn't dangerous at all,' I say.

'But, on the other hand,' Irina says, 'we're not set up as pioneers. We made no affirmation, no compact: only we two got off that ship.'

'Certainly,' I say, remembering the chicks that ended boiled. 'It's not our thing. That's what Alp said. And – we've no stall back here, for him to end his life behind. And if you cheat at poker and get caught – no book will save you, that's for sure.'

'They'll have stalls there,' Irina says. 'Why should he leave? They'll need him, if they start to build . . .'

'Not all you set up, stands,' I say. 'Alp linked himself to Seljuks – they left some memorial . . . but, the Qara Khitai – what became of them? The monuments, the ruins – in the end, they blend. The stones get reused, for building huts . . .'

'This stuff is recondite,' Irina says. 'When you set foot in history, you end with witches, stuff incredible. Blacklists, defoliants . . .'

'That's trite, Irina,' I think, but leave it for a while unsaid.

'In the end,' Irina says, 'you discover modernity. But it palls. Your big head – its size makes it ache the more.'

'And then,' I agree, 'there's your roots. If you cut those, the fruit goes rotten. Maybe anyway, it was never to your taste.'

'It's settled, then,' says Irina. 'We count Alp as a friend, although I never saw him. He'll sweeten their grey dough. And we'll stay here, and roam about.'

'We spare a thought for Indians,' I say. 'There's always some left, somewhere. Maybe – they've set up a poker game, to celebrate their luck.'

'Of course, it's not all punishment,' Irina says. 'You need relax time, from doing good. You could do lectures, on "Being happy always".'

'Oh no,' I say. 'That would be tough. Indeterminate as well. I think flying planes would be easier.'

'You need to be a Christian, to do that here,' Irina says. 'It gives the bosses confidence. They know you'll drop your load exactly where you're told.'

'No, I'm happy voyaging, Irina. You might say I'm a philosopher. They don't need a place to be in, no backcloth. They can be everywhere. A diplomatic passport usually lets them through.'

'Those stories you were telling me,' Irina says. 'Cortés, Pizarro, Fitzcarraldo – I never knew about them . . . You could make a stir. That could bring you wealth, prestige, or death. At least – a name.'

'That insider news,' I say. 'It's *vieux chapeau*. I'd rather move around. The lawyers, when you tell the tales – they throttle you.'

'Tell what you guess, suspect,' Irina says. 'Then back into the background. Or else – it's in the camps you go, doling out flour with Adnan. Or queuing for it.'

'You're hard, Irina,' I say, and we laugh.

'Your friends are settled, if they're not yet dead,' Irina says. 'We could find some Indians. Be good to them.'

'The cash, Irina?' I ask.

'Oh,' she says, 'I'm the purser. I have souls in credit. A gold ring. Being good – that's been my life. I won't tell you all in detail . . . my father, violent, roughed up by some White Guards, some Red Guards maybe . . . my mother traced – not by me – to a drinkers' paradise, redeemed, sobered and dead . . .

'Unlikely it seems – Calvinism overwhelmed me, made me good. I have a training, a speciality. I cuddle soldiers; tormented, they come back from shooting guys. They're impotent. They should've thought of that before, when they were in the fight. At the last, they could repent. Now, it's too late. Hexed over there, the dead men's friends will take ship, have revenge. You have friends for that. I cuddled them, the soldiers, and got well paid. I was a bandage. They were crazy first – then stupid, with getting things the wrong way round. First, you repent – then you don't do.'

'Is there a cure?' I ask.

'Of course not, stupid,' Irina says. 'If there's a cure, you need renounce your fee. You're paid for trying, just like all the rest.'

'It's no use looking at the floor, thinking there's written there some moral, trick, plot. We all know exactly what's gone on,' I say, fearful of travelling with Irina, who's at home only with the impotent. 'We accept, or we resent. That's democracy.'

'That's so,' Irina says. 'You sound a true reactionary. But – your friends live now, they twist and turn, they suffer. They don't need it all explained. Doubt is there to be expunged. They know when they're in charge and when they aren't. As for us – we'll find some guys who someone calls "the Indians". We'll be benevolent, and then move on.'

I don't see why: – but nothing better comes to mind.

'Before we take the ship again,' Irina says, 'I should explain. I believe in predestination. Nothing supernatural – it isn't needed. Faith. Works are irrelevant . . . but – you need do something in your life, or there's no rhythm. This way, my way – you can do anything you want. No one can tell you what to do.'

'Is this going to help,' I ask, 'with where we go?'

'Oh yes,' she says. 'Destiny – is science too.'

She takes off her golden rings, and stows them in her boot. 'We're not bringing capitalism,' she says, 'though some guys would settle for it. The stage is primitive: debts and taxes – that's how the bosses grow their stash.'

We sleep on deck. We are the only souls on board. I could be the captain, there is no one else . . . we motor on and on, until we smell the earth, the smell of guys with nothing much to do.

The guys here don't seem Indians. Their dwellings, in the 'quake – they all fell down. Rather than build them up, it's better waiting for the next – a tremor, flood, whatever comes. There seems to be a plague, of sorts. They all speak French. I'm much confused. There is no welcome here.

'Here, there's a scent of destiny,' I say. 'Of predestination, dear Irina. Maybe you are right. It seems I am the only happy one around.'

'I'll buy a bulldozer,' Irina says. 'Knock down these huts. Then someone else will come and build them up again. Better, of course.'

'And all the cash,' I ask, 'comes from those rescued souls?'

'Where else?' she says. 'I'm not like your friends who steal.'

You're harsh, Irina. That money . . . we two could spend it otherwise, and on ourselves, I think.

'Observe,' she says. 'No one's exploited, no profit's made. Besides – I told you – works leave the destiny untouched, or maybe open to abuse. You, my friend – you are a lily of the field. You watch, you comment – then you run; unlike the plants, I guess.'

I see her rings are on her wrists again. It means we're off, without the time to hear the tale about the scandals, the humanity, broken and reviled. Without the making of some friends, who'd ask us back . . .

'Don't mention it, Irina,' I say. 'The word is: *Schtum!* From slavery into poverty. Waiting for some guys to find it worth exploiting them.

Shadows of the dark continent . . . I've heard it all, and so has everyone.'

'If you do something bad – there's only repentance. Or – there's silence. Nothing else – the model's built that way. I'm immune to backward glances. I told you – I do what I can do. Wanting – doesn't come into it,' she says.

'I never had comrades,' I say. 'Not like Toni and Adnan – before they turned, and tried to love themselves. They came to think – to see – it wasn't about communism at all. Like now it's certainly not about correcting pasts, the faith, the good life. I don't know if I could stand firm like they did once, or if I stand and watch. More genocides? The guys here – they're not napalmed and the rest, and yet I see them as if they will all disappear quite soon, like ice-statues . . . Not because they're feared or hated: or can be counted. But – is that enough? Ancient things, proceeding. Their destiny?'

'Each time it's different,' Irina says. 'You must be the last to understand! You'll never find the formula. It's clear your friends – they didn't.'

'They didn't look for formulas. I hope they didn't anyway,' I say. 'And they couldn't end up humanists – that's for sure. *We* can't. You don't go that way, Irina. We humans – not a case for adulation, nor our works . . .'

I stare at her. Everything been said, or hinted at.

'You can't live this way,' Irina says. 'You'll eat yourself right up.'

*

It's better on your own. I feel an opportunity's been lost, another one . . . There's Irina's bulldozer, stuck on the slope. I'm almost a benefactor too. She said, 'You'll have to buy a ticket now.' Here's a grey ship. I have my knobbly sack.

Once you're on board, they can't throw you off if you've no cash. Can they? You're there for the trip. That guy before the war, the chef, armed – I could have . . . what? Nudged his shoulder? Shouted down, made his targets look at him? Those guys would come and get him later, anyway. Three of them – one to be sacrificed, one to go round behind and finish him, one to help hide the cadaver under stones. No one sings, no opera, while it goes on. Not that he was wrong – just a nasty looking type. His prices too! Maybe – the others – were the bad guys. You don't chop trees all day without a single bad reflection. Trees through and through like seaside rock: 'good'.

Here's a sailor. No gold rings. 'I'm the armourer,' he says. 'That's from "amorous". I love my work. We have a special room, so that we shan't explode. At sea, land does not exist. It's to be avoided at all costs. You were adept at couples: "beg or steal". So – it's land and sea: air and water. True – they don't hold, not always: space and empty. Summer winter. Peace and war. Things elide, words are made to. "Act and real". Sometimes we do a show on board, just for us. We're sailors, but sometimes it's good to be a woman, a real one,' and he takes me by the hand and leads me to the special room. There's rows of bunks. A sea-green missile lies in every one, beneath a leather blanket.

'There's pirates,' says the sailor. 'Every ship is armed. There are bad cities too . . .'

He has told me everything. I say, 'I was with a woman, she was real. Irina. She was hard to talk to, not like you. She promised nothing, but all the same, her hopes were high. She wanted to do good, tidying the people . . .'

The sailor's quite indifferent. 'I'm from Mali,' he says. 'There's no sea – but there are rivers. Everything is restive nowadays. Skittish. Your friend – she sounds invasive: the liberals say, "Do what you want, but only if it doesn't bother me." That's a creed that's gristly.'

'No, no,' I say. 'Bother wasn't on her mind. She wasn't liberal – maybe a liberal with cash. But – you don't look as if you come from Mali . . .'

'Oh?' he shouts. 'And where does it look as if you come from? North? South?' and he scuttles off, skittering down a ladder.

I hope they don't want me in their show.

Then, there's a shout. 'Sleepers awake!'

They're bringing up those tubes, like Toni's capsules, still dozing, hugging their embroidered blankets, waiting to be primed and timed. 'A warning. An outrage. Injustice . . .'

I have no doubt at all. Yes, let's shoot them off, and show them. No sarcasm, no holding back. There is a line, and when it's crossed, you arm the tubes, you post the message. No one likes it, a scrap, even the martyrs turn a goosy green. It's not being on a side. It's doing what you must.

The armourer puts on a hat, a matelot's, a cherry on the top. 'Don't put it into words,' he shouts at me. 'Your couples and your contraries. They're commonplace. You make it all sound bellicose. These tubes, they are a *pharmakon*. Enough is for a cure; too much – is poison, a bother in the tongue. Your tongue's thick like a turtle's: try croaking it – war, war, *waar*. It's like enamoration – enough's a feast, too much is sticky sweet. Nothing at all – the species dies. It's clear. There's weapons all around . . . a book, a border, a drum, a document, a threat, a promise . . . the everyday . . .'

'I know,' I say. 'It's knowing how and when . . .'

'Now and then,' he says.

The sea. This troubled scurfy oilcloth, lumpish, dowdy, hiding secrets – the duplicates of everything, they say. Unbelievable: a fantasy of mermen, submariners. Instead, there's teeming fish, each drawn original, the scaly worms, the brittle scuttling stars, the inoffensive vertically wandering *régalec* – the kingfish: the clinging arms, hands, claws, the beasts that writhe and choke when up they come, raised into our airy world to wriggle to a death, open-mouthed, uncared for . . .

and now, how hard it is, to keep my happiness aglow. Must I share the blame for what those shells are landing on? – a hut, a palace . . . Blame? Easy enough to bear. Shells. Like crabs have. How strange it seems, the skates, the flounders, dabs, the polyps and the soles, all so unlike their namesakes on the land . . . like all these officers, the fairy pipes instead of bugles, mustering armies of the landless . . .

'No, no, it's commerce, that is how it works . . .' That's what the sailors say, but every ship has its particular room, peculiar mission. The officers – their orders . . . the crew . . . souls winched up the side from trenches, their bunkers collapsed and sinking. The captain, on his mattress in the *pension* or listening to his wireless, organ arrangements – themes from Brigadoom . . .

'Hey!' shouts the armourer. 'What you feel is only words. What you say you think – is quite irrelevant. It isn't even you. You need defence and challenge. You need to make a drama of the past. It's love. That's where we're all involved, under those heavy blankets. We love one another, and we fight injustice. Be happy, go on being happy. Remember – here on the ship – no one carries cash. There's no money, nothing is exchanged. There's never been a mint at sea. The gold and silver – if they're found – go back on land. Here – there's no poverty, no one is rich or privileged. We steal our rings from dwarves complicitous. All deaths at sea are violent, none is violently caused. You fall, you struggle like it was a birth. You never make it. You are not lost. You're never found.'

Some guys cheer, as dust goes up on shore.

'We could be friends,' the armourer says. 'Where you came from, and us – we're allies. That's the future.'

Friends – allies – drag you down, they drag you in, to other bands of friends.

'Of course,' the sailor says, 'there's some on board who don't approve. And they can't swim to shore. They . . . they must eat the worm, and have it scavenge their insides. You know who they are – you hear their bellies, slurp and sludge. There's nothing to be done. It takes two sides to make a war, my friend: there is no middle. That's a no man's land – a place uncomradely and perilous.'

'Hey!' I say. 'I'm not obsessed with war. I'd rather think of other things. You're not convincing me of anything, of good or bad. It's just . . . it's not my thing.' I think of Alp, surrendering to curiosity. I'm happy, I'm not curious. 'Even the golden light – it doesn't draw me. I'd rather keep the powder on my wings . . .'

'That's right!' the sailor shouts. 'The powder must be dry. And maybe this here's just an exercise. We're too far off to see if we have hit . . . a row of stalls, maybe. Some landsmen, dangerous, marching razors, that collective guillotine . . .'

I chose the wrong colour. A grey ship. Better risk your soul in a green, a blue, an orange one.

'It's marquetry,' says the armourer. 'The politics. The bad guys – can always be redeemed. An inlay, a chisel-stroke – throw down some pearls . . . a grand design. We landscape what may be this continent, the geysers and the glaciers, volcanoes, sinkholes. At least we'll try – until they have a ship like ours.'

'Let me land,' I say. 'Go back to where we ran the stall and spoke of voyaging by bus . . .'

'You'd like to be a soul that's saved,' the sailor says. 'You – and your chatter of philosophy and German songs . . . A soul – wouldn't understand a word; the guys that count them, bind their loyalties, chant their books and tell them miracles, that they're saved, die, be bathed in honeyed light – those guys won't talk to you. The souls – they land, then flee again. But guys like you – you're safer on a ship that floats without a helm . . . without a destination . . . What we knock down – on board we have a team that sticks that stuff back up. You don't do that. You don't take part. We're nearly what you want – we have no country and no government. We're mercenaries. We serve alliances . . .'

'Land!' I say. 'It's an anomaly, sticking out the water. But . . .'

'I know,' says the armourer. 'You can't run on water . . . Well, we sailors, once we carved those narwhal tusks. Now – it's needlework:

our petit point's a marvel. Look – here's a silk sack, embroidered with a theme of wings. It took me years, from mayfly to imperial eagles, birds of paradise . . . and all the while they'd go extinct before you could draw a bead on one – the albatross . . .! I needed several specimens, though they present a profile that is easy on the arrow . . . But, here they are. Just slip inside. Over the stern you'll go. Be born again, if you get out. If not – sea burial, a silken shroud, the twitter of those little pipes – reminds you of the Aztec rites, the flaying . . . the salts all weeping, tearing at their beards . . . that's why the sea is salt, I'm sure you know . . .'

'I'll try it, sailor, though the sea's been salty long before, indifferent to my funeral . . .' I say.

He sews me in. My heart – beats like lark's wings, there is a chudder and a roar of air on feather . . . Over the side I go.

The silken bag, sewn by the tarry tar, his fingers scrubbed to leave no stain, is on me like a caul – down down I go, a squid's envelope . . . oh, I think, who'll bear me up, oh, beat beat those wings, make me a fish that flies . . .?

A prophet's rock! A miracle, or at least a foothold quite miraculous. I burst the bag. My head rises from the waves . . . a puff-fish, bladder-wrack . . .

Float to the shore. That's where Afrodite lands, on her pretty cockleshell. In a row, Rosine, Claire, Irina . . . you need your opposite, they say, who, quarrels done, becomes a complement. A crazy thought, a torment, beyond all reason, of how to live.

All gone their ways; good luck! fair winds! You think you're the subject, and instead . . . Small lives, beginning, over and over, growing wings, and then away!

5

The sand is hot. Not Syria, I hope?

'I know you,' says someone, Andreas, it appears. 'You were on the history stall sometimes: antiquities. What a terrible end, modernity made. First, killing granddads, then fathers – now, it unreels, but oh! its teeth are sharper still! and you guys sold the capsules, the memos – stashed away before they could be used – the cans of movies, cans of everything, all preserved, even the faeces, never used. Those little telephones! empty now, like always.'

I'm still drowned. I say, 'What were you in, Andreas? Something that disappointed, that's for sure.' I'm happy, after all. He's not. I go on, 'I don't think it was modernity killed them all. I – for instance – wanted to get off the ship, and out my sack True, most of them would be dead by now . . . I could have drowned completely.'

'You don't have the eye, I see,' he says. 'All you've been part of – was part of something else, and large. Where there's a ship – there is a fleet, where there's a ruined fort – there's huts built with the stones, and daggers hidden in the thatch. Where you'd your stall, and did your deals – I was the guy who parcelled up the lots, laid it all out: the fashion and the books, the music, the history, the uniforms. Each on its square.'

'The owners – all dead or needy,' I say.

'You were the owners,' he says. 'It was all yours, all the property. And all you could think was to sell it off, to poorer guys. You missed your chance. To make a buck, you rolled the ball again. Did you think it wasn't round, that your eyes distorted?'

'We never thought there could be another way. And there was not,' I say.

'If any one could cogitate,' he says, 'it was you. I just laid out the ground, divided up the surface. Everything went bad. You stopped some wreckers – but all the rampaging that you'd done – intimidation, throwing stuff around, driving out the blacks – that moulded you. and you didn't give it thought. Commerce, you thought, and stole the goods and sold them on.'

'In a way,' I say, 'that's true. And it was done that way. There was no other way, we being what we were. The place – as it was.'

'Oh,' says Andreas, picking me up, to lean on his stave, his branch. 'You had the imagination. that is evident. The prophet's rock – invisible, underwater . . . You found that. You could have given tongue . . .'

'It's high water, Andreas,' I say. 'The guys stand on it and spout when it appears, when the tide is out. All's dependent on the moon, they say.'

'Make your analysis,' Andreas says. 'You're never wrong. It is your theme, whatever follows, rests on that, expounds. There are no second thoughts, or cancellations. Remember – the "historical rotations of the sun". That is the key, the theme. Non-linear. Pasts recurring. Cycles that illuminate the natural, the artificial – all the things that meanwhile change. From your analysis comes what too is always right. It's always far too radical. Too radical for you to act upon. You know it's right – it asks too much. Remember: analysis – correct: the consequences – correct, non-doable. Maybe you'll find someone, a group, that takes the risk. But – it's then clear. It wasn't their analysis. They want to act, not on analysis – but to make a carnage . . . revenge . . . build rose-red cities, any goddam thing.'

'I agree, Andreas,' I say, 'but the task's a drastic one. If anyone has ever tried . . .'

'Of course they try,' he says.

We leave it there. You know there's genius.

'Meanwhile,' he says. 'I guess you need some cash.'

'It's always joined to work,' I say. 'The cash I need – but it's ephemeral. It has no weight, no substance. If you have a packet of it, or you're skint – life's just the same.'

Andreas looks impatient. 'I could promote you. Be a manager, that way your analysis might change. It's just a quirk – I'd like you to wear this cap, pencil behind the ear – just so.'

'So far,' I say, 'it's easy. The finest kind of work.'

'Here's the map,' he says. 'It's blank. Imagine – so, it's a marketplace. What you must do, is fill the space. Forget what I might say it represents. It's space. It's meaningless. And think up categories. They're abstract, so you'll find it hard to fill the space. Or – you may find it easy. Go to, go to!'

What I do has consequences: the spaces, the categories – those are easy. But there must be stalls. For fish, and meat, and crumbly bakelite: recordings of the opera where all who clap and whistle – they're all long long dead. Pistols, and nurses' uniforms on card, for tiny volunteers, gasmasks and white vegetables.

The fish – are all identifiable: their mothers must recognise them. How sad, resigned, they look. Each death identical. Here, there's a claw that stirs. Oysters – maybe they still live, inside those green patisseries. The meat – is chopped and bloodied. No chance there's someone that you knew, or even guess the shape it came from.

'I've done it, Andreas,' I say. 'It's a cemetery, a *campo santo*, no flowers by request.'

'No, no,' he says. 'There's flowers. Must be. The lady selling them – my mother. Crosses and crescents too – my lovers . . .'

'I want no trouble, Andreas,' I say. 'I'm not into commerce, and the hucksters – not space, nor categories. Ossuaries too – quite out!'

'I've offered you a post with great powers, a strategic centrality,' he says. 'You didn't understand.'

'It's the people,' I say. 'The traders. Their territorial demands. They sell live animals; out the back – there's humans in the trade as well. The porters. Those guys you never see – working too early and too late. These spaces and their opportunities, stall city, its fountains, the green stuff, the crumpled bronze – you think they're things, but no –

they're things that think. At least – the animals, their sellers – they're one, their brains move on click-tape. Ruling over them – who'd care?'

'You're rambling,' Andreas says. 'You abandoned my idea. You didn't play to win or lose.'

'I didn't see it,' I say, 'not that way. It was a chore. I just saw those guys – a space to live in gave them what they need to eat. To be alone in. They fought, to have more, and to be still more solitary.'

'That's their viewpoint,' Andreas says. 'It needn't have been yours. The Prince faces the mob, he doesn't love his subjects: he has to watch for other princes. He doesn't love them either. If you're not in that business, that's the worse for you.'

'I worked,' I say, 'I suffered. Now – the payoff.'

'Work that doesn't recognise its end,' he says, 'is worthless. Of course you suffered. That's because you didn't see what you were up to.'

'I'm best at travelling,' I say.

That bus said 'the Place'. It goes there every week, then comes right back.

'I'm a professional,' Andreas says. 'Your friends were drifters. Alp the prime example. Toni – power or peace: which did he want? And Adnan – his raging fire peeped out. A bang on the nose – and now he must atone – he thinks. Me – I'm big.'

He is, he has no neck. No hanging, no decapitation, then. Lord of the marketplace, lord of the stalls. The Prince who doesn't need to bluff.

He walks down the aisle, kicking the little worn-out things, stealing an orange flower, tweaking an innocent, indifferent bum.

I cancel all my lines: the map is what it was – a blank sheet. 'There,' Andreas says. 'The toil availeth not. It's faith, not works – surely you've been told?'

'I need to eat, my friend,' I say.

'The guy that draws the lines – he gets his eats from off the stalls he's favoured,' Andreas says. 'It works that way. Cash is always cash, immutable, whoever's hand it's in. Food – if you've eaten, you would see . . . it metamorphoses. You wouldn't eat it twice. Cash now, is indigestible . . .' He laughs.

'My next task, then, Andreas,' I say.

He takes the blank sheet. 'See? The market works. The stalls – are all laid out. But – the map is virgin now, again. An empty sheet, no stain, no blur, no blot. It's of no place, no limit, no line, and no memorial. Reality – is over there,' and he points. 'Potential . . . is here.' And he jabs at the empty paper.

'If I need a hand,' he says, 'I'll let you know. For now – the real is doing well.'

They give me a *régalec*, a kingfish, unsaleable, off a stall. Two metres tall, it trails wings, a dragonfly's. 'That's me,' I say in jest. 'The kingfish.' Where to give it burial? At sea, like carrion? Beneath a tree, in soil, compounding its anomalies? Here's a leather case, two metres tall, once for an arquebus . . . He fits inside, his face unearthly green and ox-blood, his opaline veils deflate . . . Docile as always. The worst has come. I can't carry him along. I stand him, safe in his case, to carry on his cycle. Life down where he was – it's a fight. You're food. Some of those monsters . . . start at the tail, don't stop. Andreas says, 'My advice is precious: you've no depth of feeling. Your happiness – it puts guys off, it makes you seem an idiot – a *pollo* ready for the pot.'

'Depth's just a metaphor, Andreas. Feelings have only length,' I say.

'Then, there's your ideas,' he says. 'Storm-tossed.'

'In the market, there's always power, and lots of sex. There's no transgression – that's just a bourgeois squib. Everybody cheats and steals – if caught, apologises. Propriety is the rule. What's the idea that I might add?' I ask.

'I can throw ideas to you. They'll just bounce off,' Andreas says. 'Everybody asks me that – "what should I think?" It's pathos, don't you see?'

Exchange: this is my trade, profession. It runs through everything I've ever said, professed. A stall.

I think – I could go, find Alp, Rosine. Rosine says, 'It's all right, I'm not monogamous.' Nursing a new white lamb, or goat. Making tea for Alp. Those new states, old as time – they always have their fortresses apart, inviolate, their monasteries, their sects that dance and smoke and drink . . . read Wonder Woman. We three – we could find a fort, a garden, out of the gaze, the order. See the sun rise that no one sees, those stars pricked out above – that no one's seen for centuries.

But I shan't.

We three – seek enlightenment. But living there, concealed – those people all around – all that's not about being right. It's about plugging into capitalism.

I must create a stall that sells . . . what you can plug in.

A space is left. I stand by my table. What can fill it? Those caves – where they painted on the lions, the rhino, mammoths, all the relics. Where did the seekers want to go? We call them forefathers. Family. Maybe they went – like the rhinos. There's no men and women round the fire with species plans. Where did they think they'd end, and what is left of what they wanted . . .? What can I sell, where would it point? Old phonograms, army fatigues, tinctures that kill or not . . . I say aloud, 'I could be a *mago* and sell lies.'

The woman on the next stall . . . my! what packets! What you wanted, as a child. Red, purple, haggis-shaped . . . 'What's in them?' I ask.

'Oh,' she says, 'it's a surprise. Like when you were young. Wooden soldiers, soft rhinos, games that let you win. Maybe a fortune. A slim body, or a friend that won't betray.'

'It's sure to make you rich,' I say.

'Yes,' she says. 'That's what I wanted, as a child.'

'I've experience,' I say. 'You can't avoid it. But – what to put here, on my stall . . . I've no idea.'

'You leave it empty, and you wait to see what people come and have you sell. On commission,' she says. 'That way, you can cheat.'

'Yes,' I say, 'but what they bring's what they don't want, can't use, or is worn out.'

'Don't see it that way, dear,' she says. 'It's what they wanted, once. Pass it on to someone else. Or take it home yourself, and let it tell its tale.'

'That sounds naive,' I say. 'Already, I've tales inside to fill a book.'

'You travelled with the wrong sort – then it was Andreas rescued you,' she says. 'That wasn't smart. Avoid rescue by evil people, even if they're dearest friends of mine.'

'I drew the map, Leda,' I tell her. 'That's why we are where we are.'

'That's metonymy,' she says. 'Didn't you do all that at school?'

'You have to watch the other guys in school,' I say. 'Class struggle. That's what a lesson's for. The information – you can pick it up – a day or so . . .'

'Another market's opening up,' she says. 'Guys off the boats. Selling poor stuff, among themselves.'

'We'd do better if they come in here,' I say. I know that'll provoke her.

'They've a better chance,' she says. 'Keeping their stuff apart, and specialised.'

Leda wears a crucifix, a little martyred figure between her breasts. She sees me staring at them,

'It's the power,' she says. 'You can feel –'

'It's made its impress, Leda,' I say. 'Reminds me of my martyred friends – self punishment, of course, but painful none the less.'

'That's foolishness,' she says. 'Big gestures – they're a way too florid.'

Her stall is flourishing. I turn away the offers that they bring to mine: it's mostly books – a Yellow book, the Colonel's Green, the Chairman's Red.

'You offer things for sale,' says Leda. 'The aim's not to keep your deck mopped clean. We could be mates. You like a couple – mine's surprise, yours could be – banality. Like – Venus's arms . . . the winged Victory's head.'

'I'd love to venture on with you, dear Leda,' I say. 'But it's static, your idea. You need a couple that can fly and twirl. Black swans. Besides – it's easy to be top of some big but insignificant place. Andreas has plans. You don't need a passport – just be voted for.'

'Why would you want that?' she asks. 'Your friends had big plans they could fail in. Your project – it's cheap.'

'It's water,' I say. 'If you're a fish, you swim in it.'

'Andreas likes you,' Leda says. 'Because you're dark. You come from the East, but you're not honest. No one knows if you've anything inside, because you hide so well.'

'Well, Leda,' I say, 'that's beautiful, but don't raise sweat on looking. I had a cat, Tiger he was called, he lay on my shoulder one night and curled round and bit my ear, the lobe, till it bled. Could you give love like that, Leda?'

Probably not. She can't respond, anyway.

'You thought they'd bring odd things,' says Leda. 'Curiosities. Instead – they preferred surprise from me, the expert. You've got nothing – but I'll buy your space. That way you'll have a capital, to buy some planks and tressles, try to sell whatever comes to hand.'

'We might have made a couple, Leda, you and I conjoined and struggling . . .' I begin.

'No, no,' she says, 'you overestimate all that. Look – there's Andreas. There's your boat! Remember what they say – this here's the place – now see how high you jump!'

'Those surprises, Leda,' Andreas laughs. 'One's in waiting for you now, I'll bet.'

'The sky's full of white sails – furling, landing – who'd have imagined . . .' Leda shouts.

Leda – farewell! We board the ship, Andreas and I. There's a piping, a tweeting, white canvas wings unfurled.

The sails look flimsy. Andreas says – 'I'll row you till we reach the open sea. I'm sure your pocket's full of wind.' He laughs, and digs his oars in deep. He's big and strong, the oar breaks, and he says, 'My friend – the answer is – you paddle us until we're there.'

He must be our lost captain. 'No!' he shouts. 'I'm the navigator, helmsman. I spin the wheel. and you – you're the philosopher who stands beside the great man, you're the guy who's paid to take the bullet.'

'The quest!' I shout. 'The navigator – knows where we're headed. Everything's fulfilled. The curiosity! Justice, compassion, novelty – and power. We're on our way! My friends – their destinies spliced in the one person . . . their purposes achieved . . .'

'Yes, yes,' Andreas shouts, his register two octaves down from mine. 'The guys we left – they're all trimmers, fascists too. They've had it all, everything's been tried on them – the myths, the legends. Now they've been told they're good, now bad. We'll go somewhere fresh and clean . . . The problem, my dear friend, is this – every hope, and aspiration that you have – shows up your method. It's quite flawed. The "couple" that you talk about's within each one of us. The peace, the war; the beg the steal; resist, comply . . . They coexist in everyone, and that is our success – the species multiplies! There's massacres, and running out of stuff, but on we go until the final precipice. Your quest – it's all been found and known. All that remains – is change the words, the tune – but make it comprehensible, so's guys can wave their arms and sing along!'

The boat is heavy, yet, it moves. Down below, there's roistering. Andreas says. 'I brought my lovely friends along – it's just amusement, nothing that can trouble you.'

He surely can't amuse them all. Here's a beauty – Sissi: she's surely Rosine, Claire, Irina – rolled into one, and then ironed out much thinner. 'Andreas dumped his crew,' she says. 'Theirs was the sin of ugliness. We were on the rocks, singing to keep our spirit dry . . . He picked us up . . . He'll go anywhere, so's not to go back to nestle with his wife.'

'So banal?' I ask. 'I thought at least we'd go to China, see how the earth is moving . . .'

'Andreas says, "Those communists are doing well. For now, their capitalism's going fine." He's rather snide, Andreas,' Sissi confides. 'But – you can't paddle us that far. You have a stash – we'll save some drifting guys, maybe you could pay them for the toil . . .'

'No, no,' I say. 'My friends have made their sacrifice. I must honour them . . . Parsimony . . .'

'How do you think you'd do them honour?' Sissi asks.

Later, she says, 'You dreamt last night. When you are in it, the dream is yours, original. But when you wake – it's dust. A powder on the floor.'

'No, Sissi,' I say. 'I didn't dream.'

She persists. 'A dream. It's bigger, by far, than any person. And it's yours, like the rhino you're drawing on the cave wall.'

'No, like the lion belongs to no one but the lion. What you draw is life,' I say uncertainly.

'We're passing by my island now,' says Sissi. 'There's trees and animals. We need another oar. New masts too – there's just four trees, so they will do. We'll eat the pigs, since no one thought to bring some food on board . . .'

'Andreas,' I say, 'is an adventurer. This is his time. And on your island – there's bound to be a stall. We won't need extinguish animals.'

'That would be friendly,' Sissi says, 'and besides – you have your capital, your venture capital, that Leda paid you for your space. You can pay for everything we need. It makes you an adventurer as well, like Andreas. I guess he's just a bonapartist . . .'

'It's all devalued, Sissi, all the currencies are worn down to their silver thread, the Bonapartes – they swarm like maybugs, napoleons are forged in bronze,' I say.

There's rows of pigs, staring out, along the shore. We hesitate. They are not welcoming.

'No hurry,' says Andreas, 'to revitalise the boat. Let's sit and drift and do philosophy. Our Master – all his books are right, and all our circumstances wrong. That's what we need, his genius, when we reach Cythera. A touch of Marx, a touch of scepticism . . .' and he lays out his plan, his dream. We've heard it all before. Andreas seems to dream a lot.

Sissi leans towards me, but there's no touch of anything.

We cut down the trees. The pigs in silence cluster round. The trees are olive – 'Crooked timbers,' laughs Andreas. They make eccentric masts. The oar is crooked too. 'No matter,' shouts Andreas. 'Wherever we might land, they'll recognise a prince. And if they don't, we'll make them study hard.'

He hugs his woman, Ondine. 'She's my fortune,' he goes on, and sets her on the prow.

There's drunken guys below. I hear them, cutting up some pigs, and whittling the olive trees. There's women too. Sissi's screaming about her island we have trashed. There's Ondine. 'Look, Andreas,' I say, 'I don't know what I have to do, or how long we'll be sailing by . . .'

'We'll maybe buy an island,' says Andreas, 'as an insurance, a refuge. You – you must set the sails. Keep the crew amused.'

I see no crew. 'Remember what I said, Andreas,' I say. 'Think of the way nomads win and hold a territory. How they too have cities, ambassadors. Not religion, or a plan. Study it, Andreas, even though others have taken the idea – it's still your lesson,' I tell him. 'Taking expanses. The desert. Or the mountain. Or the sea. No one wants the sea. You can have as much as you can take.'

'I understand,' Andreas says. 'Just ways of being emperor.'

He hugs me. 'You're a genius,' he says.

'Everybody abuses everybody. Tortures them,' says Sissi. 'Locks them up and sends them to the guillotine. The only difference is – do you do it at home, and are you in uniform? Is your boss vulnerable, if you have one? Anything else is opera, Andreas.'

'Nonsense!' Andreas says. 'It's easy enough, to make sufficient people happy. Look at you,' and he squeezes my cheek in his fist. 'He's always happy. It's not too hard to find a bunch of humans just like him.'

'My island?' Sissi says. 'You destroyed my nature. Attracting pigs – took me lifetimes: growing trees – they did it all themselves.' She flaps her cloak, rises on her toes. Her face – reddens, blackens . . .

She's angry, that's for sure. The bully boys, the goodtime girls, that's rollicking in the hold reach a crescendo – 'Give us a shanty!' Sissi shouts to them. 'Or no more rum.' She's storming up, her wrath darkens more . . .

There's quiet for moments. Andreas expounds his plan.

'Armenians, Jews, Palestinians,' he says, 'Polisario – the rest . . . we march along with them a while. And then you tire, they tire, those that are left – they've turned the things around, perhaps. They tire – of you: your ignorance. Indifference. The details, names, the dates – can't be bothered with all that. The time – ah yes, the time grinds on, and history is far behind, ludicrous, in its dogcart, or a wheelbarrow . . . here it comes, singing those old German songs, the lilacs on the bonfire, unwatered roses in the compost. Ten per cent, said Ali Pasha – the nation can't survive if there is more than that. A nation can't exist – if it's a nation that you want, like that – if there's more minorities, divided loyalties, and different songs and cakes. Well – I'll have none of that. We'll find a place where all cohere already! All lined up, neat, good, expectant – waiting for me. and the philosopher here. Not too much work for him to do – that's his priority . . .' And he cuffs me, in friendship. 'You Sissi – you thought I was your prisoner. Instead – you're bound to me, to my enchantment. You've no home left – you've taken ship with me, and on and on we'll sail, until we find that happy land . . .'

'Forget all that, you creep. You bully!' Sissi shouts. 'I'm not your prisoner. My island! Nature. Pigs and trees! All gone . . .' And in her rage, she takes an olive branch and sweeps him . . . oh no! into the sea . . . for sure he cannot swim, maybe he'll float . . .? No one moves to try a rescue, risk a plunge . . .

But no – he's on a rock. 'Sing, sing!' she screams. 'See if you'll find a rescuer, and spin your scam! Sing on the rocks. Eat seawrack, drink the rain, remember psalms and German songs, and have them resonate . . . over the desolation, and hear them die, feathering down into the black, like the albatross . . .'

She doesn't curse him. 'He has his rocky realm,' she says. 'And we are seamen. Nomads. Lords of this desert,' and she waves at the water, surging uselessly up and down, and changing colour – black blue green and mostly grey. 'Remember the manifesto,' Sissi proclaims – 'Nineteentwentyfour,' she shouts. 'Surrealism. The *poisson soluble*, those melting fish our magic masters have invoked. Not conjuring and spells, my dear,' and she presses close to me. 'But – power to the imagination! The surreal, that penetrates the real and finds – more real! "You have a world to win." Who wouldn't thrill to that? That's my trick . . .' and she laughs hugely as we drift along, dismasted, the olive trunks rolling drunk upon the deck.

'Sissi,' I say, alarmed. 'Your game was giving refuge, changing the time, changing the nature of the guys who sought you . . . All that has gone – destroyed, butchered and sequestered. Blame it on Andreas. But – please – steer the boat. Whistle up a wind. Point Odine in some direction, or we'll gyre around . . .'

'Yes, yes,' she shouts. 'That is our destiny. Our space is featureless . . . no rock, no atoll, no dull yellow strips of desert sand . . . just slop and slur. There's no direction here . . .'

I think of Alp – his curiosity firm centred on the land, on vehicles with wheels, the marching and the boots . . . Irina – so ordered, keeping her accounts. And here I am – on board a hulk without a helmsman, a nomad, no living beasts to herd, no foliage, no growth – just universal water, undrinkable, full of inedible life . . . All ours, all everyone's – a means to nowhere and to everywhere . . . A party in the hold I'm not asked to join . . .

'Find me a rock, dear Sissi,' I implore. 'And let me off.'

'There is no "off",' she says, 'unless you are a fish. But no: I caught you, landsman. You're out of your element – but there's not another one for you. This is my realm, this in-between, this nothing-nowhere, this voyaging from port to port, harbourless, import to export – where you're a good that never lands, that has no customs, just some songs that only sailors sing. Lookout. That's what you are – Look out!' she screams . . . A wave has doused poor Ondine, down we go – past the happy grinning skulls – always happy them! – into the land of fantasy – the tentacles, the worms, the mouths that chew on nothing without end, no appetite, no satisfaction and no sound – then eaten in their turn, reproduced in shell-less eggs, lighting up or going black – one evil eye awake and seeking out its lunch . . .

'Sissi!' I shout. 'This is terrible! Turn off your fantasy, and let us sink and drown . . . This horror! All eats and is eaten, rises from the mud to paradise of wrecks and mermaids – skeletal all, like marathoning x-rays . . . those songs the whale philosophers send out – incomprehensible, and pitched so high . . . a 'peep', a 'poop'. No cantilena – and no aria. Dense syllables, portending what – digestion? Excretion? Your world, Sissi – it's in no book. No God, no prophet thought of this, nor engineered these simulacra. There's no ghosts – to be a ghost you need have lived . . . No war, no precepts good or bad, no geo so no geopolitics – just the implacable eat . . .'

'Exactly so,' she says. 'You should have kept me on my island, with my pigs and nuts. Imagine – your friends with their crusades, their jihads – let them bring them down here, see what they avail. You scoop it up, this life, and in revenge – it's fish and chips. See if they care! The life breeds on and on, no mothers, mother love, no families –

just shoals. A myriad of flashing thoughts, so dense there is no sense . . . To you – it's hellish. But to me – it's my salty mind. That's all it needs – sodium and rain. No creation, and no end: just cold and claggy shapes . . .'

'Last time I drowned,' I say, 'there was a happy end. I reached the craggy shore . . .'

'You should have stayed on board your girl, your ship . . . That was before the anger came upon me,' Sissi says. 'And I showed you how it really was. you people – say there's always hope – some awful thing occurs – "Oh well," you say, "there was the Ghaznavids, but then – the Ghorids – they were lovely guys . . .", "Here come the Mongols, swallow your pearls – maybe they'll ride away . . .", "Look – those are some Tiger tanks – they'll never bother with us, nestling here . . ." I tell you – it is never so. The bad gets worse, and never worst. That's why the history's put in books – if it comes really back, you'd soon be terrified. And – think of the future. You tried to conjure it away – time capsules on your stall! As though you'd never crawl and shriek . . . But – the rest I'll spare you. It was Andreas set me off – telling the truth, showing the real. It's a rare privilege, you must enjoy it . . .'

Sissi hugs me, puts her long tongue in my mouth . . . maybe she smells or sees with it . . . it reaches down inside and roams my entrails.

'I can make it up to you,' she says . . . 'A minute. Sex. You can think it cancels out my sea, that intercourse and childbirth will reproduce your better thoughts. It isn't so, my friend . . . But don't deny me now, or I'll have you see the sky afresh. It isn't full of perfumes, German songs, and twittering. I'll spare you that for now. Reality you take in spoonfuls,' and she jiggers up and down.

'Be very careful, Sissi. What you do – it's classed as fraud – you go to jail. Or maybe – blasphemy: so, jail or worse,' I say.

'I don't do anything,' she says. 'I say what there is, and what I see. The rest is all made up.'

'What you say and see – that's even worse than sorcery,' I say.

'I lost my island,' Sissi says. 'That was the vandal Andreas. No conjuring involved. The lesson is, to stay at sea. Don't go near land, or ships.'

'Food, Sissi,' I say. 'When do we eat?'

'Oh,' Sissi says. 'There's pigs abound. If you've a hang-up over them – there's olives. We can plant some on the deck.'

'Then there's the party down below. We can't eat them, nor change them into useful fruits,' I say.

'You and I,' she says. 'Can't that be enough? We'll find a rock, and people we don't have uses for – we'll plant them. Colonies, they're called – or rigs, observatories, prisons, airports. You can choose the name.'

'Did we rise from that wave, Sissi?' I ask. 'Did we have sex?'

'There's see and say,' she says. 'You can see we're afloat, and talking in the air.'

'The party down below,' I say. 'If it's my time to be together – with you – maybe they could just go overboard.'

'Oh no,' she says. 'Next, you'll ask me to shoot them down with arrows, naughty boy! That's not my thing, my way, at all.'

Poor Claire, I think. If you had not been Adnan's girl. If you had fought for something, not only for the sake of it, the purse . . . If only . . . where might we have gone? Our friends, our real friends – they're all dead. Or missing, where they don't know where they are, and no one thinks to look for them. You're all missing, we miss you . . . Who killed you, if you're dead, Alp and Aslan? Do you care? Do I? The best weapons kill the most, and bury bodies deeper. You ask 'how'? Not why. 'Why' is something for before and long after.

'Don't get alarmed, or confident. You're not exclusive to me,' Sissi says. 'Your being not a sailor, that's attractive. Maybe you come from battle? Though – if it was a tough one, you must have waited for the dark, and run away. Survivors here are rare, and if you find one, you must cling to them, and hug them close . . .' And she does, she's all over, like a vine.

'There was no battle, Sissi,' I say. 'And I feel bad about those people, Ondine too – she was no one special, just trying out to be a figurehead.'

'Nothing to do with you,' says Sissi. 'It was nature. Besides – they'd nothing special to have parties for. Ondine – went to her element. Desolate places – that's where we meet the people who mean most. Cities are bean soup. I mean to follow the trek of the antelopes. When they die their horns stick up, two fingers at who looks at them. They're right. The ship – it was a difficult place they found themselves in, quite complex. External forces did for them,' she says. 'They should have crewed instead of crowed. They went in the big wave. Most voyages to Cythera end that way. Not your fault. You're a coward: that's attractive too. You helped sell things off a stall – that's harmless, bland as well. You're lucky that an accident didn't fall on you.'

There's nothing down below. We two – we are alone. 'They're gone, the others, like soluble fishes,' Sissi says. 'I mustn't laugh. I didn't bond with them.'

'This ship,' I say, 'I guess it's ours.'

'You see there's no one else,' she says.

We must be rich.

6

We're not so rich.

'This boat keeps sinking,' says the guy. 'It's good for refugees, not trade.'

'Just roll the cash inside this nautilus,' says Sissi, not seeming fazed.

She says to this guy, the mariner, 'Once, to feel disappointed, you voyaged for a year, and saw an earthquake, one kind of slavery, some dirty tricks. Now, in a month you see a swarm – volcanoes, trafficking, disease. You mustn't feel a disillusion though. You didn't have illusions at the start. You must keep happy, like he is,' and she shakes me, to impress the guy.

He fills her shell. 'We could go look for your friends,' she says to me. 'But that would be your autobiography – especially if we never find them. Self-indulgent. It's about them. Their first person. They must find themselves – that's what it's about: not you. If it's my choice – I can lope along for days. Three without water, eight with no food. Even then – not a banquet. A handful. A shellful. A song of the green grass. My mind – grows bigger and bigger, as I keep my pace. Then it goes back, into its carapace, when I've stopped. Its bonecase. Like a nude crab, finding an empty home, folding its pink, naked legs and going in. No name, no door. Life, with a window.'

'Yet – there's been people,' I say. 'The island. The ship. Inveigled.'

'Oh yes,' she says. 'They interrupt, they stagger, reel over the rocks and down the anchor-chain, on, up, the trees. I can't stand them. I need reduce them – something useful, inoffensive. Their true nature.'

'They were all round,' I say. 'You gathered them in. It must have been your aim, a project. Then you distinguished – on some basis. They all partied. And you dumped them all . . . The people; the gathering – that's not me at all.'

'You've no patience,' Sissi says. 'Think of the Revolution – the Russian. Or the French. In a day – it was all over – except . . . there was a civil war, that went on and on. Decades. The Russians – maybe they've found the superficial thing they want, they wanted. The French – they're philosophers. It'll go on for ever, they won't breed, but others will – they'll immigrate and on and on . . .'

'No, Sissi, forget the revolution. It's the partying I can't stand,' I say. 'If I'm not invited.'

'Forget the partying,' she says. 'It's not about that – it's the weighing in the balance. Reducing the loud and raucous people. Being alone again. Following the antelopes, and getting first to the waterhole. Then trekking on.'

'Yes,' I say, 'I see some of that. It seems perverse, though – the social part.'

'It's about patience,' she says. 'Your friend Toni – he wanted to be chief cock. Then he saw it meant he stood for ever on the dungheap. Better to climb the tree of life, perch there on the top. See who comes to feed you.'

'Your "real", Sissi, your "nature". I don't trust you with them. There's a catch . . .' I say.

'Don't worry,' Sissi says. 'I'm flexible. They mean what I want them to.'

'That's exactly it,' I say. 'My real nature – can't be open to interpreters.'

'Your happiness,' says Sissi, sharply. 'It gives me a pain. Especially when it creeps on your foolish face. People who are punished and despised – they'll take to arms, and disrespect. They won't care for your happiness. Expect their rampage, and their victories.'

'I wish I'd partied,' I say, 'when it was heating up.'

'Don't wish for anything,' says Sissi. 'I'm the only one who's wish comes right. Leda wished for freedom. She got passion. In a whirlwind. She's forgotten you, for sure.'

'It's not all sex and water, Sissi. It's not like the antelopes. There's the speculation, and the carpentering. The singing too . . .' I say.

'Yes, my dear: the singing. When I was on the rocks, I did a lot of that. Look who fell in to my open jaws,' she says. 'You. Andreas – he's got his own rock now. I hope he bellows, and gets heard. You're not worried it'll come to roost on us? He has his own devices. All is up to him.'

'There's the soluble fish . . .' I say.

'They didn't invite you, you don't even know their names. Their bourbon gives you acne. You don't feel for them, you don't want to be caught and punished,' Sissi says. 'If it helps – imagine they had violent thoughts. They probably marooned scores, garrotted hundreds. Relax.'

'You settled those people. Turned them into oxen, toiling on your rock. Consumed. Digested. Me,' I say. 'I'd give the order – life and death, they're shaken together in the cup. How it turns out – is chance. For that, there's no responsibility.'

'Nonsense,' she shouts. 'They had their sex, their whisky and their smokes. You heard them stamping. That was flamenco, not death throes.'

You have to study, follow on – or else it's all a puzzle. Taking your mind off your friends, their modest lives. Sissi – her culture, her determination – those could be attractive. Being with her, though, you need protection. There's a scent of deaths unnecessary, guys after you with axes. She knows about the French, their manifestoes, guys with red spade beards, standing around and partying, charging the galleries thousands for their pics . . .

'Don't make that gesture when you're near to me,' says Sissi. 'There's no need.'

'Just harmless superstition, Sissi. New dangers surface, new chants and prohibitions. Everybody shouts something when the bombs come down, and everybody bombs. That's all,' I say.

I peer at her: from neck down, she's all golden scales.

'It seemed the right thing on the day,' she says. 'The gold is cadmium. It kills you, and it settles in, right to your bones. It won't come off. It makes us shine a green, a yellowy submarine, when there's no other light.'

'That's terrible. A curse, Sissi,' I say. I'm terrified. Alas, it simplifies my quest . . .

'It's like the faith,' she says. 'It's visible, and irreversible. It is my body, see? Unto death. Yes, you're right. All my lovers too. They die. The poison. Head to toe . . . those shining scales. That's what it means, I guess – the "weighing in the balance". I thought the balance had a spring – but no! It's "me and you", that kind of scale. Me and you, close as close. You understand – I cleave to you, so's not to pass it on. No suitors.'

Maybe it's just an idea she has from a book. What ideas aren't in them?

I don't feel good.

I'm hers, for a short life.

'I'm disappointed, Sissi,' I say. 'I know all about you, and it all comes from mustiness. Pamphlets. A crackling of bombast with a peppery smell.'

'Well,' she says, 'you want to have a profile, make some kind of name. Boss people. Is it the village fascism that tickles you? The full church, the big bully, eccentricity and suicide? Or town fascism? Order, murder, the dreams of the mad clerk?'

'I guess I rather drift,' I say, annoyed.

'No, no,' she says. 'You've a great purpose in you. It's just – your happiness is fucked.'

'No,' I say. 'Happiness is an attitude, not a circumstance. It doesn't change because you tinker with the clock.'

'Someone will find a cure for us,' she says. 'The Americans? They're perfidious. They invent a bomb and say it cures a fever. China? Now it's births, then deaths . . . you can't be sure what's simmering in their pot. Then – there's the Arab nation . . . It's continental: when it's sorted out . . .'

'Men are warriors, Sissi,' I say. 'And women too. They haven't yet decided – if they approve of drawing on the body, or maybe it's unclean.'

'There's Alp,' she says. 'He's the intelligent type. If he read some books, he'd sort us out.'

'Whatever he decides he is,' I say, 'he isn't Arab.'

'Stay as you are, then,' Sissi says. 'Best to be happy, like you say. At least, covered as I am with scales, I can sing to myself, lounge here naked on these rocks. It's natural, I'm happy too, and no one can object, or stare.'

About the author

John Fraser has lived in Rome since 1980. Previously, he worked in England and Canada.

www.ingramcontent.com/pod-product-compliance
Lightning Source LLC
Chambersburg PA
CBHW072051170626
46813CB00004B/1303